Someday Isn't Far Off

TO LOVE A COWBOY
BOOK ONE

JAN HALEN

Plot Twist Publishing

For romance-obsessed
readers everywhere

CHAPTER 1

Cody

BETWEEN SPRAWLING ACRES of pasture and the limitless expanse of blue sky, Cody Schafer was trapped. Bound in on all sides by his circumstances, unable to rise or sink, he was simply doing what needed to be done. He lowered the brim of his baseball cap against the glare of the afternoon sun and sat deep in the saddle. Scowling at the stubborn calf—the last to be separated and corralled—a muttered curse escaped his mouth. He and the horse edged themselves into the herd and took a position between the calf and the rest of the cows.

The calf resisted being pushed out of the herd; Big Red plunged into action. His hooves pounded against the ground and sent clumps of dirt into the air. The calf bolted right, then left, in an effort to rejoin the others. Cody lowered the reins to give Big Red plenty of slack as he changed directions. Darting back and forth between the snorting calf and the herd, Cody and Big Red cut away the calf and drove it into the corral.

"Good work, Big Red." Cody patted the horse on the neck.

Beads of sweat plastered his hair tight to his head and dampened his forehead, soaking the edges of his cap. More annoying though was the moisture that trickled down his back. He reached behind him to scratch where the perspiration caused a maddening itch. Sweat had never bothered him much on the football field, but on the ranch, it brought out strings of curses.

He should have convinced Mom to sell the ranch two years ago, but between his grief and her illness, he wanted to hold onto anything that was Dad's. Before long, the life insurance benefit had been depleted, and Cody was in over his head. He'd had no choice but to beg Wayne to come out of retirement to help him as foreman.

Wayne, red-faced with exertion, swung the corral gate shut and latched it.

"What do you think, Wayne?" Cody asked.

"About the calves? Prices are a bit low right now, but these yearlings should bring in enough to keep you afloat through the summer, until you sell the two-year-olds in the fall." Wayne took off his hat and wiped the sweat from his balding head with a bandanna. His hand shook with age when he tucked the faded fabric back into his chest pocket. Deep lines creased his face as he looked over the acres of green grass with a practiced eye. "You're gonna want to let the land out to graze other cattle. Every bit helps. I don't have the connections your dad had: Boyd made friends everywhere he went. But I can ask around who's interested if you're up for it."

"Okay, if that's best," Cody said. "We'll need another hand if we're caring for more cows. Think we can afford it?" He rubbed his throbbing forehead under the brim of his hat. At twenty, he was too familiar with the worries of a much older man.

"Well, that'll stretch the money thin, but we can cull a few more cows if need be." Wayne sighed. "How's Rosie today?" He asked about Cody's mother every day. The answer never changed, despite her worsening health.

"Same."

"Have you looked any more into getting some help?" Wayne asked.

"Can't afford it. She ain't old enough for Social Security. I thought about applying for disability benefits … but I just don't know," Cody said.

The idea of dependence on assistance programs soured his stomach. The voice of his father echoed in his mind like a rooster that just wouldn't shut up. *A man takes care of his family.* Cody had heard that counsel his whole life, and he didn't dare dishonor his father's memory by going against it now. If Mom had a need, it was his responsibility.

"Besides, she won't go. She can't even step out into the yard. How am I going to get her to a care center?" Cody's voice cracked as he flung a hand up in the air. There was never an answer, only the same questions. He calmed himself before the frustration could take over. It would never do to appear out of control. He sat up straighter in the saddle. "I can take care of her. I *will* take care of her."

"What can I do?" Wayne asked.

"Just keep this place going, and don't let me do anything stupid."

"All right, then. But *you* can turn this around. Just gotta find what works. Keep the good, and move on from the rest."

"There ain't nothing good about this place."

"If you say so." Wayne tipped his hat. "But Cody, if there's something you don't like about your life, change it.

Because no one else can." He rode off toward the barn and left Cody alone at the corral.

For a man who grew up on this ranch, he knew next to nothing about being profitable. His father had made it look so easy—keeping the cattle, the books, the employees. He was a natural. Cody, however, made so many mistakes.

Dad had never pushed him too hard about ranching. He always knew Cody wanted a different life for himself, and he'd almost had it. If his dad hadn't died, Cody would've been halfway through a bachelor's degree by now.

He looked over the calves in the corral, penned in to await the arrival of the stock trailers in the morning. They were docile and content to stand together with their noses in feed troughs, oblivious to the fact that there was no way out. Cody was as penned in as they were, with the cows on one side and his ailing mother on the other. He envied their oblivion. If only he could forget the well-laid plans for college that had vanished into the horizon two years ago.

Cody glanced up at the sun's position in the sky. Mom wouldn't need him for another hour or so. He turned the chestnut quarter horse toward the treetops in the distance.

"Come on, Big Red." Cody rode to the northern border of the ranch under the clear early-summer sky. The only clouds were the ones that hung over him in his mind. They grew heavier and darker as he and Big Red headed for the creek.

He slumped in his saddle and guided the gelding along the beaten path through the lush field. Out here, away from the herds and manure, the air was fresher with the smells of grass and soil. There was so much green grass—plenty for the cattle to graze, even if they took in cattle from other ranches as Wayne had suggested.

Wayne had good ideas about the ranch. Cody would have liked to hand it over and just walk away, but it wasn't up to him. Mom owned the place now. All Cody could do was keep it running so she could stay in her home.

He urged Big Red to pick up the pace as they got closer to the creek. As much as Cody depended on spending time at the creek bottom to take deep breaths of the moisture-laden air and sort his thoughts, the directions his mind wandered frightened him. He nudged Big Red to a gallop until they arrived under the shade of the trees.

Cody dismounted and led the horse to drink from the creek before looping the lead around a low tree limb. Then from the saddlebag, he pulled out the book that stood between him and the dangerous path his mind took. He smoothed the bent corner of the paperback cover. *Romeo and Juliet*. Old friend.

Long ago, before her mind had cracked, Mom had borrowed it from the bookmobile that passed by each month. Cody had intended to return it to the library for her, but as he'd walked out the door on that dry autumn day, he'd dropped it in the dust at his feet and it had fallen open to the back cover. Someone had used a purple pen to cover the page in alternating jagged or loopy cursive and had signed it *A.G.* The words "three days" had pulsed and stood out from the rest of the script. That was the first day Cody had read the book at the creek bottom. The first of many.

Cody sat on a large rock under the sycamores and propped his feet in their work boots on a neighboring fallen log. The sun filtered through the leafy treetops and scattered splashes of golden light. The creek flowed by with a lively gurgle as he grounded himself by breathing deeply of the humid air.

He opened the book to the inside of the back cover. Cody had read the new ending so often, he'd practically memorized it. A.G. hadn't liked that Romeo and Juliet had killed themselves for the sake of their star-crossed love, so they had written a new ending, one in which Romeo waited three days before making the fatal decision to drink the poison. Those three days allowed Juliet time to wake up. Three days had made all the difference.

Three days. Things were terrible, and nothing would change in three days. The ranch would still be struggling, his mom would still be wobbling at the edge of her mind, and he would still be a high school dropout with no future.

Cody looked down at the page. He had already waited three days, again, and again, and again.

He gripped the book, white-knuckled and weary, and lowered his head to rest on the edge of the pages. He hated feeling trapped and useless. He hated that no matter what he did, he would always be here doing the same things day after day. "But maybe my ending can change."

There had to be more to the story, something stronger than merely holding on for three more days. There *must* be more. Holding on had kept him here, that much was true. But it had *kept* him here. A.G. must have been suffering something terrible, given the distressed penmanship and tear-stained ink. But where Cody only saw problems, A.G. had seen hope; enough hope to last three days at least.

With his eyes shut tight, he dared to imagine a life away from the ranch, a life that so far had no shape. If only he could meet A.G. and ask them what had happened.

What had made them write the new ending, and where the hope came from. Maybe then his own path would become clear.

He wasn't sure how he might go about finding A.G., but the book itself was a clue and was where he would start. On his next trip to town, he would visit the library.

Cody was hanging on to the echo of A.G.'s hope by a thread. Tightening his grasp on that thin lifeline, he tucked the book back into the saddlebag. The creek seemed a little more cheerful than when he'd arrived. He'd had a lot of practice at taking life three days at a time.

CHAPTER 2

Lina

SORROW OOZED from the sister-shaped hole in Lina Grant's heart. After nine years, the loss still throbbed with phantom pain. Especially at times like this when the stack of pancakes towered higher than two people could eat, when the aroma of sizzling bacon filled the air, and when they should all have been greeting each other around the breakfast table.

The ache was too much. Lina pressed a fist to her chest as if she could stuff it into the void and let her imagination do the rest. Today's version of a cork had broad shoulders, a captivating smile, and just enough stubble to leave a mark when he ravished her. She closed her eyes and shivered as the dream man pulled her close, nuzzled her neck, and whispered, "We're together now, my darling." He smelled like scorched grease.

The burning bacon jerked her away from her fantasy.

"Dang!" Lina set the skillet in the sink and opened the window above it.

She waved the smoke out of the room with a dishtowel as her dad entered the kitchen with a cheery, "Good morning, pumpkin. Trying to burn the house down, or is this another science experiment?"

"Hilarious." She lifted a cheek to receive his kiss. "No, just distracted." Picking through the greasy disaster with a pair of tongs, she raised a slice for his inspection. "A few pieces are not totally ruined. Do you have time for breakfast?"

"If you've got the food, I've got the time. Load me up." He set his briefcase on the kitchen island and held out a plate for her to pile high with pancakes and partially edible bacon.

Her dad always had a smile for her. But Xander Grant, the overprotective father, expected everyone else to earn his good humor, and the price for that favor was steep.

Still a young man, his generous head of hair was speckled with premature gray. The ordeal of the last decade had left him with crow's feet and had burned the twinkle from his eyes. He straightened the knot in his tie and sat down at the table. "So, what do you have planned for today?"

With an eager smile, Lina took a seat beside him with her own stack of pancakes. "I spoke with Mrs. Paul at the library. They don't really need another page right now, but she said I was welcome to come putter around."

"Does the puttering earn a paycheck?"

"Yes, Dad." She flooded her plate with maple syrup. "Just not very much, and I'm not sure how many hours I'll get. I'm still on the lookout for something else."

"Well, I'm glad you have work to do. Somewhere to go," he said over a steaming cup of coffee.

A long summer lay ahead, and Lina looked forward to the break from her nursing studies at Washburn University. While she loved the independence of her apartment in Topeka, she couldn't help feeling obliged to spend the summer at home with her dad. That also meant a return to his rules, which were designed for a much younger daughter. No amount of persuasion could convince him otherwise, and who could blame him for his caution?

Ever since Ruby had disappeared nine years ago and their mom had died shortly after, Dad had held on to Lina more tightly than was necessary. She didn't mind, not really. They only had each other left, and a curfew was a small price to pay for peace of mind.

"Well, I'm off to the bank." Her dad wiped his mouth with a napkin and rose from the table. "Thank you for breakfast." He grabbed his briefcase and keys and walked to the front door. "Have a great day, pumpkin. I love you, and I'm really glad you're home."

Lina followed him out to the front porch. She stood in the morning light and waved until he was out of sight. Despite the chirping birds and the possibilities of a new day, a heaviness built up in the pit of her stomach. She crossed her arms over her abdomen and pressed hard to keep it from growing too big to manage.

Her dad had taken a step down in his career to move her to a safer town, and now she didn't even live in Harton full time. He used to be a hot-shot financial advisor in Kansas City. He still worked remotely with a few clients, but here in Harton, he spent his time as a loan officer at the local bank. His talents were underutilized, but he never complained.

Lina shrugged free of the guilt of her dad's choices as best she could and went to her bathroom to get ready for the day. Under the neglect of study and finals, her hair was longer than she was used to and showed signs of damage.

In an effort to conceal the split ends, she gathered it into a braid and let it drape forward over one shoulder.

As she primped, a few snapshots tucked into the edge of the mirror frame caught her glance. Pictures of Mom and Ruby were always present. The lineup of boys' photos rotated too frequently.

Three photos of boys smiled at her today—two she'd put up when she was home for Christmas and the third she'd added during spring break. A soft smile crossed Lina's face as she looked at the first two pictures. Dating was exciting when it started out, and she always hoped she'd found The One, but nothing ever lasted.

The first photo showed her at a basketball game with a blond named Todd. He had friend-zoned her right from the start. "Just friends" was hard for her to accept, but it wasn't his fault she had imagined a chemistry that wasn't there.

The second photo was of her and a pre-med student, Brandon, on a hiking trail. He had wavered back and forth on what he wanted. She should have moved on from him sooner, but she'd kept hoping things would blossom between them.

And that left Gary. She plucked the picture of him off the mirror and, in a sudden flare of irritation, tore it in half. He didn't deserve any fondly remembered moments. Not after she'd confessed her feelings for him and suddenly his idea of a fun date had become a parked car. As quickly as her anger had surfaced, it ran its course and fizzled out, an emotion management technique she'd learned from Dr. Bowman. Looking back, she had more imagined the feelings than really falling for him.

All three photos fluttered into the trash. Lina looked at the forlorn pile of crushed possibilities with a heavy sigh.

Someday, a guy would want her as much as she wanted him. He wouldn't lead her on, or keep her at arm's length, or try to score on the first date. Someday.

"Someday isn't so far off." In the quiet of the bathroom, she ignored the lonely echo of her words.

In the meantime, the library was her happy place, crammed full of stories about true love and happily ever after. By the time she had pedaled her bicycle across town, she could barely contain herself. She had worked for Mrs. Paul the past two summers, but her excitement wasn't about her boss, or even the work. Lina was excited to read. A boring job at a library that didn't need the help meant that she could keep a book under the counter and read bits throughout the day. There wasn't much time for pleasure reading in a college student's life, at least not in hers. While not a bookworm exactly, Lina couldn't help losing herself in a heated romance.

She bounced in her skinny jeans and Converse All Stars and twisted her hands together as Mrs. Paul gave her a name tag. Her fingers itched to get into the pages of something juicy. Hopefully she was old enough now that Mrs. Paul wouldn't raise an eyebrow at her reading choices.

Lina arranged her reshelving task to take her to the romance section where she searched for new titles as she worked. The welcome feel of a book in her hands and the smell of ink and paper as she thumbed through the pages sparked her imagination. With each book she placed on the shelf, she told herself a story that it might contain.

A thick volume had a traitorous stepsister. The thin one was about a cheating husband. It was a short book because the wife shot him before much else happened. Guessing was more fun than reading the summaries.

She rounded a corner and heard a familiar voice.

"Woo wee! This one here is spicy! I ain't never read spicier; should be in an adult only section."

"Good morning, Miss Fayla," Lina said.

Fayla O'Dell was a fixture at the library. She came in nearly every day and always sat in the same chair. Her silver hair formed a prim bun at her nape, but her taste for amorous reading material was far from prim. Her worn, knee-high stockings sagged to her ankles and made her look as though she'd dressed in a hurry after a passionate rendezvous.

"Which book are you talking about?" Lina laid an arm around Fayla's shoulders in a brief side hug.

"Never you mind, honey. You just stick to those nursing books and let me deal with this." Fayla tucked the book out of Lina's view under her handbag.

Lina laughed. "How will I know which title to avoid if you don't warn me?" She and Fayla were kindred spirits in their mutual attachment to romances. This game they played was one of her favorite things about the library.

"I'm gonna help you." She poked her index finger in Lina's direction. "I'm gonna check out this book myself to save you from your own curiosity."

"How very selfless." Lina offered her arm for support as the older woman heaved herself up from the chair and waddled to the circulation desk. She took her place behind the counter and scanned the book. "There you go. Will I be seeing you tomorrow?"

"Most likely."

When Fayla reached the exit, she turned as though she had forgotten something. "Glad you're back in town, honey," she called across the lobby. "Your dad ain't the same when you're away."

Lina waved with a tight smile. The lightness in her heart dropped to her belly where it formed a tight lump.

It stayed with her all morning as she put away books and dusted the tops of the bookcases. At last, she gave up trying to push Fayla's comment from her mind. With a deep breath, she pulled out her phone to make an appointment with her therapist.

CHAPTER 3

Lina

LATER, after Lina finished reshelving, she sat on a stool behind the counter and chewed on a fingernail. With her nose in a book, her mind was in a carriage with a handsome scoundrel of a duke. She turned the page and her breath hitched, a flush creeping into her cheeks. Her eyes widened at the duke's brazen advances; she skimmed the page faster to find the juicy part.

"Ahem."

Lina dropped the book to the floor and nearly tumbled from her seat. She pressed a hand to her chest to calm her racing heart.

"Sorry, ma'am, I didn't mean to startle you."

It was the broad-shouldered duke, or darn near close to how Lina had imagined him. A young man stood before her with fervent brown eyes fringed by thick lashes and a dimple that flashed only for a moment before he became serious once more. In that moment, a glimmer of happiness was born, lived, and died on his youthful face.

Heads up, heartstrings! He has a dimple.

The duke ran a nervous hand through his toffee-brown hair, smoothing it into place, and cleared his throat again.

Lina had seen that dimple before. In fact, there was something familiar about the whole man. A quick check of the book cover where it rested on the floor assured her that he was not the duke.

"No, you didn't startle me. How can I help you?" Lina asked.

"You always throw books when you're not startled?" There was the dimple again.

She climbed off the stool, bent to pick up the book, and laid it aside. He glanced at it, so she turned it over to hide the image of the bare-chested duke on the cover. Her cheeks burned with a flustered blush that he'd caught her with such provocative reading material. "It seems that I do," she said with a warm smile. "Don't I know you? You went to Harton East High, right?"

"Yeah, I'm sorry, I don't recognize you."

"I went to West High. I remember you from the football games. What's your name?"

"Cody."

"I'm Lina." She extended her hand. Callouses brushed against her soft skin as his warm grip enveloped her fingers. Her heart skipped a beat in a way that could not come from reading about a scandalous duke. Tearing her attention away from his dimple and her hand away from his, she swallowed and asked, "How can I help you, Cody?"

He set a copy of *Romeo and Juliet* on the counter. "I have questions about this."

Lina scanned the bar code. "It's checked out to Rosie Schafer."

"My mom."

"There is a late fee of thirty-eight dollars."

Cody slid the book back to his side of the counter. "How much if it's a lost book?"

"Thirty-eight dollars. The late fee caps off when it equals the cost to replace it."

His downward gaze was intent on the book. He released a heavy sigh and began to drum lightly with two fingers on the worn cover.

"Do you need a minute alone to say goodbye?" Lina teased, but her joke went unnoticed.

"Can you tell me who else has checked out this book?" he asked.

"Our database should have that information, but there's a privacy issue. Why do you want it?"

"Someone wrote in it."

"Are you sure it wasn't you?" She squinted at him, hoping to coax that adorable dimple out of hiding.

He gave no sign of understanding her humor.

She cleared her throat. "Sorry, that was a joke. Did the damage ruin your reading experience?"

Cody shook his head.

"Is it inappropriate, or vulgar, or ..."

His head shook more slowly.

"You'd better let me have a look." Lina wiggled the book out from under his fingers. She remembered this book, but it couldn't possibly be the same copy. She thumbed through the pages looking for damage, her heart sinking as page after page was clean. Lina jumped ahead to the inside of the back cover. And there it was, the alternate ending she'd written during a meltdown in her therapist's office.

Her breath caught in her throat. The sister-shaped hole that usually oozed now gushed with a tidal wave of heartache. With weak knees, she braced her hands on the countertop and the writing went blurry to her eyes.

"Ma'am?" He waited.

Lina blinked hard, swallowed the lump in her throat, and entered a code on the keyboard. "I'm waiving the fee." Her voice was strained. She barely pushed the words out. "You're clear. Please come again."

Cody picked up the book again. "I need to check it out again."

She reached over the counter for the book, but Cody held it tight.

"Do you even have a library card?" she asked through clenched teeth.

"Yes, ma'am. I do."

Neither released their grip on the book suspended in the air between them.

"We have other copies of *Romeo and Juliet* available. This one is damaged." Lina's voice raised in pitch.

"I'll pay the thirty-eight dollars, but I need this one."

Lina glared at him with determination and pulled on the book with both hands. She had already lost too much —there was no way she would give up this particular battle.

Cody surrendered, slowly easing his hold on the book. She was quick to set it out of his reach on a cart behind the counter.

"Please, just tell me who had it before my mom?" he asked.

"That's private." With arms folded across her chest and a challenge in her glare, she concluded their business, duke or not.

His eyebrows knit together as he searched her face.

Eventually, he yielded. "Sorry for the trouble. Have a nice day." He turned to walk away.

As soon as he was out of sight, Lina snatched the book up again and opened the back cover. She blinked rapidly, pressing a hand to her heart to keep it from leaping through her ribs. The words appeared foreign to her; she only remembered the gist of what she had written so long ago. She had come a long way since then, but deep inside, under layers of positive self-talk, she was still the same scared, lonely girl.

Mrs. Paul chose that moment to join Lina at the front counter.

"You and that boy seemed to have a bit of excitement."

"It was nothing." Lina put her back to Mrs. Paul and pretended to sort through a stack of books.

"Nonsense. It looked like it started off well, at least."

"Yeah, but it doesn't matter."

"I can't have you getting into tugs-of-war with library patrons. Your shift is almost over anyway. Go find him and apologize. Hurry—you might be able to catch him before he drives off."

Without thought or argument, Lina hid *Romeo and Juliet* under the counter. She hurried to the exit and ran out into the parking lot.

CHAPTER 4

Cody

CODY SAT on a bench outside the library entrance, unable to bring himself to go back to the ranch just yet. He propped his elbows on his knees and lowered his head to his hands. He had only thought about finding A.G., not the possibility of losing the book. What if he needed it again? He should have paid the thirty-eight dollars without mentioning the writing in the back. And he hadn't even been able to find out who wrote the ending that had saved his life so many times. The loss weighed his shoulders down into a pathetic slump.

Lina. That was her name. She sure had rattled him. He hadn't been prepared to be disarmed by such a beauty at the library. When he first saw her eyes, they'd been a deep, intense blue, but when he challenged her for the book, they had flashed violet sparks. The piercing jabs from their daggers still stung. He almost wished for another book to return, if only to see her face and let her rattle him again.

Cody didn't remember ever seeing her before. He had never mingled much with the kids across town, or even with the kids at his own school; only the football team, and not even all of those guys. No, he had never met her before. A guy wouldn't have forgotten eyes like those.

The library door slammed shut and Lina ran past him into the center of the parking lot, her long dark braid bouncing against her shoulder. Perfume lingered in the space she passed through, and Cody, from his seat on the bench, inhaled deeply to catch the delicate scent of open meadows and sunshine.

She stopped between the rows of parking spaces and turned a full circle with her hand up to her brow to block the sun. Then she dropped her hand and let her shoulders fall as she dragged herself back toward the library.

Cody stood when she came near. He shoved his hands into his pockets and hoped she couldn't tell that he was just thinking about her.

She spotted him with a visible sigh. Out of breath, her cheeks were pink, probably from her hurried search. But he preferred to believe she was just as affected by him as he was by her. He weakened in the kryptonite of her pink lips when she smiled at him.

"I'm sorry about what happened … in there." She brushed a few stray hairs off her face. "I need to …" She lowered her head and looked at her hands, clasped and twisting at her waist.

Cody could help her. He could say something to put her at ease, but this was too adorable.

She found some words: "Would you like to have coffee with me? There's a café around the corner." She smiled again.

Kryptonite.

"I'm trying to apologize …?" Her eyebrows lifted as she asked again.

"Yes, ma'am."

They walked together along the sidewalk in the bright sunshine. Cody broke a sweat that could not be blamed on ranching nor the heat of the day, but on the presence of Lina at his side. The sun couldn't take the blame for the riot of butterflies that swarmed in his belly, either.

"You know, you don't have to call me ma'am," she said.

But that was the one thing he knew he could say without getting tongue-tied. He was out of practice when it came to girls. Tessa, his high school girlfriend, had been easy to talk to, but that had been ages ago. Now that he and Lina weren't in the library anymore, they might not have much to say.

"Yes, ma'am, I do," he said. "It would disappoint my mom if I didn't. She's whooped my hide for less."

Her laughter filled the air. He smiled to himself and stood a little taller. If he could keep her laughing, maybe he could manage coffee without her realizing he was as awkward as a three-legged horse around her.

The coffee shop was busy, but they found an empty bistro table outside on the sidewalk where they could talk. Lina got right to the point before he even took the first sip of his iced coffee. "Why did you have *Romeo and Juliet* so long? And why is it such a big deal to you?"

The alternate ending had played an important role in his life. In living. Now here she was, a stranger to him and his problems, asking why. Cody took a deep breath and chose to disclose things he had never spoken about to anyone.

"The new ending. It's gotten me through some pretty dark times. I had thought about … about … well …" Cody cleared his throat and looked around before settling his focus on his clear, plastic cup. "Every tough day, the new ending convinced me to keep going. I wanted to find whoever wrote it, so I could thank them. Or something …"

His gaze darted upward in time to see her blink away the moisture glistening in her eyes. Cody ran his hand through his hair. He didn't want her to feel sorry for him. He shouldn't have said anything, but he couldn't take it back now. "Never mind. It's not important anymore."

"You know it was written by a thirteen-year-old?" Lina asked, her voice soft and defeated, having lost the challenge that began their conversation.

"You know it?" he asked.

"I wrote it."

Cody leaned back and studied her. The wrought iron of his chair, warm from the sun, pressed its swirls into his skin. She wasn't very old—younger than him, if he were to have guessed. In the lull of the conversation, he imagined a girl like her being in enough pain to rewrite *Romeo and Juliet*.

"You?" His voice was so rough and throaty, he could barely croak out the word. He swallowed down his surprise and rubbed at the stubble on his chin. "But your name is Lina," Cody murmured and pointed to her library name tag. Of course she knew her own name, idiot.

"Adeline Grant. I go by Lina now, but I was called Adeline until a few years ago. I'm A.G." She stopped talking to sip from her straw. Shifting in her seat, she glanced around the patio. What was she looking for? Eavesdroppers or a quick exit?

"I'm sorry that I was so rude back in the library. I, um …" She fiddled with her straw wrapper as two teenagers rolled past on their skateboards, their wheels bumping out the rhythm of the seams in the pavement. One of the boys waved to Lina. She didn't pay him much attention, only fixated on the wrapper.

"You were thirteen?" Cody had not expected someone so young could have written the heartfelt appeal in the new ending, the desperate plea for patience.

Lina nodded into her coffee.

"*Why* did you write it?" Cody stood on the edge of a precipice, as though everything hung on her answer.

"It was a therapy exercise," she said. "My mom took her own life. At the time, I thought if she had waited three days, maybe she wouldn't have."

Cody looked down at his hands. "I'm sorry. The book is yours. I had no right to ask for it."

"I'm sorry too." She clasped and unclasped her hands. When she finally rested them on the table, they trembled. "The alternate ending helped you?"

"Yeah, many times." He tried not to look at her shaking hands. "When things felt too hard and I didn't know how much more I could take, I read the alternate ending and knew I could take at least three more days." Cody resisted the urge to take one of her hands in his. He could hold her hand and keep it safe until the trembling subsided, maybe even longer. "I know things were hard for you too because I could feel your pain whenever I read it. But something else too: a possibility. I couldn't let go of the 'what if?' I mean, how do you turn 'what if?' into something real?"

Cody lifted his gaze to meet hers and found a reflection of his loss in the stormy depths. Here sat a girl who might really understand him. It was a vulnerable connection, a link to another person that was so revealing and intimate. He blinked first.

"Do you mind me asking what difference three days would have made for your mom?" he asked.

"My sister is missing." Lina shifted in her chair again. "She disappeared on her way home from school. After nearly a year of searching, the police found a body. My mom went ballistic. She took pills that weekend. She couldn't bear the thought of living in a world where Ruby was truly gone." She sipped her coffee again, her gaze darting to a pair of sparrows hopping about the ground at their feet, pecking the pavement for crumbs.

He searched for the right words, knowing from experience people didn't often say helpful things when faced with sorrow. He kept it simple. "I'm sorry, Lina." He hung his head. He could never compare his pain to hers. His dad hadn't made the choice to leave him and his mom.

"By Monday they had confirmed the identity. It wasn't Ruby. There is a chance she's still out there somewhere. But the tiny hope we hold onto came too late to keep my mom from making things worse."

"And your sister …?"

"We won't stop looking for her." She glanced from her coffee to the people sitting at other tables, to Cody, and then up to the sky where she squinted against the sunshine.

He should have taken her hand when the impulse had struck him. The beautiful girl across from him was clearly uncomfortable. His mother had taught him about making polite conversation to put people at ease. It was no longer a burden; every detail about Lina fascinated him.

"Is she older than you or younger?" he asked.

"She's older by eleven months, so we're Irish twins. We were always very close. Best friends."

His brow furrowed. "What are Irish twins?"

"Siblings born less than a year apart." From her kryptonite smile, he was on the right track in distracting her from her heartache.

"I bet you two were a handful." Cody smiled with her, picturing two little girls running around causing trouble for their parents.

"Yeah, we are named for our grandmothers." Her expression became thoughtful, on the verge of sad.

"Do you have a picture?"

She opened her phone and as she scrolled to a photo, the heaviness behind her eyes lifted. She passed her phone to him. The case was worn and had a sticker of a flower peeling at the edges. He held it at an angle to reduce the glare. Two little girls with dark hair and eyes of the deepest blue sat in a wheelbarrow full of water, wearing swimsuits.

"It was our swimming pool."

"That's real nice." Cody said. "Is this one you?" He pointed to one of the little girls and she nodded.

He divided his attention between the photo and the sparkle that entered Lina's eyes as she spoke about Ruby. She laughed and gestured with her hands to punctuate her stories. He folded his arms on the table and leaned in. The three-legged horse faded away as he relaxed into Lina's charm.

The sun shone brightly on Lina's side of the table. She had been squinting for a while, and her cheeks and forehead were turning pink.

"Trade places with me," Cody said. "So your back will be to the sun."

"But then you'll have the sun in your eyes," Lina argued. "We can sit together."

Cody moved her chair and they sat side by side. She was close enough that he could have laid his arm across the back of her chair if he'd known her better. What was her favorite color? What music did she listen to? Did she have a dream for the future? What would her perfect, pink lips taste like? Learning more about her became the best idea he'd ever had.

"What have you been doing since high school?" he asked.

"I go to Washburn University in Topeka. Do you know it?"

"Yeah, I got accepted there."

"Well, are you home for the summer too?" she asked.

"No, I didn't end up going." He turned his near-empty cup, watching the melting ice swirl with traces of watered-down coffee.

Lina waited for him to elaborate.

"My dad died. Plans changed."

She grabbed his forearm with both hands. "Cody …"

It took all of his control to sit still with her touch on his arm. His muscles flexed and clenched with electricity. Awareness of her hands on him flooded every part of his mind and body. Instinct told him to bring her onto his lap and bury his face in the curve of her neck. He was scared to act on it, and it would likely scare her too. This was exactly why he needed to call her ma'am.

"Please don't …" He was almost too breathless to say even that. Don't feel sorry for him.

She didn't persist in questioning him about it but let go of his arm and shook the ice in her cup before giving the straw one last slurp.

"Do you want to come with me to The Bad Bronco?" Lina changed the subject without warning.

"What's The Bad Bronco?"

"It's a cowboy bar about forty-five minutes from here, near Copper Creek on the way to Topeka."

Cody hadn't dated anyone since Tessa, and if that weren't reason enough to hesitate, this was the first time he'd been invited to a bar. He wasn't twenty-one yet, and neither was she, but she leaned forward, grinning from ear to ear.

"It'll be fun," she said. "We can go either Wednesday or Thursday—those are the nights they are open for eighteen and up. We can sing karaoke and line dance. And I want to see you ride the bull!"

"Ride the bull?" He laughed. How could he say no? It would've been easier to bust a wild bronco than to disappoint those oceans she had for eyeballs.

"Where's your phone?" Lina held out her hand. Better to not swim upstream against her whim; he didn't even want to. Cody pulled it from his pocket. She called herself from his phone and let it ring before she disconnected. Her ringtone was a Sam Hunt song that he had heard before but couldn't remember the name. "Now we have each other's numbers."

Cody checked the time before tucking his phone back into his pocket. He needed to get back soon.

"Can I ask you something?" he asked, toying with his empty cup.

"Sure." Lina pulled up a knee so that she sat sideways in her chair to face him. She blinked and waited.

Cody couldn't speak while he drowned in her oceans. He had to look away but lowering his focus to her lips gave him another image that stole his words. He settled on the empty cup in his hand.

"With everything you've been through, how are you so hopeful?" he asked. "I mean, you talk about Ruby as though you are certain she's still around somewhere, and you're cheerful and … happy."

She tilted her head while she thought about her answer.

"Hmm. As for Ruby, there's no other option. And as for the rest …" Lina shrugged. "It's been nine years since I've seen my sister, and eight since my mom died, but I've learned how to live more happily. The people who say 'time heals' are full of crap. Time hasn't fixed anything. I didn't start to feel more cheerful"—she used air quotes around the word he'd chosen—"until my second year of therapy. That's what heals …" She finally looked away. "… in my opinion."

"Therapy," Cody repeated after her. "What's the most useful thing you learned in therapy?"

"The future is better than the past. It's kind of something I adopted as a mantra. I actually have a couple of those."

"What does it mean? The future is better than the past," he said, trying the words out on his tongue.

"To me, it means that I will live tomorrow better than yesterday. I know I can't control everything, but if I don't hope that tomorrow is better, I'll stay stuck in the misery."

Cody leaned back in his chair. He pressed the heels of his hands over his eyes while he let her wisdom soak in. He was stuck in misery, but her trick wouldn't work for him because he could not escape a tomorrow that was already laid out. His tomorrow was going to be exactly the same as his today and his yesterdays. He finally sat up to find that she'd been watching him sort out his thoughts.

"Thank you for telling me all of that. I mean it," he said. "But I need to be going. It's taken me a *really* long time to return a library book." They both chuckled at his double meaning and once again, Cody stood a little taller for having amused her. "Can I walk you back to the library?"

"Sure." She rose from the chair and they began to make their way back.

They walked slowly, like a lazy Sunday stroll during which neither of them wanted the moment to end.

Cody measured her up next to him. He was taller than average at a hair over six feet, and the top of her head might just reach his nose. He walked a little closer to her than was necessary, and when her arm accidentally brushed against his elbow, he once more fought the desire to take her hand.

"Thank you for the coffee," she said when they arrived back at the library.

Cody didn't want to say goodbye. Meeting A.G. hadn't carried the satisfaction he'd thought it would in regard to the alternate ending, but the author had intrigued him in an entirely different way, and that could be enough.

"It was really nice to meet you, Lina."

"You too. I'm looking forward to The Bad Bronco with you." Lina backed in through the door and looked at him as she entered the library, then she smiled and waved until the door swung shut between them.

A whistle escaped under Cody's breath. The book was gone, but he had a new friend. A fair trade.

CHAPTER 5

Cody

ALONG THE THIRTY-MILE drive from Harton to the ranch, Cody played a dangerous game. He imagined what his life would have been like right now if his dad were still here. His mom would be well. He might have been home from college for the summer, like Lina. He wouldn't have been needed so heavily around the ranch, so he would have been free to take a girl swimming at the lake, horseback riding, or to get a burger in town. He could have planned to stay out late at The Bad Bronco without worrying about an early morning tending animals.

Clouds that had been high in the sky earlier now rolled in low for an evening shower. Fat drops landed on the windshield, just a few, then more. The wiper blades smeared the dust until more rain fell to wash it away. Cody drove faster. Mom could get agitated when it rained. At least there was no thunder.

At the ranch, Cody hopped out of the truck to get a stack of bills from the mailbox before continuing to the house. Mrs. Bauer's Jeep was still parked out front. He had been gone longer than he'd planned. No doubt his mom's friend would be wondering what had kept him.

He entered the home he'd lived in his entire life. His parents had moved here before he had even been born, but they'd updated nothing indoors. Built in the nineteen-eighties, the kitchen still wore country geese wallpaper and builder-grade oak cabinets.

At a small table in the entryway, he slapped the mail down to join several other bills waiting to be paid. Cody came into the main living space, an open floor plan with the kitchen at the near end, separated from the family room by the dining table.

A mouthwatering aroma came from the kitchen. His stomach growled. Breakfast was a long time ago and lunch had only been the iced coffee.

His mom sat in her rocking chair at the family room window. A lime-green scrunchie held her cinnamon brown hair in a ponytail, and she smelled of shampoo. He knelt next to her and took her slim hand. She was serene, in spite of the rain.

"Mom?"

She kept her gaze out the window but stroked Cody's hair off his forehead. "Wash your hands, little Cody. Dad will be in for dinner soon."

He hung his head and sighed. "Okay, Mom."

He went into the kitchen and scrubbed his hands. The towel bar nearby was bare, and the drawer was empty too.

Mrs. Bauer emerged from the hallway that led to the laundry room carrying a large basket of towels. Her gray hair was cut short, and freckles peppered her face from a lifetime in the sun. She was getting on in years but still had the energy of her more youthful days.

Cody chose a towel and dried his hands. "How'd things go today?"

"Fine. Just fine. I got her showered and fed her a sandwich for lunch. She's been calm today, just sitting in her rocker."

Mrs. Bauer came over a few times a week to help with his mom. The two ladies had been best friends for years, and when his dad died, Mrs. Bauer had taken it upon herself to help care for them both. She always cooked dinner when she came and made sure there was enough for leftovers.

Cody rubbed Skippy, the house dog, on the head, and poured kibble into the mutt's bowl.

"How was your errand in town?" Mrs. Bauer asked. "You were gone a good while."

"I met a girl." Cody turned away so Mrs. Bauer couldn't see him smile or turn red.

It didn't do any good. She came around him to look for herself. She put a hand on each of his cheeks. Cody could not restrain the grin any longer, letting it grow from ear to ear under her inspection.

"A girl …?"

"Yes, ma'am."

Mrs. Bauer leaned against the kitchen counter and waited for more details. "Tell me about her," she said.

"Her name is Lina. I met her at the library, and we went for coffee."

"What is she like?"

His cheeks ached from smiling. "She's got blue eyes."

"Blue eyes. Well now … Are you gonna call her?"

"Maybe. I don't know."

"Well, keep me posted, hon. I'm happy to come sit with Rosie if you need me to." She lifted a casserole dish from the oven and set it on the table before returning to the kitchen and starting the dishwasher.

Cody helped his mother up from her rocking chair and led her to the kitchen table for dinner. She came willingly, her eyelids tired, and thankfully didn't mention his father again as he scooped chicken and creamy noodles onto her plate.

"Well, I'm off." Mrs. Bauer gathered up her handbag. "You enjoy your dinner, Cody, and call me if I can help you out with your new girl." She squeezed Mom's shoulder as she passed by on her way out.

"Yes, ma'am, and thank you." Cody helped himself to the casserole. He was about to take a big bite when his mother spoke.

"Should we wait for Dad?"

"No, Mom. Dad ain't coming tonight. Eat your food."

"Ain't? Please, Cody, use your education."

Cody lifted an eyebrow. "Sorry, he *isn't* coming tonight." Even in the depths of her muddled mind, she was still his mom correcting his grammar.

She picked up a forkful of food and held it in midair. Sometimes Cody had to feed her because she wasn't always interested in food. He might have to do that tonight. He ate quickly. He was too hungry to feed her first.

"What girl?"

Her question caught him off guard. He never knew when his mom was paying attention, but she must have heard him tell Mrs. Bauer about Lina. He lowered his fork and smiled at her.

"The prettiest one."

Mom smiled too and took a bite.

"I'll talk to your father about giving you a day off to go see her."

Cody nodded. Even with how out of touch she was, she was still right. The ranch kept him too busy with work to go out with a girl. Now that he trudged about in his father's oversized shoes, he spent all his time trying to not screw it up. His heart sank and the dark clouds outside were nothing compared to the ones that gathered inside him.

CHAPTER 6
Lina

LINA TUCKED *Romeo and Juliet* between an old journal and her high school yearbook on the bookshelf in her room. She'd thought she would never see it again, but here it was. Six years and thirty-eight dollars later, she finally had the evidence of her meltdown back in her custody.

Six years ago, in Dr. Bowman's office, Lina had lost herself in a rant about the play her English class was studying. While her fellow students swooned over the blossoming romance between Romeo and Juliet, Lina had grown more and more angry over the tragic end. Amid the tears, the shouting, and the clenched fists, Dr. Bowman had encouraged Lina to reimagine the story.

The alternate ending had taken shape that very afternoon as Lina scribbled out a new possibility inside the back cover. Dr. Bowman had guided Lina in creating a future for Romeo and Juliet that was now filled with hope, if not happiness. Even all these years later, Lina still would say that hope was more important than outright happiness. She probably should have said that part to Cody earlier.

The book looked at home on her shelf, as if it had lived there all along. All this time it had been missing, Lina wondered who might have read it, who had been witness to her private thoughts and searing pain. And now, the worry over laying her heart bare to anyone who had read all the way to the last page was over. Only, she couldn't help but wonder if the handsome cowboy who smiled with a dimple needed it more than she did.

She sat cross-legged on the foot of her bed and inhaled deeply and exhaled slowly, over and over, to calm her jumbled thoughts and guilty selfishness. This day had been full of the fluttering of a new crush mixed with the sorrow of loss. Though it wasn't easy, she suppressed the fluttering, as she'd been taught by Dr. Bowman. No sense in rushing into anything, not with her history of diving in headfirst with guys.

Even so, Cody competed for headspace with all the memories of Ruby that had been brought to the surface. Well, they hadn't just resurfaced, they had been dredged up on purpose. Lina didn't mind talking about Ruby, but she didn't do it very often. People became uncomfortable when she mentioned her sister, and when she was just getting to know someone, Lina never brought her up.

Things had been different today. Cody had asked questions and kept her talking. When she'd been ready for a new topic, he had only dug deeper instead of moving on. Lina reviewed every detail of their conversation, especially things he'd shared about himself. There hadn't been much, just that his dad had died, and the alternate ending had helped him through hard days.

She had been moved to put her arms around him when he told her about his dad, had wanted to hold him close and assure him that he wasn't alone anymore. But she barely knew him, and what promises would that gesture have implied? She hated when guys did that to her. She would not be the girl who did it to him.

Cody was exactly the kind of guy she fell for overnight without really knowing. Well, when they went to The Bad Bronco, she would fix that. She would ask questions until she knew every little thing about him. But, as Dr. Bowman would say, more important than knowing his details was giving him a chance to figure out if *she* was *his* type. She just couldn't survive another one-sided flirtation.

She scrolled on her phone to the newly made contact, which she named "Cody the Cowboy Duke," and typed a text message.

I'm glad we met today. Does Wednesday or Thursday work better for you?

She sent it before she could doubt herself.

The front door banged shut. Her dad was home from the bank. Lina found him in the kitchen unpacking a take-out box of salad and a pizza.

"Hey, Dad." She slid under his arm and hugged him around the waist.

"Hi, pumpkin. How was your day?"

She opened the lid and inhaled the aroma of spicy pepperoni. Her stomach rumbled. "Fine. The library is the same. But I ran into somebody from high school, and we got to talking about Ruby."

Dad stopped dressing the salad, the spoons held frozen in the air, and raised his eyebrows.

Unfazed, she began to set the table.

"Are you okay?" he asked.

Lina kept her head down and smiled while she

arranged silverware next to plates. "Yeah, I think I am," she answered with a nod. "And just a heads-up, I'm going to The Bad Bronco this week."

"All right, and a heads-up for you—even though you're technically an adult, I still want to meet the kids you're going with."

Lina had never minded her dad knowing who her friends were. He didn't get to meet the people she hung out with up at school, but he would if he could. She'd be embarrassed, though, if he knew how often she changed romantic interests. It was better that he hadn't met *all* of them.

"Okay, Daddy," Lina teased him with her sweet, innocent voice as they sat down to dinner.

"So, who's the friend you saw today? Do I know them?"

"His name is Cody. He actually went to Harton East, played football. Mrs. Paul told me to take off early—they barely have enough for me to do—and Dad, we talked for hours. Well, may be only two. But he was really interested in me … like, as a person."

"That sounds about right," he said around a mouthful of pizza. "You are a very interesting person."

"Yeah, but hardly anyone wants to know about Ruby and that part. They only care about Today Me, if they care at all. It was nice to have someone interested in where Today Me came from."

He sat back and searched her face, prompting a blush to rise in Lina's cheeks. "So you two hit it off and you're going out?"

"Yeah. He's kind of reserved though, so when you meet him, try to be more friendly …?"

"I'm friendly," Dad defended himself as he took a bite.

"Less of an interrogation then, please." She had been an hour late to prom because of his intimidation ritual, and that hadn't been the first time her date had been scared silly.

He chewed his food and directed a mock glare over his pizza slice at his daughter. "Anything else happen today? How's Fayla?"

"She's the same. She protected me from a kissing book again."

Her dad raised his water glass in the air. "To Fayla," he toasted and then took a sip.

Lina groaned and rolled her eyes. "Oh, brother." She toyed with her fork and twirled a bit of lettuce around on her plate. "I'm going to see Dr. Bowman on Friday."

"Talking about Ruby was that hard?"

"No, I made the appointment before that." Lina snuck a glimpse at her father. "Have you been doing okay, Dad? When I'm away at school, are you okay?"

He wiped his mouth with a napkin and reached across the table to take Lina's hand.

"I miss you when you're not here, but I want you at school. And I already know what Dr. Bowman would say: *Get a hobby.* Now, finish up. There are a few episodes of *Family Feud* on the DVR." He cleared his place and set the dishes in the sink. "Do you want popcorn?"

"You have to ask?" Lina stuffed the last of her pizza into her mouth.

After clearing the table, she reclined on the couch and waited for her dad to change out of his suit before watching their favorite game show. Her phone had been so quiet. She made sure the ringer was turned on, then checked to see if she had missed any messages. Only one mattered; there was no word from Cody. She could not message him again. In her experience, appearing too eager was a fast track into the friend zone. She'd already taken a risk by texting him first. She set her phone aside with a huff. Maybe she had already blown it with him.

CHAPTER 7

Cody

CODY LEFT the chicken coop in the dim morning light with ten eggs in an old bucket. His mother had always used a basket to collect eggs, but he felt silly carrying her dainty egg basket around, so he used an old utility bucket from the laundry room. It shouldn't matter—no one ever saw him bring in the eggs. *Does Lina like eggs?* Never mind that. What Lina liked was none of his concern. He waded through the tall grass back to the house, morning dew wetting the hems of his jeans.

He was almost to the house when Spence, one of his two ranch hands, arrived and waved from his truck as he drove around to the garage. Cody needed to hurry. The day's work would begin soon.

In the kitchen, he cracked the eggs into a bowl, whisked them with salt and pepper, and put a pan on a burner to heat. He was not a great cook, but Cody could manage eggs. *How did Lina like them cooked?* He shook his head free of the thought and was about to pour them into the pan when a shrill scream came from his mother's room. He turned off the flame and careened down the hallway.

Mom stood in her nightgown at her bedroom window, her forehead and the palms of her hands pressed against the glass. Her breath fogged the dawning view of open fields of grass.

"I don't see him. Do you see him?"

The panic in her voice sent chills through him. He didn't try to answer her. In this state, she wouldn't listen to him or acknowledge anything but her fears. Cody laid a robe over her shoulders and guided her arms through the sleeves one at a time.

"Do you see him? Do you see him?" She would stand there repeating herself all day if nothing broke her rhythm. She needed her medicine.

He left her there reciting her worries and returned to the kitchen to crush a pill into some applesauce. If she knew about the pill, she would fight him harder. It was easier to sneak it in.

Then he turned on his mom's Carrie Underwood playlist and went to get her from her room. The familiarity of the music sometimes helped settle her down when the hysterics crept in.

She was still at the window. "I don't see him. I don't see him."

He took her elbow to guide her away from the glass, but she lashed out at him. She shook her head and swatted him away. "Do you see him?" she wailed.

He whispered the lie, "I saw him outside," because saying it aloud felt more wrong. It was enough to get her attention. "Come eat breakfast. He wants you to be healthy."

Her gaze stayed locked on the window until she

couldn't see it anymore as Cody led her from the room and sat her at the table.

"Eat the apples, Mom, then I'll cook your eggs." The sooner the meds started working, the better. This morning's behavior was fairly typical. She wasn't always this panicked, but sometimes she was much worse. Something about waking up in a world where her husband was gone brought all the pain back like it was yesterday. She remained still, her face drawn into a frown.

Cody brought a spoonful of applesauce to her mouth and placed a hand on her cheek. She finally looked at him and opened her mouth. He was able to get it all down her, then he returned to the eggs.

His mom's warm brown eyes followed his movements with growing interest. As he set her plate in front of her, she became aware that it was mealtime and began to feed herself.

He gobbled up his own breakfast. There was a lot of work ahead of him, as always, and he needed to get started as soon as his mom was settled.

He guided her to the bathroom and waited outside until he heard the flush. Cracking open the door, he saw she was washing her hands on her own—a good sign. He put toothpaste on her toothbrush and handed it to her. She brushed in a daze.

Finally, he eased her into her rocking chair in the family room. Cody brushed her hair, working through the tangles gently so as not to upset her right when he needed to leave her alone for a while.

"Mom, do you need anything before I go do the chores?" Chores were something she still understood.

Her only response was to hum along to the music as

she rocked back and forth. That was the best he could hope for.

"Skippy! Come." The little dog jumped up to sit in her lap. "I'll see you at lunchtime. Love you," he said. He didn't expect she would ever say it back again.

Tay, the second hired hand, was at the garage with Spence and Wayne by the time he got there. While Cody had been getting his mom settled, the three men had discussed the work that needed to be done and had divided the tasks among them all. As the last to arrive, Cody was left to the most undesirable job—digging out a blocked irrigation ditch while Tay and Spence doctored a few cows in the near pasture. Wayne would take care of the horses and fill water troughs. Then they would all move cows from the grazed north pasture to the thick, green grass of the south.

The UTV rumbled to life, and Cody started out to where the morning's work waited for him. A few scattered clouds shaded him from the morning sun for the moment, but they didn't protect him from the encroaching heat and the humidity.

A younger Cody would've planned to steal away to Mrs. Bauer's farm for an afternoon plunge in the swimming hole on the far side of her property. Gone were those days. He'd have to settle for dunking his head under the hose beside Mom's neglected garden patch.

He arrived at the place where the blocked ditch caused water to pool up and flood the pasture. It looked like a hard, messy job. A trickle of sweat left his hairline and dripped down his face. He hadn't even started yet, and he already hated the day.

His phone buzzed. He wrestled it from his pocket and saw another message from Lina. A single question mark.

She wanted to know which day they would go to The Bad Bronco. He hadn't responded last night because he hadn't known what to say.

It would've been smarter to tell her some excuse right in that moment at the coffee shop. He worked the night shift, caring for Mom: true. He didn't care for nightlife: could be true—how would he know? He didn't want to spend time with her: lie. Big. Fat. Lie.

Who was he kidding? He couldn't have said anything different if he'd had a week to practice.

Those blue eyes …

He'd been at her mercy and would have agreed to anything. She wasn't looking at him now—perfect time to text her back with his excuses.

Those pink lips …

But how could he possibly cancel over text? Especially when all he wanted to do was spend every minute with her. Not shovel mud on the ranch, not care for a grown woman. His whole situation was upside down and backward.

What Cody wanted to do and what he actually *could* do were different things. The worst thing would be to lead her on, and the more he thought about his life, the more he realized that he was not boyfriend material. He had nothing to offer her. He was nothing but a high school dropout. Lina would go back to college at the end of the summer, and he would still be here trying to keep the ranch from circling the drain. His life was stuck in work from dawn to dusk, and on top of that, he had his mom to care for. There wasn't much left to give.

He tossed his phone onto the seat of the UTV without responding to the question mark. Tearing his t-shirt over his head, he knocked his baseball cap to the ground.

"Damn," he muttered. He piled his t-shirt next to his phone and snatched his cap from the dirt, tugging it low over his forehead. Cody yanked his shovel from the back of the UTV and stabbed it into the muddy blockage. After a dozen scoops of sloppy earth were heaved away, the water began to trickle free and make its way along the ditch. He stopped a moment to watch the trickle gain momentum. What kind of shovel would it take to free him?

"Damn." He wished someone had heard him curse that time—he'd even take Mom and her scolding. Anyone. A witness. He had dreamed for two seconds about cooking eggs for Lina, and that was more than enough for the crash of reality to flatten him. He would never cook eggs for her. He would probably never even see her again.

Every plunge of the shovel into the ground reminded him to just forget about her. It was for the best, right? To never dream at all.

CHAPTER 8

Cody

CODY SCRUBBED at his forehead again with his discarded t-shirt. For all the sweat he wiped off his face, he smeared on twice the dirt. From the heat on his shoulders, his skin was likely burning, and he'd long since guzzled down his water bottle. The curses escaped more frequently. His pace slowed with the sticky, sucking mud.

He'd made it through three-quarters of the blockage when Wayne pulled up in another UTV and joined him.

"Looks good, Cody." Wayne had brought his own shovel, which he hoisted over a shoulder before picking his way through the loose mud.

Cody wasn't in a talkative mood after spending the better part of the morning focusing on mud, on the invention of the shovel, on how much digging it might take to reach liquid-hot magma—on anything but Lina and her dark-as-night braid, Lina and her teasing lips, Lina and her lost nearly-twin sister. Lina, the girl who wouldn't fit into his limited life. The only effective distraction had proved to be the alternate ending. He'd been reciting it over and over again in his head. "Shoulda' kept the damned book."

"What's that?" Wayne asked.

"Nothing."

Wayne didn't deserve his poor temper.

"Almost ready to help move the herd." Cody tossed a shovelful of drippy mud to the side and scooped some more. The water gushed along the ditch where he had already dug it free. It pooled wide over the remaining area.

He moved aside, making room for Wayne. Together they made short work of the task in companionable silence. He dug two shovelfuls for every one of Wayne's. The man was old. How old, Cody wasn't sure, but more and more often, his age showed. He worked faster to lessen the burden on Wayne. Finally, he lifted the last scoop of earth from the watery mess and threw it aside.

"I ran across Mrs. Bauer out by the house," Wayne said. "She brought some apricots from her trees, and she told me about your lady friend."

He hadn't pegged Mrs. Bauer as a busybody. "Don't have a lady friend. Mrs. Bauer is mistaken." Cody rested, standing the shovel on its blade and leaning on it.

"Well now, that's a shame." Wayne wiped the mud from his own shovel on a patch of wet grass. "A man can't have too many friends, but he only needs one that's pretty."

Enough. Cody rammed the shovel into the back of the UTV. "Let's go move the herd."

He drove back to the barn to trade the UTV for Big Red, but on the way, he stopped in at the house to check on his mom. She still sat in her rocker, but now Skippy napped at her feet and she held half of a grilled cheese sandwich. Mrs. Bauer had left more sandwiches on a plate in the kitchen next to a bowl of apricots. Cody's stomach growled as he washed up.

He spread an old magazine open on the mismatched ottoman next to his mom's chair to keep his dirt off the furniture and sat on it to eat a sandwich with her. He needed to get a weight off his chest, but he started with the easier topics. He told her about the irrigation ditch and the need for another ranch hand. She focused out the window, but she stopped rocking. Not even sure she was listening, he told her the harder things.

"Mom, I want something else for my life. Not ranching. I want …" Lina's name teetered on the tip of his tongue, but he'd already tortured himself enough today over her. He dropped his head into his hands as he said the part that made him a monster. "I want you to not need me so much."

She crunched into the crust of her sandwich and resumed rocking. The rhythmic squeak of her chair against the floor grated on his nerves.

"All right then." He squeezed her shoulder before he left, no lighter than when he'd arrived.

Cody gathered the sandwiches in a paper towel and continued on to the corral where Big Red waited. He balanced on the fence rail and ate the rest of his lunch while he more effectively unloaded his burden to the horse.

"You think tomorrow is gonna be better than yesterday, Red?" Big Red nuzzled his hand, looking for a treat.

"Yeah, that's what I thought too. Only thing I'm sure of is that I ain't gonna be reading that book again." *Ain't … won't.*

He finally figured out what to say to Lina, so he drew his phone from his pocket and typed.

I can't go to The Bad Bronco, sorry.

He looked at the words for a long moment, then pressed send. It was over.

CHAPTER 9

Lina

MUSIC BLASTED in the small bathroom where Lina scoured the shower tiles.

She leaned over her phone when an incoming text interrupted the song and read the message. "So that's it?" she said aloud. Her hands were slippery with water and cleanser, so she wiped them on a towel and lowered herself to perch on the edge of the tub. She picked up the phone and turned down the volume of the music before she typed a response.

That's too bad. How about we just go get a pop or something?

Did that sound desperate? She deleted it and tried again.

Bummer. Well, I'll be here all summer so let me know if you change your mind.

No. She was not going to wait around for a guy to decide if he liked her or not. Delete.

I'm sorry too. I think you're totally hot and I would've made it worth your while.

Her mind went wild with what that would be like, and

her face flamed. She couldn't delete it fast enough, but she allowed the images of the two of them in a torrid embrace to flit around in her head while she finished cleaning the bathroom. Eventually, she thought of a more neutral response.

Okay, have a nice day.

Having lost enthusiasm for housework, she wasted the rest of the day binge watching YouTube videos on her laptop.

A FEW DAYS LATER, Lina sat across from Dr. Virginia Bowman, a cold bottle of root beer in her hand. There had been a mini-fridge full of root beer in the office since Lina's very first visit to the therapist. As a kid, it had helped take the sting out of difficult emotions. Maybe she was conditioned, but it helped now as well.

She kicked off her sandals and crossed her feet on a plush ottoman, the soft nap of the charcoal velvet marking the shape of her heel. A new photo sat on the desk. Dr. Bowman had gotten married since Lina had last been here.

"I've been taking responsibility for my dad's feelings again," Lina confessed.

"I'm glad you recognize that. Do you remember what to do about it?" Dr. Bowman asked.

"Yeah, it's just hard. I want to help him adjust to me growing up and moving out."

"That's not your job," Dr. Bowman said. "Focus on things you can control, and he'll do the same. Last time we met, we talked about—"

"You were telling me to not get too excited about guys."

"Right. Gary, was it?"

"Yeah"

"How is that going?"

"It was a disaster." Lina groaned. With her heart resembling a stretched-out and deflated balloon, she closed her eyes and dropped her head back against the couch cushion.

"Want to tell me what happened?"

"Uh, okay, so it went exactly like you said it would. I liked him so much, and I told him so, and things got way out of hand, and … He didn't even like me. Not really."

"I'm sorry to hear that. Would you like to explore that today?"

"No. I'm pretty sure I know where I went wrong. I'm just, I'm just so …"

"Is it the empty space?"

"Yeah. I tried to shove him into the empty space." The empty space had a name. *Ruby*. Knowing that no one could ever take her place didn't stop the primal urge to try, in spite of the inevitable tears. Lina couldn't even count how many boys she'd cried over in this office, and she was about to add another. "And it might be happening again."

Lina had been one of Dr. Bowman's first patients when she set up her practice in Harton. Their relationship was one truly forged by fire. Dr. Bowman had been eager to listen and help; twelve-year-old Lina had only sat there and cried. Weeks of crying eventually led to talking, and finally, Dr. Bowman had been able to teach her some coping tools. Over the years, as Lina became better able to process her family situation and deal with those feelings, their discussions had tipped more toward boys and romantic issues.

Dr. Bowman crossed her legs and smoothed her pencil

skirt over a knee. She tucked her sandy-blonde bob behind her ears while Lina decided what to share.

"I met a guy, and I thought he liked me. We had that vibe, you know? But the very next day, he totally blew me off. I can't stop thinking about it. Him," she corrected. "Thinking about *him*." She took a long pull on the root beer. The carbonation scratched its way down her throat with sharp prickles and gave her something to focus on other than the tenderness of her lifeless, deflated balloon.

"What's different about him?" Dr. Bowman asked.

"Well, for starters, he had *Romeo and Juliet*. My *Romeo and Juliet*!"

"The one you changed the ending to? Goodness, that was a long time ago."

"I know! And he asked me about Ruby, and he let me go on and on," Lina continued.

"So, he had your book. He was kind to you and showed an interest in your sister. Is there a chance you confused courtesy with romantic interest?"

"There's *always* that chance." Her free hand flew up in the air. More than a chance, given her track record. But everything had truly felt real with Cody.

"Lina, what are you in charge of with this guy?"

"My thoughts. I made our conversation mean something more by getting carried away." Whatever the situation, it always came back to the same thing. Lina had already learned this, but it helped to be reminded. "It was just a conversation."

"Right, you cannot *make* him call you, or like you, just as he didn't *make* you think about him romantically. You chose those thoughts all on your own, and your thoughts led your feelings to jump the gun. Slow down and let him show you how he'd like you to feel about him, or not feel, if that's the case."

Dr. Bowman was right. Her thoughts had put her and Cody together in dozens of fascinating ways. No wonder she felt broken up with. It was all her own doing.

"Practice some restraint. Give yourself time to get to know a guy before you call it love. That's how we filter out the ones who aren't into us. I promise you, Lina—when you find the right person, you won't have to force it."

Practice restraint? Practice? She'd been trying that for months now. Granted, she was getting better at it all the time, but still. There was something very wrong with the universe if meeting a guy like Cody had been just like meeting the others—just for practice.

CHAPTER 10
Cody

NOTHING COULD BE WORSE than helplessness. How could Cody make sense of something if he couldn't even see it? Technically he was a man now, capable of voting, joining the military, purchasing a rifle, but not capable of managing his financial situation.

From his seat across the desk, Cody watched the banker's thick dark eyebrows move up and down as they scowled between the computer monitor and himself. Sadness etched around the man's eyes and his pursed lips. After several attempts to convince the banker to let him access the ranch's accounts, Cody leaned back in the chair and crossed his arms over his chest.

"I'm sorry," the banker said. "Your name isn't on the line of credit account or any of the loan documents. I can't speak to you about these details without your mother."

"My mother is sick. I'm just trying to help her out."

"Do you have a power of attorney?"

"No."

"Then if you don't bring her with you, I can't help you." The banker stood and guided Cody out of the office.

It could have been sympathy behind his weary eyes, or plain old frustration. "Bring Mrs. Schafer with her ID, and I'll be happy to answer your questions."

The door closed behind him with a thud, the sound of the final nail in the coffin. He would lose the ranch to debt before the year was out if he didn't get some help. His mom would lose her home, and it was his fault.

Cody climbed into his truck and slammed the door. He'd never had a good visit to the bank, but this was the worst yet. All his questions about the mortgage on the ranch and the line of credit against its equity were still unanswered. It probably wasn't even legal to get a sick person to sign over power of attorney. What a pointless trip into town.

He drove too fast and blasted angry rock, his hand slapping the steering wheel to the beat. Several choice lyrics exploded from his mouth. The profanity and the anger didn't sit well, so he shifted his thoughts to Lina's pink lips. The memory of her softness unraveled his tightly wound springs until he no longer wanted to punch that banker. She was never far from his mind. Ever since the library, her ocean-blue eyes had invaded his quiet moments, and her perfume had distracted him in his work. He kept her close for moments like this, when nothing went right and he needed to feel like the world wasn't a giant waste. Maybe he couldn't be her boyfriend, but he'd probably think about her until the day he died.

A few miles outside of town, Cody slowed. A girl on the road ahead of him was pedaling a blue bicycle with a basket on the handlebars. Long dark hair billowed behind her on the wind, reminding him of Lina. He steered the truck wide around her. A quick glance over his shoulder as he passed was all it took to turn the day from rotten to heaven-sent. It *was* Lina.

Thinking of her had conjured her appearance here on this remote country road. What luck! It had nearly killed him to put her off, but here he had a chance to talk to her again. Not thinking twice about it, he pulled over onto the shoulder a short distance in front of her.

In an instant, Lina turned her bike and pedaled fast in the opposite direction, crossing to the other side of the road. She rode farther and farther away in his rearview mirror. With a furrowed brow, he turned around in his seat, unsure what had just happened. He made a U-turn and caught up with her. He just wanted to talk with her, maybe apologize for how he'd broken their plans, so he again stopped on the shoulder in front of her. Cody stepped out of the truck and approached her, unable to keep an eager grin from growing on his face.

Lina's bicycle slid on the gravel. She put a foot down to keep from following it into the ditch and pushed it away. Standing strong in the road, she braced her feet wide and aimed pepper spray at Cody.

His smile vanished. Something was wrong.

The wind whipped at her hair from behind, flipping it forward around her face. Power radiated off her in waves, crackling in the air around her, halting him in his tracks and forcing him to question what was actually happening. Their time at the coffee shop had gone well, and she hadn't seemed mad in the least when he'd canceled going to The Bad Bronco. But maybe he was wrong about all of that because here she was, pointing a weapon at him.

"What do you think you're doing?" she shouted. Her eyes flashed with wild sparks that threatened to burn him if he came any closer, so he remained where his feet were planted.

"What am I doing? I saw you and wanted to say hi."

"Are you crazy?" she yelled at him. "On a lonely road? No crossroad, no mailboxes, no flat tire. There's no reason to stop here." She caught her breath in Cody's stunned silence. "You pull over for no reason? *Right in front of me!*" The strength of her stance faded, and the arm that threatened him with pepper spray began to shake.

The pieces fell into place, and it dawned on him how this looked. "I'm sorry, Lina. I didn't even think about how it might seem to you." He took two careful steps forward. "You're right to be cautious, but I ain't going to hurt you. I won't ever hurt you."

She looked unwell, her cheeks red and her ribcage heaving.

"Are you okay?" he asked.

She shook her head.

"Will it help to shoot me with the pepper spray?"

She looked at her hand and the weapon still pointed at him. Lowering her trembling arm, she released the pepper spray, and it clattered to the ground. The shaking spread from her arm to her whole body. Lina looked as though she might collapse to the asphalt, but instead, she sobbed. Great racking sobs shuddered through her and threatened to unbalance Cody as well.

He'd done this. He'd frightened her. He'd made her cry. *Look away? Go to her? Get back in the truck?* Indecision trapped his feet to the ground like a thick puddle of sticky tar.

"Lina …? What should I do?" Other than *not* scare her with the thing she feared most?

She closed the space between them until her forehead

rested against his chest. As she leaned into him, he enfolded her in his arms and stroked the tangles of her hair, the hair he'd ached to bury his fingers in. Her hands crept around his waist and clasped behind him.

They remained there, wrapped up in each other on the side of the road until she had a grip on herself. But while she regained her composure, Cody lost his. Like on the day they'd met, the smell of her perfume took him to an open meadow with glorious sunshine. He dropped his face to her hair to breathe it in. He held her softness against him as his heart raced and he became less interested in comforting her and more distracted by her nearness. Her warm body pressed so close. The best feeling in the world had to be her breath on his chest through the fabric of his t-shirt.

He was a fool to imagine he'd be okay without her. Whatever he'd told himself out by the irrigation ditch was a load of bull. There *was* something worse than working a limping ranch, and it was missing out on dating Lina. He wouldn't fight it. Let the world crumble around him; he would do anything to be hers.

Her breathing slowed. She no longer made the weird, gurgle sound of a sob held in. Loosening her clutch around him, she brought her hands to rest on his biceps. His muscles tightened under her touch and she squeezed.

Cody lifted her chin and studied her face. Ruined mascara around the eye that had been pressed to his shirt fascinated him almost as much as her parted lips tipped up toward his. Forbidden fruit, her mouth promised to be soft and sweet. However, he'd already made the huge mistake of frightening her today, and he didn't care to add another by tasting her before he knew if she even liked him.

She seemed to have recovered from her fright, but he wasn't ready to let go of the protector role. He glanced at her bicycle, only the handlebars visible above the ditch. Sunflowers and larkspur spilled out of the basket and all over the shoulder of the road.

"Can I give you a ride somewhere?" He stepped back to put some space between their bodies. The loss of that closeness may as well have ripped him in two.

"Yes, please." She released him and pushed her tangled hair from her face. "But I think I need ice cream."

Cody tilted his head and raised an eyebrow. What did ice cream have to do with anything?

"It's a girl thing. And it's the least you can do after scaring me to death," she teased with an uncertain smile.

"Yes, ma'am." He sighed and returned her smile as the tension left his posture. He'd never been forgiven so quickly. It was refreshing, and though he deserved nothing from her, he couldn't help wanting everything.

As they walked over to her bike, Cody felt his back pocket for his wallet. Did he have money enough for ice cream? He'd sell a kidney if necessary, and they'd eat ice cream until they were old and gray. Lina retrieved the spilled wildflowers from the ground, and he retrieved the bike.

"Those are nice," he said, gesturing to the flowers. "What are they for?"

"They're for a neighbor. Her cat is sick."

"So, you're going to give her flowers?"

"Yeah, maybe they'll cheer her up."

"I'm sure they'll be appreciated." He inspected the front tire alignment on her bicycle. "Sometimes it helps just to be thought of during a hard time." There had been many kindnesses offered to him and Mom in those early days after Dad had died. Now it was mostly just Mrs. Bauer and Wayne who seemed to remember the Schafers were still suffering.

"I try to help, even in just a small way."

Cody lifted her bike into the bed of the pickup and then opened the passenger door for Lina to climb in. As he drove back toward town, he had trouble keeping his eyes on the road. He kept stealing glances at her.

She looked lovely with a bouquet in her lap and a flush in her cheeks from crying. He looked down at his shirt and found the match to the smudge of mascara that blackened her eye. Like a shared secret, the mascara marked them both.

Lina turned up the volume on the radio and sang along to a song he'd never even heard before. She belted out the lyrics like a shook-up Mountain Dew, unrestrained and unafraid, reaching every far corner of the cab.

With the windows down and Lina's bright energy next to him, Cody could've lived in that moment forever. He drove slower than necessary to draw it out.

As they reached a crossroad at the edge of Harton, he turned the music down. "Where would you like to get ice cream?" He definitely didn't have enough cash on him if she chose the gourmet ice cream shop in the town square. He had the ranch bank card, but ice cream was not a business expense, no matter how he spun it.

"Dairy Queen, please."

"Yes, ma'am," he said, but what he really meant was thank you, and take my heart while you're at it.

Cody came around the truck to open her door in the parking lot of the Dairy Queen. Lina slid down and was about to walk into the restaurant when he grabbed her elbow. He pulled her close until her face tilted upward.

Lifting the hem of his shirt, he used it to wipe the ruined make up from her face.

The smile faded from her lips. "Thanks," she whispered.

Cody grinned, and she did too. He cleared his throat and led her away from their goofy-grin moment and into the Dairy Queen.

CHAPTER 11

Lina

STICKY in the heat of the afternoon sun, they licked around the tops of their cones to keep the melting ice cream from dripping onto their hands. Lina could not look at Cody without obsessing about his lips, so she sat cross-legged facing outward on the open tailgate. He sat next to her, his long legs dangling over the edge. Now was a perfect time to dig into him, or filter, as Dr. Bowman called it.

"So, what would you have majored in if you had gone to college?" she asked.

"Not sure. I thought I'd figure it out when I got there."

"Well, what sort of things do you like to do?"

"I don't know anymore," Cody said. "I liked sociology class in school, and I was pretty good at math. But these days I'm always ranching."

"But it doesn't sound like you want to be a rancher."

"Nope. Never did. It was my dad's thing, but I guess it's mine now."

"Well, if it matters… A cowboy is a lot sexier than a mathematician." She cringed. The flirty thought in her head had sounded too forward when it came out in words. *Let Cody lead the sexy part of the relationship!* She looked away and busied herself with her cone to hide her telltale blush.

"Maybe you haven't met the right mathematician." Cody's magnetic laugh pulled her focus off her embarrassment, and his dimple had her undivided attention.

"Okay, so now I'm picturing you with a calculator, and a pencil tucked behind your ear."

Cody lowered his cone and posed, almost as a challenge to imagine him in his new look. "What do you think?"

"Hmm. Cowboy mathematicians are smoking hot." Dang, there she went again. Would she never learn?

The tips of his ears reddened, and his Adam's apple bobbed. He nudged her shoulder with his own.

Lina laughed and crunched into her cone. Melted ice cream gushed out and splattered all over her jeans, pooling in the triangle space created by her legs. Cody's eyes grew wide with surprise, but she only laughed again. She took his offered hand and let him help her down.

"Sorry to mess up your truck." She tossed the remnants of her cone into the nearest trash can and came back with a handful of napkins to wipe up the puddle.

Cody took the napkins from her. "Don't worry about the truck. Do you need a new cone?"

"No, that was a rookie mistake. I don't deserve another." Lina wiped at her soiled jeans with a napkin.

"Do you want to finish mine?" He held his cone out to her.

Lina stared at the cone and gulped down what she dared not say—that she could think of a more fun way to get his germs than from his ice cream. Doctor Bowman would be so disappointed. She had lost her battle to control her thoughts concerning this guy. The heat stole back into her cheeks. Her voice cracked as she said, "No thanks."

Before these crazy ideas about making out with him or love at first sight carried her away, she still needed a few answers. "Can we talk about what happened last week?"

"What do you mean?" he asked.

"Why did you cancel The Bad Bronco?"

Cody looked at the ground where his ice cream dripped onto the pavement. He went to the trash and threw it away. By the time he returned, Lina was put out and bristling at his delay. Filter. It was time to find out if he was one of those guys who wouldn't say what he means.

"Do you have a girlfriend?"

Cody shook his head, not meeting her gaze. "No, no girlfriend."

"Did something come up? Or did you just change your mind about hanging out with me?"

"Lina, no," he said. "It's not anything like that."

"Then what happened? Because after that text, I was pretty sure I'd never see you again." She paused, embarrassed by her tirade but needing to know. Enough with guys who didn't say what they were thinking or didn't do what they said they'd do. Enough of getting her hopes up, of letting herself care. She was tired of being toyed with and crushed by her crush. She was willing to let him mean something to her, but only if it went both ways.

She waited for him to speak, one breath, then two. That was it. She climbed into the truck bed and dragged her bicycle over to the edge. Cody took it from there and lowered it to the ground. She lifted her knee to straddle it.

"Wait." He put the kickstand down and looked at her

with a bright gleam in his eyes. "I want to see you, but I have responsibilities on the ranch."

Lina's heart softened. Hopefully that was true, that it wasn't her but some other reason he wouldn't sweep her off her feet. *Slow down, girl.* Patience sucked. "So, you work a lot?"

"Yeah."

"Do you get any free time?"

"Not often. I only came to town today because I had to run an errand, but I'll do my best to make time for you."

"What about evenings?" *Ugh, stop pestering him. Let him make the move.*

"Lina …" A muscle clenched in his jaw. He took her elbow and let his fingers trail along her arm until he held her hand. "When would you like me to take you to The Bad Bronco?"

She interlocked her fingers with his, her heart skipping a beat. "Can you get away on Thursday?" she asked, unable to raise her gaze from their joined hands. His was sun-darkened and calloused, large enough to swallow up her pale and delicate one.

"I'll arrange it," he said when she finally met his eyes. She believed him.

Lina was reluctant to remove her hand from his. He had to be the one to let go; he did, to close the tailgate. She collected the flowers she'd left in the cab and returned them to the basket of her bicycle, gulping deep swallows of air in an attempt to calm her racing pulse. "You know, even if you don't have time to see me, you could still call." *Stop! Just stop already.*

"Yes, ma'am." His dimple flashed, daring her to abandon caution further.

After a momentary debate, she rose to her tiptoes and

kissed his cheek. Perhaps that would make sure he showed up. *Oh, so not cool to dangle kisses like a carrot.* Self-correction always came too late.

"So, I'll see you Thursday, but we'll talk sooner?" Lina climbed onto the bike before he could react to her impulsiveness. "Thanks for the ice cream!"

She pedaled down the street and out of sight before she finally slowed. Misgivings entered. Had she been too hard on him? Had she tricked him into taking her for an ice cream? Had she pressured him into agreeing to take her to The Bad Bronco? She'd been out with too many guys who weren't with her for the right reasons. She hadn't known it at the time, but they had, and she was always the one whose feelings were trampled.

Lina turned into a residential area and rode the long way home. If her relationship with Cody was going to be different, she couldn't push, or it would crumple. He didn't seem like the kind of guy to spend time with her without really wanting to be in it for the long haul, but she didn't know him very well yet. What was wrong with her? All her resolve to get to know him before investing her affections had melted faster than the ice cream. With Cody, she couldn't make the same mistakes she'd made before. Kissing him was exactly that—a mistake. But, oh! She wanted to do it again. And next time, when it was his move, she wouldn't settle for a cheek.

CHAPTER 12

Cody

THE ENGINE WAS at least as old as Cody was and needed constant maintenance. He laid out the pieces of the UTV's carburetor on the workbench in the order they went back together and began to clean them one by one. He wiped a part with a shop rag and held it up in the light. The garage doors were rolled open to let the sunshine pour in. A mild breeze blew through the open doors and brought with it thoughts of Lina with her hair a mess. She liked to ride her bike—maybe she'd enjoy horseback riding. They should do it soon, before the summer blazed too hot.

Rebuilding the carburetor was mindless enough that his thoughts could wander far afield. He had been stupid to pull over when he'd seen Lina on that country road. She'd been so scared, and he didn't blame her for that. She probably always had her guard up after what had happened to her sister. He would have done better to just roll the window down and wave as he drove by. But his mistake had brought her into his arms—the last thing he would've predicted, but the best reward for a stupid decision. He rubbed his cheek where she'd planted her kiss and smiled to himself.

"Cody? Meet Elijah Trygg." Wayne's intrusion on Cody's thoughts was like a needle scratching across one of his dad's old Kenny Rogers vinyl records.

He left the carburetor and wiped his hands on a rag as Wayne brought a man into the garage.

"Eli is our new hand, a brand-new graduate—got a degree in animal science." Wayne put his hands on his hips and smiled as though he'd had something to do with Eli's success. "He can start right away."

Cody shook Eli's hand, sizing up the clean-cut cowboy and feeling smaller by the second. Eli had a confident handshake and an open smile. He was a little older than Cody, taller, and stronger too. Probably smarter; definitely friendlier. All Cody could hope for was that Eli had mountains of student loans to offset his imposing attributes.

"Glad to have you, Eli," Cody said, remembering his manners. "Where are you from?"

"Montana." Eli pushed his cowboy hat further back on his head and grinned at Cody. "I grew up on my grandpa's ranch."

Cody had never been as excited about ranching as Eli seemed to be.

"What brings you to Kansas?" Wayne asked.

"I'm the youngest of seven sons. Wanted to go some-where where I'm not living in all those shadows."

"You got a horse?" Cody couldn't help digging for something about the guy to not be perfect.

"Yes, sir, I'll send for him. In the meantime, Wayne said I should borrow your Delilah."

Delilah belonged to Mom, not Cody. Ha. Though it

wasn't fair to revel in the mistake—Eli had just arrived. He couldn't have known who owned the horse.

"Call me Cody."

"You own this place?" Eli asked.

"You could say that, but Wayne is the boss around here."

"All right then, Cody it is." Eli surveyed the view from the open garage doors. "You've got quite an operation here for someone so young."

It was Boyd, his dad's operation. He had been the one who built this structure behind the barn and across from the house. The garage, large enough for twelve cars, served as the hub for all ranch work. Age aside, Cody hadn't done anything to add to the splendor of the place.

"I'm not that young." Cody felt a thousand years old, on the inside at least.

"No? What year did you graduate?"

"Didn't graduate," Cody mumbled. He looked out to see Tay approaching the garage, just in time to take the focus off him. "Tay, you want to show Eli around?"

The two men left the garage, but Wayne hung back. Cody returned to the carburetor and fiddled with the pieces.

"Something bothering you?" Wayne asked.

Besides the golden boy? He wanted to like Eli. He seemed good-natured and genuine, but the Montana cowboy was everything Cody was not—experienced, educated, and excited about ranching. Working with him side by side would only accentuate his own shortcomings. "Can we afford someone with a degree?"

"Can't afford not to hire him. He's forgotten more than I ever knew about the business side of managing a ranch. But there's a rancher outside Falls City looking for pasture for a hundred head. If we lease him the acres, we can afford Eli. And the rancher, Frank Chancer, also has a nephew looking for work. He ain't got a ton of experience —just a few summers working for Frank—but he'll be cheap, and we can train him on how we do things here."

Cody furrowed his brow and twisted the rag around his fingers. Having two more hands sounded too good to be true. He would be able to both tend to his mom better and see Lina. However, something about this perfect deal smelled like charity. "Is it good business for both us and Chancer?"

"It's not a kindness he's doing. He's gonna lease pasture somewhere, might as well be ours." Wayne placed his huge hand on Cody's shoulder like Dad used to. "One more thing. I know it rubs that you left school. Do yourself a favor and go back." He left Cody to his thoughts and hurried to catch up with Tay and Eli.

LATER THAT AFTERNOON, Cody showered and shaved. He brushed his work boots clean as best he could, but they were too far gone. He resisted all things cowboy: boots, hat, belt buckle, all but the horse. But The Bad Bronco was for country dancing, so there was no help for it.

He rolled back the door to his dad's closet and rummaged around until he found the proper cowboy boots. They fit perfectly, unlike the rest of Dad's life he was trying to fit into.

With one last check in the mirror, Cody tried to picture himself as Lina might see him. His hair was too long, but slicked back off his forehead it looked okay. Butterflies bounced around in his belly, but at least they were on the inside, invisible to everyone but him.

Out in the family room, Mom stood at the window and nibbled a chocolate chip cookie. She turned and smiled when she saw him. "Boyd said we should stay out of the wind."

Heaven knew what she meant. There wasn't much wind today, but she was happy, so Cody didn't worry too much about it. He grabbed her into a hug and swung her around.

"Have fun, little Cody." His mom followed him to the kitchen and swiped another cookie.

"She's been repeating that about the wind," Mrs. Bauer said from the kitchen sink where she dried a saucepan. "You look handsome. Excited for tonight?"

"I'm nervous." He fumbled with the top button of his shirt.

"Nerves are good," she said. "They'll keep you from getting too cocky. No girl likes a cocky man, not really."

Mrs. Bauer scooted a plate of cookies closer to him and took over his button. "No more than one left open." She laid his collar flat and nodded with satisfaction.

"Mmm …" He sank his teeth into a cookie and loaded a couple more into a napkin.

"You got enough pocket cash?" Mrs. Bauer asked.

"Yeah, I think so."

She handed him a stack of cookies wrapped in a cellophane bag and tied with a yellow ribbon. "For Lina. You can't show up to a first date without a gift for the lady."

Cody should've thought of that. Saved by Mrs. Bauer. "Thanks, Mrs. B. I gotta run."

"I'll sleep over tonight, so you stay out as long as you

need to." She shooed him out the front door. "And make sure Lina has a good time at the honky tonk!"

"Only old people call it that."

"Cody!" Mom whipped toward him. "Manners!"

"Only old people call it that, *ma'am*." He threw a flippant smirk as he left the women to their cookies.

CHAPTER 13

Cody

Cody stared at Lina's text in surprise. He had expected to meet her father before he took her out, but he was willing to meet her anywhere. Pulling out onto the highway, he drove toward town gripping the steering wheel tighter with every mile. He drove a little too fast. The butterflies continued to rage.

When he walked through the library doors, he was greeted by a round, elderly woman with a tight silver bun and a few books tucked under her elbow. She would probably call The Bad Bronco a honky tonk.

"Are you Cody?" She eyed him up and down. Her careful perusal left no detail unnoticed.

"Yes, ma'am." Cody shifted uncomfortably and worried that he'd forgotten something in getting ready for his date. He smoothed his hair back, only to realize it was still in place.

"Mmm-hmm …" she said when she finished her inspection. "Well, you'll do nicely. Lina'll be right along." She squinted to look up at his face and pointed an index finger at him. "You bring her back in one piece. I ain't having her cry on my shoulder tomorrow."

"She'll be safe with me, ma'am. I promise you that."

"Now, Miss Fayla, don't scare him off." Lina came up behind the woman and wrapped an arm around her shoulders. She wore a blue dress with flowers on it, with a denim jacket and a pair of boots. Like Cody, she had taken extra care with her appearance tonight. Her hair cascaded down her back in loose curls, and she wore heavier makeup than usual. A gloss glistened on her lips. Kryptonite ... again. He couldn't pull his gaze away. Miss Fayla cleared her throat to get his attention.

Cody shook off the spell and smiled at his beautiful date. "You ready?"

Lina nodded and stepped closer to him. As they walked out the door, he placed a hand at the small of her back to guide her. He caught a glimpse of Miss Fayla glowering at him. She shook her head until he removed his hand.

In the library parking lot, he opened the door of his truck for her and was treated to a whiff of her perfume as she climbed in past him. "You look nice," he said before he closed her door. He exhaled and shook the tension from his hands and fingers as he moved around the truck. Some nerves might be necessary to keep him from getting cocky, but not this many. He cleared his throat before climbing in himself.

It was a long drive to The Bad Bronco, and he had to make sure they actually got there, but he would've rather taken her to the pond to watch the sunset and make out. First date ... *first* date. A guy good enough to call her "ma'am" would not take her to the pond on a first date.

Lina found the bag of cookies. "Are these for me?" she asked, toying with the ribbon.

"Yes, ma'am." Cody winked at her. "In case the night doesn't meet your expectations, at least the cookies are good."

"Nonsense," she said with a laugh. "I'm already having a good time."

Lina chatted the whole way. She told him about her roommates, her life away at school, and the nursing career she hoped for one day. When she wound down, Cody asked her another question that got her going again. He could listen to her talk all night.

She navigated with rights and lefts until they arrived at a Mexican restaurant where they would have dinner before they went to The Bad Bronco.

Mariachi music blasted out as Cody opened the door. The hostess led them through the brightly decorated restaurant and seated them in a booth. Wait staff surrounded a neighboring table singing *Feliz Cumpleaños* over a candle stuck in fried ice cream. Their server set down water glasses and chips with salsa and left to give them a few minutes to look at the menu.

"You have to tell me about your life now," Lina said, laying her napkin in her lap. "I've talked the whole way here. You can't possibly be that interested in mine."

"I am. But I'll take a turn if you like," Cody said. "What would you like to know?"

"Are you able to talk about your dad?"

"Yeah." Cody pushed his menu away. If she was ready to order, so was he. "He and my mom bought the ranch before I was born. I've lived my whole life in the same place. Dad taught me to ride a horse when I was little and gave me chores around the ranch since I could walk, practically. I played football in high school because I'd rather have been at practice than working on the ranch after school."

"I saw you at a couple of the games," Lina said. "I first noticed you standing on the sidelines. You dumped a water bottle over your head to cool off."

"You must have a good memory."

"I remember some things *very* well, like a cute football player." Lina bit into a tortilla chip that crumbled to pieces and fell to the table. "Ice cream cone flashback." A nervous flush pinkened her cheeks as she laughed it off. "Please don't think I'm always a messy eater. Stuff like this only happens when I'm trying to make a good impression."

Cody picked up a chip and crushed it in his hand. He scattered the crumbs on the red tablecloth until his side of the table was messier than hers. "Are you impressed with *me* yet?"

Her answer was swallowed up when the server came back for their order.

"They have giant portions here; want to share something?" Lina finally looked at the laminated menu. "I love the enchiladas."

"Sure, whatever you think is best." He was normally hungry enough to want his own meal, but between the nerves and the expense, sharing was smarter.

The server moved on, and Lina tried again at the chips and salsa. Dark hair framed her fair skin, a curl hung over her shoulder, and her eyes sparkled. They were the color of the sky in that fleeting moment after sundown but before the stars appeared. Dark blue, endless, a wormhole he might be sucked into and lost forever.

She licked a bit of salsa from her lips and looked at him expectantly. Wasn't there a princess with her coloring? The one who ate the apple. Cody tried to remember the fairy tale, but all he could recall was that the princess needed to be kissed. *Whoa.* He refocused his thoughts from kissing her lips and caught the tail end of her question.

"… how you lost your dad?"

Cody cleared his throat and sipped from his water glass. Too late to go back to kissing the princess—Miss The Future is Better Than the Past waited. He hadn't shared this part of his story with anyone in a long time.

"He and my mom were out with the cattle. Something happened. The horse spooked. Who knows for sure? My mom thinks it might have been a snake. Anyway, the horse threw him. He got up and came around to make sure Mom was okay, but the horse hadn't calmed down and kicked him in the head. Mom saw the whole thing happen right in front of her and couldn't do anything to stop it." He dipped a chip into the salsa and left it there. "She called an ambulance, called me out of school. By the time I met her at the hospital, he was … Well, they tried to save him. Had him on life support for a while. Cost a fortune, but we would've paid anything to get him back."

Lina sat white-faced and speechless across from him.

"The day after the funeral, I shot that horse."

Lina clasped his hand in hers on the tabletop. "Sorry."

"That was the first of a long series of bad decisions. You know you've got to pay a service to come and remove a dead horse from your property?"

Lina shook her head.

"Yeah, I didn't know that either. They're not cheap. I could've used my dad to warn me about that." Totally the wrong conversation for a date. He withdrew his hand from Lina's as the server set their meal between them.

"I'm so sorry," Lina said one more time.

"You still hungry after that sad story?"

"Yes, and so are you."

"I am?"

"Of course! We are here together, celebrating Random Guy's birthday"—she gestured to the party nearby—"and you have to eat at least half of this so I don't look like a greedy pig."

"Okay, no problem."

Lina cut the entrée in half and scooped her share onto her plate. Cody savored a bite in his mouth. The spicy, creamy enchiladas tasted like the kind his mom used to make before she lost interest in cooking and everything else. It tasted of happier times.

"Please don't get weird," Cody said into the silence between them. "People usually get weird after they know what happened."

"I know! Same with me. You are the first person I've ever told about Ruby and my mom who still treats me the same after."

"Okay then. For us, no getting weird with each other." His enchilada was half gone. Lina was right; this food was delicious. "Do you have enough to eat?"

"Yeah, but if I run out, I'll distract you with my womanly wiles and take yours."

Cody laughed. "It won't be too hard. One smile and you could steal the floor out from under me."

She slapped a hand down on the table. "So, you *do* know how to flirt! You should do it more often. A girl might wonder if you're really interested in her."

He looked away while the tips of his ears heated. "How's this one?" He leaned toward her. "Do you know CPR? Because you just took my breath away."

"Nice try, but I've heard that one before. Do you ever get tired of running through my dreams all night?"

"Oh, you're smooth." He laughed. "But your hand looks heavy. Can I hold it for you?"

"Do you believe in love at first sight? Or shall I walk by again?"

She hit a little close to home with that one. He hadn't been the same since he first saw her in the library. "Kiss me if I'm wrong, but dinosaurs still exist, right?"

"If you let me borrow a kiss, I'll give it right back."

"Have you ever used that one, like in real life?" If she said yes, he'd have reason to wish he'd met her first.

"No, but I've been dying to see if it works." Lina stifled a giggle when the server came to refill their drinks.

"You kids need anything else? Maybe some dessert?"

They both shook their heads, then talked and laughed as they finished their meal. Lina shared a story about a prank she'd pulled on her roommate with the bedsheets, and the prank they'd pulled on her in retaliation. Something about walling off her bedroom door with popcorn. Cody couldn't remember the last time he'd laughed so much.

Lina checked her watch. "Let's go. If we arrive too late, we'll be really far down on the karaoke lineup."

Cody suppressed a small shudder. He'd sung with his mom since he was a little kid, never in public, never karaoke, but he *had* given a speech in eleventh grade. He wasn't cut out for the spotlight.

CHAPTER 14

Lina

LINA SHOULD'VE GIVEN up on the idea of a perfect date long ago, but tonight reinforced the belief that it was possible. Kind of like seeing Santa Claus with her own eyes. Waiting in line to get inside The Bad Bronco with Cody was perfect. Absolutely perfect. The moon shone full and bright overhead, and his hand captured hers while they edged closer to each other in the night air.

A rowdy group of college kids behind them bounced around like they were in a mosh pit. One of them bumped into Lina and sent her crashing into Cody. He caught her against his solid frame.

"I've got you. Come here." Cody put himself between her and the punks.

She leaned back against his chest and wrapped his arms around her waist. Turning her head, she pressed her cheek to his chest. She couldn't be sure, but it felt like he planted a kiss on the top of her head. Accepting it as real, she smiled, breathing in the scent of his laundry detergent. Neither of them minded the slow line to get into The Bad Bronco.

When they each had an under-twenty-one handstamp, they stepped inside. Blaring music surged from the DJ booth under the flashing lights above the dance floor. Lina led Cody by the arm past the restrooms, through a hallway, and into the soundproofed karaoke lounge. Three women were halfway through "Dancing Queen" on an elevated platform while the crowd ignored them.

Lina made a beeline to the sign-up clipboard, dragging Cody with her. "What do you want to sing?"

"I want to hear you sing."

"Come on … please sing with me?" She grabbed fistfuls of his shirt to bring him close and batted her eyelashes at him. "We can do a duet. I'll be with you the whole time."

"Are these your womanly wiles?" A muscle twitched in his jaw as he avoided her eye contact.

"That's just a taster sample." Gone was her earlier resolve to let Cody lead, to resist pressuring him in any way. What was wrong with her? In the excitement of karaoke, she was back to her old tricks.

No, the excitement was Cody himself. He smelled delicious, not like the frat boys doused in cologne, not like animals, which was how she had imagined a rancher would smell. Just soap and what could only be pheromones, because all restraint had melted into a puddle at her feet. Forgotten.

Finally, he looked at her. Cody slid an arm around her waist and drew her up tight against him. She was trapped, nearly nose to nose, her chest pressed against his. The last time she was this close to him, his pecs had been the furthest things from her mind. Now, her world revolved around every bulge and indent. Her heartbeat pulsed in her chest and in her head. It was happening. She rose to her tiptoes and lifted her lips. *Wait for it, wait for it …*

He looked at her with a furrowed brow and loosened his hold. "Pick a duet, hopefully one I've heard before," he said, then stepped away.

Lina whirled around with her face on fire. Once again, she'd been caught up in her own fantasy and believed something that wasn't true. In need of a timely distraction, she picked up a clipboard with a list of song titles and chose one that had been on the radio a thousand times: "Need You Now."

She signed their names half a page down from the top of the list, so it would be a good hour before they had their turn. She turned to ask Cody what he wanted to do while they waited, but he wasn't there. People had poured into the room since they'd entered. She scanned the crowd in the dim light but couldn't locate him.

An older man with a thick mustache spotted her. "Hey, doll, you here all alone?"

Lina opened her mouth to say something just as someone grabbed her elbow. She almost jumped away before she realized it was Cody. He stared down the mustached man who shrugged his shoulders and approached a different lady.

"Dance with me," Cody said.

Lina followed him back through the hallway, the music growing louder with every step. They found a place among several other couples circling the dance floor with a two-step before he took her hand. Within the safety of his arms, she responded to his lead as he pushed her into motion, and they joined the tide of dancers.

"You can dance!"

"A little." He spun her out and back in again, his

dimple on full display. "My mom likes to dance. She taught me a little bit."

There was no way she wasn't going to lose her heart tonight. Why fight it? Her hair flipped over her shoulder as she twirled, and every time he brought her close, she melted into his warm brown eyes. Too soon, the music ended, but she couldn't step away from his spell.

"Do you want something to drink?" he asked.

Her spellbound feet lagged as he urged her to a small table near the corner. Cody left to get them some pop at the bar, which allowed Lina a few moments to puzzle out the mixed signals. First, he hadn't kissed her when he'd had the chance. Then on the dance floor he'd looked like kissing her was the only thing on his mind. She'd seen that look before, most recently on Gary, the guy in the torn-up picture in the trash. But with Cody, she really wanted it. She imagined Dr. Bowman's disapproving eyebrow raise.

The Bad Bronco was heating up. Lina shed her denim jacket and draped it over the back of the chair just as Cody returned with their drinks.

He held her chair as she sat, then joined her at the table and extended an arm across the back of her seat. Touching her bare shoulder with a fingertip, he leaned in to say in her ear, "You look really pretty." He twirled one of her curls around his index finger and studied it in the flashing lights.

He was so close—close enough to spot a small scar on his chin. It wouldn't take much to close the distance and kiss that scar, or better, his beautiful lips. How nice it would be, even for only a moment, to forget herself. She needed a signal—a loud, clear, unmistakable sign that it was safe to fall in love with him.

Furrowing his brow, he dropped the curl and eased

back in his chair. Wow, he sure knew how to hook a gal and reel her in. Lina sipped from her Coke and fidgeted. The DJ played a line dance and she jumped up. "Do you know this one?"

"Everybody knows this one." Cody smiled and took her back to the dance floor where they joined in.

The dance rotated, putting Cody in front of her, and Lina indulged in the view of his back as they grapevined. His broad shoulders tapered to a trim waist and his shirt clung in all the right places. He moved with an ease she envied, confident and almost lazy, yet hitting each beat with precision. She glanced at his butt. It was a fleeting glance, but poorly timed, causing her to miss a direction change. She missed another step in her confusion and glanced at him as the dancers moved on. Left behind in the ever-progressing line dance, Lina freestyled. He laughed at her wiggles and robot, and freestyled with her for a few measures until they picked up the sequence again.

The song ended, and a ballad began. Lina stood in a moment of uncertainty. She'd already made embarrassing assumptions tonight and didn't want to assume he still wanted to dance. She moved toward their table, but he shook his head, his jaw set, and slid an arm around her.

"You know," he said into her ear, his chin a caress against her cheek, "there's only one reason why a guy line dances."

Keep it light, girl. "Because it's fun?"

"Because of a woman."

Falling, and that was all there was to it. The Bad Bronco was a terrible idea for a girl denying her impulses in favor of taking things slow. Lina should have suggested a 5k race, or a barn raising, or anything else that didn't require touching. She attempted to keep space between them, made room for the Bible and all that. But Cody guided her arms up and placed them around his neck. They swayed to the music wrapped around each other.

Cody lowered his face to the curve of her neck and inhaled her perfume. "You smell nice."

She barely heard him and convinced herself that she'd imagined it. But then his breath against her neck supercharged her pulse and left her in a panic, trying to suppress the sensation. Eventually, she decided—she could not slow dance with him without also wanting to jump him. Definitely *not* Dr. Bowman-approved behavior. As soon as the song ended, she steered him back to the table to get her jacket and their pops.

They carried their drinks through the crowd to the karaoke lounge and found another table where they could watch the performances. The mustached cowboy from earlier was butchering a Garth Brooks oldie on the stage. There were still a few people ahead of them, so Lina settled in, grateful for the small table between them.

"Have you done this much?" she asked.

"Never."

"Really? Well, I wouldn't worry—you can't possibly be as terrible as Mustache up there."

"His voice is pretty bad, and I think he's getting the lyrics wrong, but he does have a fine mustache." Their heads came together as they laughed. "Seriously though, this is fun for you, subjecting your ears to this?"

"Not everybody sucks, but I've heard it's easier with alcohol. Actually, for me the fun part is being up there." She nodded toward the stage. "I like to imagine I'm shooting a music video. Me and Ruby would use Dad's old video camera to film all kinds of videos. My mom taught us "Girls Just Want to Have Fun," and boy, did we sing the heck out of that one."

"Karaoke seems like a pretty special way to keep them around."

He hit the nail on the head. That was exactly why she loved it so much. She pressed her lips together in a tight line to avoid planting a juicy one on him. He understood her. He understood her in a way that melted her, that tied her to him, that … *Stop. Just stop.*

Meager applause leaked out of a crowd only half paying attention to Mustache. Lina used the distraction to change her thoughts. If Cody had never sung before, who knew how this would go? He might have a bad voice, or terrible stage fright, or maybe he would ham it up and be ridiculous. That would be fun. Awesome. *Please, Cody, ham it up.*

After a few more acts, it was their turn.

"What song did you choose?" he asked as they made their way to the stage.

"'Need You Now.' Is that okay?" She accepted two microphones from the DJ and passed one to Cody.

He nodded. He ran his hand through his hair and tapped the handle of the mic against his thigh. Yeah, he was nervous.

"Don't worry. I've got you." Lina showed him the computer monitor with the lyrics. "Look here. Your lines will be in blue and mine will be that purple color. Watch this indicator as it bounces above the lyrics. It will help you keep the timing."

He raked his hand through his hair one more time as the introduction played. His nervous tic was adorable.

The duet started with Lina's part. She had a fair singing voice—it wouldn't shatter any glass, at least. Then came the chorus and Cody joined in to sing with her. They sounded good together. Lina loosened up once she wasn't so worried about Cody's ability to manage.

When Cody's verse began, his rich baritone rang out clear and sure. Her jaw dropped. He ignored the monitor and completely focused on her. He was so good! Lina missed the place where she was supposed to join in. It wasn't until Cody touched her arm that she remembered what to do.

As she sang next to him, she watched his face. His Adam's apple vibrated. He never looked at the audience, only at her. *Ruby would totally love this guy.*

They returned the microphones, retrieved Lina's jacket off her chair, and made their way from the room.

"Cody, you were really good up there."

He shrugged. "But somehow, you stole the show."

"Oh no, you're the star!"

"Well, you were all I could see. All I …" His words were lost in the noise of music blasting and people talking. Lina filled in the blank: *wanted to see.*

They passed the dance floor, passed the bar, and continued to the mechanical bull.

They got in line and watched others ride while they waited for their turn. A few people were good at it, but many fell after a few seconds. The gathered crowd cheered for their friends and whistled or yelled.

When it was Cody's turn, he boosted himself astride the bull amid the cheers and hollers of the crowd. It started off slowly, then accelerated with twists and turns, faster and faster. He kept his seat for a while, arm flying about overhead, as the operator turned up the intensity, and then turned it up again. Cody fell face up on the mat with a great thump.

He pushed to his feet, and with a modest wave to the applauding crowd, returned to Lina's side. Laughing, he swung her in a circle. Lina laced her fingers behind his neck and smiled into his twinkling eyes.

"That was fun, right?" she asked.

"Yes, ma'am."

CHAPTER 15

Cody

CODY DIDN'T WANT the night to end, but damn if it wasn't killing him. Ever since they arrived at The Bad Bronco, Lina had been under his arm, holding his hand, leaning against him, wrapping her arms around him, and presenting her shiny, candied lips like a gift for the taking. Aside from being on high alert in Lina's presence, Cody's face had worn a smile more often than not, and he hoped against hope that her perfume would stay with him.

After another karaoke song and another line dance, she tugged on his sleeve. "Just a heads-up, but I have to be home by midnight."

"Oh. Okay, then we should get going." Cody fetched her abandoned jacket from where she had thrown it aside near the karaoke lounge. They walked out into the parking lot, into the welcome chill of the night air after the heat of The Bad Bronco.

"Sorry, but my dad is really overprotective. It's annoying sometimes, but when I'm home, I try to respect the curfew. He waits up for me." She took the denim jacket from him, wadded it into a ball, and tucked it under her arm as they made their way to his truck.

"It's okay, really." Cody opened the door for Lina, then he got in and started the engine. "I bet it feels nice to have someone care that much, making sure you get in safe at night and stuff."

"Yeah, I guess you're right. But when I'm away at school, no one waits up for me. I kind of like that too."

As they left The Bad Bronco behind them, Lina unfastened her seatbelt and slid over closer on the bench seat.

"Whoa, you need a seatbelt—"

"I want to wear this one." She clipped into the lap belt in the center seat.

Well, that was a whole other kind of dangerous. She was soft and warm against him. He tensed up. For their first real date, she seemed comfortable enough to be so familiar. He loved how familiar she was, but he was far from comfortable.

"Is this okay?" The thigh contact was more than okay, as long as he didn't lose focus and drive off the road.

He nodded and imagined himself stretching his arm over the back of the seat to nestle her in close. The whole night had been a battle like this—the proper thing to do up against what he'd rather do. Cody dug deep for hidden reserves of self-control and changed the subject.

"Did you have fun tonight?"

"Yeah, I think you did too, right?" Lina asked.

"Yeah, if you call being scared to death fun."

"You were scared? But you're such a strong, brave man," she teased. "Seriously, though, you were amazing. You're good at everything—you dance, you sing, you stay on El Toro."

He shifted in his seat, checking the rearview. The years

of being beneath everybody's radar had conditioned him to deflect compliments. "Well, I *was* scared. Is there such a thing as adrenaline poisoning? 'Cause I definitely over-dosed tonight."

"Okay, tough guy, what part was the scariest?"

The part where he wanted to find a dark corner, push her up against a wall, and kiss her until she begged for mercy. He would've killed Mustache for trying something like that, but damn if he didn't want it for himself.

"Meeting Miss Fayla."

Lina laughed and Cody grinned. Singing and dancing didn't matter much. As long as he made her laugh, he felt like a man who could do anything.

"Thank you for the cookies." Lina untied the yellow ribbon from her bag of cookies and tasted one. She had the same response as Cody earlier. "Mmm …" She held it up to his mouth so he could take a bite while he drove.

"Can we stop at a Gas 'n' Sip for some pop?"

"Yes, ma'am." Cody pulled over at the next convenience store they came across. They used the drive-through and were back on the road in plenty of time to get her home by midnight.

"You don't still have to call me ma'am, you know." She stabbed a straw through the lid of her drink and did the same for his.

"Yeah, I still do." Cody glanced at her. She wore a small pout and studied a cookie way too intently. "It reminds me to treat you as a gentleman should." He took his eyes off the road one more time to see her shove the whole cookie in her mouth.

"So then"—her words came out garbled past the mouthful—"I should be a lady?"

It was Cody's turn to laugh. She joined him in the hilarity and handed him another cookie.

"Tell me more about your life at Washburn," Cody said when the humor had died down. "What are your favorite classes, what do you do in your spare time, who do you hang out with … You know, all the stuff."

"Why do you want to know about Washburn? Do you think you might want to go to college someday?"

"Yeah, maybe someday."

"Well, someday isn't far off."

It was to him. Someday hovered on the horizon.

Lina didn't get tired of chit-chat. She talked and joked all the way back to Harton. Asking about her life at school had opened a floodgate and she had so much to say. Cody drove and listened, responding when necessary. She sucked him in with her stories and the journey flew by too quickly.

They pulled up in front of her house a few minutes before midnight. Cody came around the truck to open her door and she slid down, shrugging into her jacket. He was about to walk her to the front porch, but she held his arm and kept him there.

"Can we say good night here?"

"Ma'am, I gotta walk you to the door."

"Please. My dad is waiting up, and I'm not ready for you to meet him."

He squared his shoulders, attempting to hide the arrow through his heart. "Am I not good enough?" The previously smooth timbre of his voice faltered.

Lina's hands flew to cover her cheeks; her eyes went as wide as the moon overhead. "No! That's not what I meant." She moved in closer and placed both palms on Cody's chest. "My dad asks a lot of questions. A lot. I need you to be head over heels before you meet him, so you don't run."

Immediate relief washed over him. She engulfed him in a tight hug and he squeezed her right back, resisting the urge to slide his hands between her jacket and her dress.

"Good night," he whispered into her hair.

"Thank you for tonight. Call me tomorrow?"

"I'd be happy to."

Lina let go of him and hurried up the driveway.

He watched her walk away and waited until she was safe inside the house before he pulled away and headed home.

Head over heels? That wasn't a stretch, and not as far off as someday was.

On the long drive back to the ranch, he counted how many times he'd almost kissed her tonight. If he had taken her to the pond to watch the sunset, he wouldn't have been able to resist.

Cody's last first kiss was three years ago, with Tessa, the silly cheerleader. They had casually dated right up until his dad's funeral, then he never saw her again. No emotional breakup scene, no goodbye at all. He'd heard she had gone off to college. Theirs had never been a very deep relationship.

He wanted something different with Lina. He wanted their first kiss to mean something. Not in a sweaty honky tonk. It should be in private. It should be sincere. It should come with his heart. Only with heroic effort had he resisted grabbing a frivolous kiss from Lina.

When he arrived home, the house was quiet. Mom and Mrs. Bauer would've gone to bed hours ago. Cody knew he should lay down too, but the Mountain Dew from the Gas 'n' Sip had kicked in. Wide awake, Lina's stories about college played out in his head. That should've been his life too.

He opened his laptop and searched for local continuing education options. Harton School District's website advertised a couple different options, but which was best for him? He was too old to re-enroll in high school. The night classes were not an option because evening tended to be Mom's most unpredictable time. He clicked a small button at the top of the screen. *Make an appointment.* He used the online scheduling system to make an appointment for Wednesday with someone at the district offices to determine which was the best route for him and his circumstances.

Now that Wayne had pointed it out and they had Eli to pick up some slack, his diploma was more important than it had been yesterday. But Eli was probably going to do more than pick up slack. He would probably be awesome at everything, and then it would be even more obvious that Cody was out of his element. Out of his element and years behind schedule. How could Cody be a good match for Lina? She should probably date Eli.

The possibility he'd felt earlier in Lina's presence hovered on the horizon next to someday. No matter how hard he rode toward it, it would always be out of reach. He recited the alternate ending to the empty room. Knowing the author gave new weight to the ending. A weight he didn't mind carrying now that he understood Lina and how hope had lightened her load. He would need more practice for himself, because as he lay there on his bed, his burden didn't feel any lighter. His burden had multiplied simply by daring to want more.

CHAPTER 16

Cody

CODY SHONE a flashlight on the path to the garage in the early morning hours. He had slept fitfully after getting home late, worried whether he was doing the right thing by dating a college girl. When it was almost time to get up anyway, he gave up trying to rest. He switched on a few lights in the garage and got to work tidying up the mess he'd left yesterday with the carburetor. He put a few tools away and wiped down the workbench.

A door on the far side of the room opened a crack. Eli peeked into the main space of the garage, then wandered up to Cody wearing pajama pants, a t-shirt, and flip flops.

"Hey, Cody. You're working early."

"Yeah, couldn't sleep. What are you doing here already?"

"I heard the door and the rattling; thought I'd come check it out."

"You're sleeping in the bunk room?" No one had used it in a long while. Tay and Wayne had homes with their wives, and Spence still lived with his folks closer to town.

"Are you okay in there? Did Wayne get you some clean linens?" Cody asked.

"Yeah, it's fine. And temporary. I'm looking for a place in town. Can I help you with anything since I'm up?"

Cody handed Eli a push broom.

"Hey, I didn't mean to poke a sore spot yesterday about school," Eli said. "I was just trying to get to know you a little." He began sweeping in the far corner.

"It's fine. I don't talk about it much." Cody returned to sorting and organizing tools. "Nobody even asks about it anymore."

"Wayne told me about your dad. I'm sorry. You've traveled a tough road, my friend."

Are we friends? Cody could use one, but maybe one who didn't make him look like a screwup by comparison. "As soon as it's light, we'll tend the animals." It was cowardly to dodge difficult conversations, and maybe someday he'd be comfortable talking to Eli about his dad, but for now, his head throbbed from lack of sleep. "Tell me about yourself," he said to dispel the awkwardness of working in silence with a total stranger.

"I'm pretty simple," Eli said. "I come from a ranching family, trying to make my own way in the world."

"You're like, twenty-two, twenty-three?"

"Twenty-five. I deferred college for two years so I could go on a mission trip for my church."

"I used to go to church," Cody said. "With my parents. Haven't been since the funeral."

"God's always glad to have you come back, no matter how long it's been."

Oh, brother. Cody rolled his eyes. He grumbled and stacked boxes of motor oil in a corner of the garage.

"Don't worry," Eli said. "I'm not gonna preach unless

you ask me too. The point is, I was a little older than you are now when I started college. There's nothing wrong with waiting until the time is right. But I recommend *not* living in the dorms, because a couple years makes a difference. I was the oldest one there, and it's pretty wild living with eighteen-year-old guys. My first night there …" Eli pantomimed pulling a blanket back from a bed to get in. "I'm trying to get in my bed, but my leg only goes halfway under the covers." Eli hopped around on one leg and laughed as he relived the difficulties of that night.

Cody laughed too. Eli looked ridiculous.

"I pushed and fought, but I seriously could not get in my bed. Then I thought I better turn on the light, see what was going on, you know? But my foot was tangled in the sheet by then. So I fell … Timber! Right across my room-mate who was pretending to be asleep. His bed broke when I landed on it."

Cody laughed so hard he had to put down the supplies he had been moving into a cabinet.

"The other guys came in to see what was going on. They had so much ammo for poking fun the rest of the semester." He shook his head. "They thought they were so funny. Stupid freshmen—they're practically babies. At least I'd been out on a date that night instead of staying in with video games on the Xbox, like them."

"I'm sorry." Cody gulped deep breaths in an attempt to stop laughing. "It's only so funny because last night my girlfriend told me all about how she short-sheets her roommate all the time. I never even heard about it before. How many times did they get you with it?"

"Just the one. They moved on to other pranks." Eli counted on his fingers. "There was the popcorn above the door, the bucket of water in the stairwell, the kefir in the milk carton, and my favorite, using my phone to ask random girls out. Joke was on them with that one; I like to meet new people." Eli smiled. "But I'd warn you, if you ever feel like pranking me, I know how to return the favor."

"I am going to choose to *not* take that as a threat."

"We can decide right now to just play nice."

"Fine by me."

"Keeping it friendly?" Eli held his hand out.

"Keeping it friendly." Cody shook it. He wasn't quite ready to call him a friend yet.

"It's getting light, and I'm done with the floor." Eli leaned the broom in the corner next to an old mop. "I'm gonna go get dressed, then I'll see to the horses if that's okay?"

"Yeah," He nodded at the tidied garage, satisfied that yesterday's work was cleared away to make room for today's chores. "I've got to check in on my mom. I'll meet you in a bit."

CHAPTER 17

Lina

THE MORNING SUN blasted through Lina's bedroom window. She buried her face under the pillow and groaned. As she came to awareness, she threw the pillow to the foot of the bed. She dreaded coming out of her room to see her dad off to work. He hadn't been happy last night about not meeting her date, but he had been tired.

"We can talk about this in the morning," he'd said.

Dawdling in bed gave her guilt time to build until she admitted to herself that she might be making too much of it. Cody had accepted her reason for not introducing them as soon as she explained it, but her dad would be harder to convince.

She stumbled from her room and found him with a bowl of cereal at the kitchen table.

"Good morning," he said. "Did you have fun last night?"

Lina nodded and got a bowl from the cabinet, considering what to tell her father about her date that would present Cody in the best possible light. "We went to dinner, then we sang karaoke and danced. We talked a lot and got to know each other. He brought me straight home and didn't try to kiss me."

"Okay. That's what you did. Now tell me about the guy." He slid the carton of milk over to where she sat across from him.

"He works on his family's ranch. His dad died a couple years ago, and he lives with his mom." She poured milk over her cereal and used her spoon to dunk all the flakes. "He's kind of quiet. He thinks a lot, especially before he speaks. He's curious, even about the stupid parts of my life."

Dad pointed at her with his spoon. "There are *no* stupid parts of your life."

"Well, he listened for half an hour about how I think it's funny to short-sheet Izzy's bed while she's in class."

Dad chewed a moment. "Do you connect over the fact that you've both lost a parent?"

"Absolutely. That's a big part of it. I haven't met very many kids my age who get me."

"If he's so great, then why did you hide him from me?"

There was nowhere to hide from his questioning stare. She pushed her mouthful of cereal into her left cheek to make room for her reply. "Dad, you know I date a lot of different people, right? But it never works out. I just want to be sure there's something there before I subject him to your inquisition."

"It's a parent's right. You'll feel the same way when you have children."

"I'll never get to have children if you scare off anyone who's thinking about being my boyfriend." She raised her voice on that last word and threw her hands in the air. Her response would have been more convincing if she hadn't been talking with her mouth full. All she had done was reinforce the fact that she was his little girl.

"If they scare that easily, they don't deserve to be your boyfriend."

"Dad …" Lina rolled her eyes. "If it matters, he wanted to meet you too. He was actually more than disappointed about it. It's not about him, or you. This is about me." She pushed her messy hair out of her face and sighed. "He doesn't drink, or womanize, or even drive too fast. He's a good guy."

"Fine, because nothing less will do." Dad carried his cereal bowl to the sink. "I have to go to work."

"I'll introduce you when I'm ready, I promise."

"Okay." He ran water into the bowl. "When you're ready." Facing her, he offered a wink and picked up his briefcase. "Have a good day, pumpkin."

"I love you!" she called after him as he walked away.

Dad's voice carried to her from the front porch. "I love you too!"

CHAPTER 18
Cody

THERE WAS a bounce in Cody's step as he made his way to the chicken coop, and he hummed the melody of "Need You Now." Talking about college pranks with Eli had lifted him from the dumps. Maybe things could still work out for him and Lina. He would know more after his appointment with the school district. Until then, there was no point in assuming a change of circumstance was impossible. He was still humming when he entered the house and set the egg bucket in the kitchen.

"I gather it went well last night?" Mrs. Bauer was up, knitting on the couch.

"Yeah, Lina is … she's … she's …"

"You get back to me when you find the right word, okay, hon?" Mrs. Bauer came to the kitchen and tied an apron around her waist. "You got time for breakfast?" She cracked eggs into a bowl.

"I should take food to Eli too," Cody said. "He slept in the bunk room last night." The bunk room didn't have a kitchen or even a microwave, only two sets of bunk beds and a bathroom.

"That's no problem, just give me a minute."

"How were things here last night?"

"Well, hon, we got on just fine, but I think it may be time to get Dr. Pace out here again."

"What happened?"

"You know how she was talking about the wind yesterday? Well, she seemed so worried about it, kept saying 'Lay down in the wind,' and 'Get out of the wind.' Might want to have Doc look at her."

"Okay, I'll call him today." It had been a while since Doc had visited. Mom's prescription didn't have any refills left anyway, so it was time.

Mrs. Bauer had made sandwiches of ham, eggs, and cheese on toast by the time Cody was ready to head back out. "I'll tend to Rosie before I leave. You'll need to check on her this afternoon," she said.

"Thank you, Mrs. B." He hugged her and wrapped the sandwiches in a few paper towels.

When Cody got to the barn, Eli was almost done mucking out stalls. He worked fast, and he was thorough.

"Better take a minute to wash up and eat before the others get here," Cody said. "Wayne usually likes to get us working right off the bat."

"You brought me food? Rock on." Eli set the pitchfork aside and washed his hands at the utility sink.

They sat on a fence rail and watched the sun climb over the treetops on the horizon while they ate. Mrs. Bauer had made four sandwiches, two for each of them. They were still there comparing life with six siblings to life as an only child when Wayne pulled up, Tay and Spence right behind him.

"We're moving cows today," Wayne said. "A hundred head from Nebraska are arriving tomorrow morning. So we're taking the herd from the south pasture and bringing it west. Then we gotta ride the fences and make repairs to keep these cows separate."

Later, Cody loaded his pickup with tools and supplies to check the fences with Eli. They found a post that was cracked. Only a slight push would bend it over. Cody clipped the wires while Eli wrapped a chain around the base.

"How long have you and your girlfriend been together?" Eli asked.

"Not long." *Clip. Clip.* "Actually, last night was our first date." Cody draped the lengths of wire around the next post in line to hold it until it was time to connect it to the splice.

Eli attached the chain to the nose of the farm jack and started cranking the handle. "Does she know she's your girlfriend?" He raised an eyebrow.

"No, but that's how I think of her," Cody said. "You have a girl?"

"No, not really." The post started to budge from the ground. Eli put his back into it. "That's why I want to live in town. Unless you've got any single gals here at the ranch. Do you? Have any single women?" The post was loose enough. He wrestled it free and tossed it aside.

Only Mom. And that wasn't happening. "Ah, man, you ain't seriously asking me that," Cody said. "I can't find you a girlfriend—barely found my own." He dragged the new fence post from the bed of the truck over to Eli, drawing deep tracks in the soil.

"Hey, don't get me wrong. I can get a gal for myself. Just need to be where they are." Eli grinned as he steadied the new post in the hole while Cody poured crushed gravel into the gaps.

Tall, strong, educated, friendly, happy … Eli was every-thing Cody wished to be. Of course, Eli could get any girl he tried for. Because he would be where they were, working the ranch, but *living* in town. That had been Cody's problem. He had been busy on the ranch day and night since they'd lost his dad. With Mom and the cows needing him …

Still, he'd held Lina close. He'd had her in his arms, felt her silky hair and smelled the floral freshness of her skin. He needed to be where she was.

CHAPTER 19

Cody

TIRED, sweaty, dirty, and hungry after the fence repairs, Cody stopped at the house to check on Mom. Skippy met him at the door. The little dog ran back and forth and wagged his tail. Cody scooped him up and made his way into the family room where his mom paced in front of the window.

"The wind is flat. Is your father still out there?"

"No, he's not outside." Cody filled a glass with water and drank it all. He filled it again and got another for Mom. There were a few cookies left from yesterday, so he brought that plate, too, and set it on an end table where Mom could reach it. He was too dirty to sit, so he stood with his water and cookie.

"Mom, are you thirsty? You should have a drink."

"The wind is …" She looked at Cody and drank a little water. Her fingernails were a bright shade of pink. Mrs. Bauer must've painted them last night. "Did you kiss her?"

"What?" Cody lifted his eyebrows. He never knew

how much she was aware of, but clearly she remembered that he'd gone on a date last night.

"Did you kiss her in the wind?" She gulped down the rest of the water and placed the glass back on the table.

"No, I didn't kiss her. We took a picture. Can I show you?" Cody opened his phone to a selfie Lina took of them on the karaoke stage and turned it so his mom could see.

She gasped and covered her mouth with her hand. "You sang?" Her wide eyes glistened, and she lowered herself down to the rocker. Skippy leapt onto her lap, which helped calm her.

Cody shoved the phone back in his pocket and knelt at her feet.

"Mom? What is it? Did the picture upset you?" He leaned forward and hugged her.

"You sang and I missed it," she said as she gripped his head to her chest and rocked back and forth.

It was the most uncomfortable rocking he'd ever endured, but he remained as much in her lap as a grown man could get while still making room for Skippy. He let her rock and remembered how she used to be.

"Kisses in the wind," she said at last, and nudged him away.

Cody hung out on the floor until he was sure she'd settled back into her routine of staring and rocking. He couldn't take a shower if he might miss a lucid moment.

After he cleaned up, he heated some leftovers and served Mom an early dinner. She was as tired as he was and allowed him to put her to bed as soon as they finished eating. There were a couple hours of light left, and Cody should've gone back out to get more work done, but he lay down on his bed with his laptop and his phone instead.

Dr. Pace's receptionist didn't answer, so he left a voice

mail: "My mom could use a visit if the doc has time to swing by. Her medicine isn't working like it should." Dr. Pace had delivered Cody. He was not only their family doctor, he was the only one in the area willing to make house calls.

Cody examined the photo of him and Lina for something that might have triggered Mom. He looked normal. It could have been the microphone in his hand. Mom had always loved music, but she hadn't played her guitar since they'd lost Dad.

In the photo, he was smiling at the camera next to Lina. She was looking up at him, so her eye color didn't come across in the photo. He might never understand why him singing would have upset his mom, but he couldn't have two women upset, and Lina was waiting to hear from him.

Cody took a deep breath and placed the call. Lina answered after two rings.

"Hi," he said. "Thank you for last night."

"I had fun." The lilt in her voice reminded him of the smile she'd worn on the karaoke stage, like everything was right in her world.

"Can I see you again?"

"Tomorrow?" she asked.

Shoot. "We have cattle arriving tomorrow. I'm needed to help get that squared away. I can probably get away for a little while Sunday afternoon." He should be able to endure the two days until then, however difficult.

"My dad wants me to hang out with him on Sunday."

She didn't sound that bummed to put him off in favor of her father. As much as he wished his own dad was still around, he'd never chosen him over a girl.

"I'll miss you." Cody said it quietly, almost hoping she wouldn't catch it.

She continued after a pause. "How about Monday? I have a haircut appointment, but we could meet for lunch after that."

Cody ran a hand through his hair. It was overgrown. He hadn't had a trim in months, maybe even a year. It bothered him sometimes, but he usually just slapped his baseball cap on his head. "Yeah, I'd like to. Maybe I'll get a haircut too," he said, "and I'll let you choose the style."

"Maybe we should get the same haircut."

"Would you look like me, or would I look like you?" He'd rather wear long hair than have her in a crew cut—he would miss her long, silky locks. Choosing to imagine she was teasing, he burst out laughing.

When she heard him lose it, she laughed too. As their mirth died out, her voice, soft and meek, raised another worry. "I would do it if I thought that was what you genuinely wanted. That's always been my problem."

His heart wrenched. There was much to learn about this girl who had captivated him, and why she would get a crew cut for him was just the beginning. "You never have to do anything you don't want to do. I only want you to be you."

There was silence over the phone, but if their hearts could've held hands, they would have at that moment. Held hands and accepted each other. Only the distance found on a phone conversation kept him from begging her to choose him forever.

CHAPTER 20

Cody

MOM TOOK LONGER to calm down than usual, so it was well past noon when Cody made it to the barn. Any trace of morning dew had long ago evaporated, leaving only the heat of the sun pressing on his shoulders. If he ever made it to college, he would spend his time in air-conditioned classrooms and lecture halls. It wouldn't be the worst thing.

He revved up a UTV rather than saddle Big Red and raced to the pasture that had been prepared for the Nebraska cattle. The stock trailers had come and gone, and a hundred head now grazed on green grass.

He drove up to Wayne at the far end of the pasture where the cattle hadn't spread out to explore yet. The animals blended into each other, the deep brown hides camouflaging the individual from the herd. "Sorry, Wayne. Mom was having a bad one."

"Never mind that. She has to come first."

Wayne held a bundle of papers tucked under his armpit. He passed them to Cody. They were the health certificates and inspection paperwork for the cattle and their tag information. Cody glanced at it, appreciating the courtesy, but Wayne was better at managing that side of the business, so he gave it back after a cursory scan.

"Eli is a kid in a candy store." Wayne pointed across the pasture where Eli was looking into a cow's ear. "He's counting them all and checking for signs of virus. Come, the Chancer kid arrived with the herd. I'll introduce you."

They made their way through the tall grass toward the fence line where Tay was explaining something to the new guy as they loaded up the portable chutes to take back to the garage. From a distance, the new guy wasn't much to look at.

"His name's Silas Chancer but just goes by Chancer. He's gonna stay in the bunk room with Eli, so I'm looking into putting a fridge and microwave out there. Can't risk upsetting Rosie with strangers."

In the old days, hired hands staying in the bunk room would come to the house where Mom fed them.

"Do you want me to do that? I can go into town tomorrow and pick up that stuff."

"I'd sure appreciate that." Wayne put a hand on Cody's shoulder. "Inexpensive, okay? No need for anything fancy."

Tay and Chancer fell quiet when Cody approached with Wayne.

Chancer was a small man of about thirty, a few inches shorter than Cody and slimmer. He wore a long goatee held together in a skinny ponytail. When Cody shook his hand, he was the stronger of the two.

"Glad to have you, Chancer," Cody said. More help equaled the possibility of more free time for him and Lina.

"I appreciate the opportunity. I'll do my best to learn

the job." Chancer slid his thumbs through his front belt loops.

"I'm going to show Chancer around, give him the grand tour," Tay said. "Cody, you mind bringing Eli back when he finishes up here?"

"Yeah, I'll wait for him."

Tay and Chancer took the truck back the long way on the road. Spence and Wayne cut across on horseback. Cody took the UTV to the other side of the pasture. He parked it a distance from the cows in case the engine sounds spooked them and walked the rest of the way to meet up with Eli.

"Looks like you've got a roommate," Cody said.

Eli peered up from the cow nostrils he was inspecting. "Should I short-sheet his bed?"

"Nah, he doesn't seem very good-humored."

Eli scanned the cow's ear tag and then tapped on a tablet. Cody took the reader from Eli and they wove their way through the animals, Cody scanning tags and Eli checking the information that came up on the tablet.

"My grandpa is old school," Eli said. "He's intimidated by technology. My brothers use a lot of the newer toys, but I still needed to catch up quick when I got to college."

"I'm behind the times myself, mostly because I haven't cared to learn about the business side of ranching."

"You haven't cared to learn how to run your own business?" Eli asked.

"It's my mom's now that my dad is gone. My name isn't on it anywhere."

"I haven't met your mom yet."

"You probably won't. She's got some health issues and doesn't leave the house much." *Or ever.*

"That's a shame. Is that what kept you this morning? Wayne said you were needed to help your mom."

"Yeah." Cody didn't care to discuss his mom. "I'm going to town tomorrow to pick up a fridge and microwave for the bunk room. That should make staying in there easier."

"Maybe I could catch a ride with you? I'm headed into town for church."

"You want to carpool?" Cody hadn't carpooled anywhere since he was fifteen, but he wasn't opposed to the idea.

"Yeah, you drop me at the church, run your errand, then swing back in time to pick me up. Then I can give you a hand unloading when we get back here. Sound good?"

"What time?"

"Church starts at eleven, over by one. Does that give you enough time?"

"Should be plenty." Cody pushed a cow out of his path. "You about done here?"

"Yeah, I've been done. We scanned them as they were coming through the chute, I'm just playing with the toys." Eli grinned and waved the tablet. He loaded the tablet and reader into a small duffel bag and walked with Cody back to the UTV.

Eli sure was cheery, like Lina. His came across like a natural cheer, unforced and genuine. Cody only felt naturally cheerful when he spent time in Lina's presence.

CHAPTER 21

Cody

THE NEXT MORNING, Cody spotted a bowl of fresh apricots. Mrs. Bauer must have brought some more over because Cody had finished the last of the other bunch. He washed and split a couple for Mom. She smiled and rocked, rambling about the wind but leaving out the part about the kisses. Cody had a much easier time caring for her than the day before, so this would be a good day to leave her on her own for a while after his chores.

Cody tended the chickens and helped Chancer and Eli with the horses, then he took some time to read to Mom from her Bible. He used to do this for her more often, but the longer her illness went on, the further he'd gotten from the habit. Perhaps it was because Eli was a church boy that Cody remembered he used to be one too.

He put a few apricots into a paper bag and wrote on the outside with a marker before he met Eli at the truck for their trip into town. Eli wore a suit and tie.

"Look at you. You ain't messing around, are you?" Cody asked as they climbed in.

"I give the Lord my best. But this looks more interesting than my suit." He took the bag of apricots from the center seat and read what Cody had written there:

"What do you call the time in between eating apricots? A pit stop." Eli laughed. "Clever. Is this for your girlfriend?" When Cody nodded, he continued. "Do you trust me?"

Cody nodded again. He trusted Eli at least enough to handle a bag of apricots.

Eli pulled a pen from his chest pocket and drew a doodle on the bag. A cartoon apricot with arms and legs and a silly face juggled pits over its head.

He entertained Cody all the way into town with stories from his missionary days before he went to college, and true to his word, he didn't preach. The more Cody learned about Eli, the more he liked him, even though he felt like a little boy in Eli's presence. But between him and Lina, Cody had laughed more this week than in the last two years.

He dropped Eli off at the church and headed over to the Home Depot. One swipe of the ranch bank card and the orange vests loaded a refrigerator and a microwave into the back of the pickup. With time to spare, he took the opportunity to cruise by Lina's place.

Her house looked different in the daytime, but he was certain it was the right place because her bicycle was parked on the front porch. He assumed she was inside, hanging out with her father, and he wanted to respect their time together. He left the bag of apricots on the doormat.

Next, he filled the gas tank, picked up several cheeseburgers, and drove to the church parking lot to wait. He listened to the radio with the windows down and ate a burger and fries. Eventually, people in suits and dresses filtered out of the building, and several kids started a game of tag on the lawn outside.

Eli came out with a few other people. Two were young ladies. Eli must've been happy about that since he wanted to meet girls. He spoke with them for a few minutes before he came to the truck, a grin plastered on his face.

"Good day at church?" Cody asked.

"Yes." He climbed in and buckled up. "Salvation … and a phone number."

"You want a cheeseburger too?" Cody pointed to the bag. "Gotta save one for my mom, but the rest are for you and Chancer." He backed out and waited behind a minivan to leave the parking lot.

"Thanks, I'm hungry. Is it okay to eat in your truck?"

"A better question is, is it okay to eat in that suit?" Cody looked both ways and merged into traffic.

"Are you kidding? I wore a tie every day for two years. I think I can handle myself," Eli said, two seconds before secret sauce dribbled onto his white shirt. "Ah. No …" He wiped the shirt with a napkin. "But hey, it didn't get on my suit!"

A text pinged on Cody's phone in the console compartment as he drove.

"Want me to look at that for you?" Eli asked.

"Sure."

"It's from Lina. *Thanks for the apricots, you're very punny* and the kiss emoji."

CHAPTER 22

Lina

LINA WAS WANDERING BACK and forth along the sidewalk in front of the salon when she spotted Cody's truck circling the square. The town hall, surrounded by green landscaping with shady trees and park benches, occupied the center of the square. Shops and restaurants lined the four sides of the square facing the center, and at one o'clock, street parking was in high demand. Cody got lucky his second time around as a van full of soccer players backed out of a parking spot in front of the gourmet ice cream shop.

She started down the sidewalk to meet him. He wore jeans, a spirit t-shirt from Harton East High, and his baseball cap, which shaded his eyes. She couldn't get a read on his mood, but his swagger screamed confident cowboy. As she neared, he spotted her and waved. Despite the grin that grew across his face, her worries erupted. What if she had pressured him into leaving his work and driving all the way into town to see her, and now he didn't think it was worth it?

"Do you think those are any good?" he asked as he joined her on the sidewalk.

"What?"

"The flavors. They sound terrible."

Lina glanced around to find what he was talking about. On the ice cream shop's chalk board were written the flavors of the week: Lavender Vanilla, Cereal Milk, and Honey Jalapeño.

"Eww. Maybe Lavender Vanilla, but I'd almost always rather have Dairy Queen."

He looked at her, shifted his weight, and lifted one arm in hesitation. She hated the do-we-shake-hands-or-hug polka, so she grabbed him by the shoulders and pulled him in. As her arms went around him and he entered her space, he gathered her in close. "Hey," he whispered near her ear.

She dug her fingers into his hair, unseating his hat, and grasped a handful. "You don't have to do this, you know. You could just tell me no."

"Do what?"

"Get a haircut." She let go of him and started toward the salon.

"Yeah, I should. I've let it go for long enough." He pulled the ball cap back into place and followed her.

"Only if you truly want to. I think you are so handsome just the way you are. Do you believe me?"

He stopped walking and looked at her long enough to make her worry again before he finally answered. "I believe you." His gaze sparkled with humor. "I *want* to get a haircut today, just *not* matching styles. And if it means I can get off the ranch and spend time with you, that's all I care about."

Lina warmed. He was saying all the right things. "Okay, the salon is right down here."

Once inside, they sat in neighboring booths and caught each other's gaze in the mirror, over and over again, while the stylists clipped and cut.

When they left the salon, they stopped at a mom-and-pop deli on the square to order lunch.

A short while later, Lina flipped her freshened up tresses over her shoulder as she and Cody settled onto a bench in the sunny town square with their sandwiches.

Lina set half of her turkey club sandwich on Cody's wrapper and took half of his pastrami. She expected some pushback, some mild teasing at least. Instead, he wordlessly spilled half of his bag of nacho chips onto her wrapper next to her barbecue chips.

She searched for a sign of his boundaries. They only had the summer to figure out if there was enough of a connection between them for a relationship. While Lina agreed that Dr. Bowman's recommendation to give it time to unfold was smart, she also needed to cut to the chase. Did he like her, or not? He liked her enough to show up and get a haircut, enough to trade sandwiches, enough to give up half of his chips. He'd already done more for her without asking for anything in return than anyone she'd ever dated before.

After they ate, they lingered on the bench in the warmth of the sun. The town square had become uncharacteristically deserted for mid-afternoon. The lack of commotion lent a feeling of privacy, but much of their conversation was spoken in low, soft voices just the same.

"You kind of surprised me at The Bad Bronco," Lina said as she settled herself cross-legged in the corner of the bench. She raised her face to the sun and soaked the warmth into her cheeks.

"How so?" Cody toyed with a napkin from their lunch.

She nudged him with a Converse-clad toe. "You can sing. You're, like, really good."

"I used to sing a lot with my mom. She was a songwriter."

She would have believed he was proud of his mom if not for the wistful, faraway look in his eyes. "Really? I'd love to hear some of her work."

"Yeah, maybe someday."

"Well, someday isn't far off. In fact, it could even be today."

"Nah, it's not today." He crushed the napkin and stuffed it into the sandwich sack.

"Why not? Someday is *always* sooner than you think." She tugged him by the arm, drawing him in. He reclined against her, his head in her lap. "Please, just share your favorite. You don't have to sing it, just tell me the lyrics."

Cody's eyes fluttered closed as she cradled his face. She had complete control. She could lower her face and kiss him. It seemed like a good idea, a cozy kiss in the town square park. His mouth was right there, the distance short-ening. Only her resolution to let Cody instigate their first kiss stopped her. Instead, she put her finger on the place where his dimple would appear if he was to smile. "The song?"

CHAPTER 23

Cody

THE LYRICS FLOATED on the surface of Cody's memory, easy to recite from his childhood days.

> *When the clouds gather low,*
> *and the sun sinks below,*
> *he looks toward the horizon.*
>
> *That's when my cowboy,*
> *my heart, my joy,*
> *heads for the horizon.*
>
> *Look at him set,*
> *upon ol' Big Red,*
> *he rides along the horizon.*

He gave in to the music and softly sang the last phrase.

> *Just to find his dream,*
> *lofty, yet unseen,*
> *just beyond the horizon.*

He opened his eyes and met hers; they danced with violet flecks amid the deepest blue he'd ever seen.

"That's so sweet. Your mom wrote that for you. You're the cowboy, right?" She stroked his shortened hair.

Earlier, she had asked if he believed her that she thought he was handsome. It was easy to believe so now. She was holding him close and treasuring his mom's song, her lips hovering and waiting for the kiss he had yet to give her. Yes, he believed her.

Cody's cell phone rang, the default ringtone. He wiggled it from his pocket and checked the caller. Doctor Pace. "Sorry, Lina, I've got to take this." He sat up and moved to his own corner of the bench.

"Cody?" The voice on the other end was a familiar one. "This is Sandy from Dr. Pace's office."

"Hi, Sandy. Does the doc have time to come see my mom?"

"I'm sorry to tell you this, but Dr. Pace has sold his practice and retired. We've got Dr. Hilderbran now, and he won't do house calls. That's a dying tradition, I'm afraid. But I'll get Rosie on the schedule for a week from this Friday, and we can see her here in the office."

"All right. Thank you for letting me know. I'll do my best to get her there. Thanks." It would take a miracle to get Mom out of the house and into a car, but if that was the only option, he had to try. As he hung up, Lina eyed him curiously.

"Is everything okay?"

"Yeah. My mom's not feeling well. That was her doctor."

"Is there anything I can do?" Her brows furrowed.

"Thanks, but no."

"Do you have to go?"

"No emergency. I can stay a while longer."

She intercepted his phone as he tried to put it into his pocket and held it farther from him like a hostage. "I'm getting the sense that music has been a big part of your life, so that default ringtone will never do." She tapped her way into his settings.

"You're just going to make yourself at home in my phone?"

She batted her eyes and captivated him with her sweet lips gently curving into her smile, inspiring thoughts of a picnic blanket by the pond. Those thoughts were definitely for a someday, but not today. "Dang, those womanly wiles. Okay, you powerful siren, fair is fair. Let me see yours."

She gave it over. With her phone in hand, he tried not to acknowledge her pouty frown, which was just as sexy as her smile. He sat in his corner of the bench, and she propped her feet up on his thigh. The contact, though distracting, was a welcome assurance that she wanted to be there with him.

As Lina had her way inside his cell phone, Cody browsed her photo library. She had a lot of friends, and many of them were guys. There were selfies of her with friends at basketball games, concerts and fairs. She'd been on a hike and there were photos of her surrounded by friends on a mountain peak. There were a couple of pictures of her wearing a swimsuit on a speedboat with a tall, scrawny boy. Her in a shopping mall at Christmas time with a slick, well-dressed man who looked too old for her. Lina, dressed as an angel at a Halloween party with a guy dressed as a devil. She was so lovely, but Cody wanted to punch that guy.

How would he ever stand out among these other men?

They had her time and attention most of the year, and he only had a couple of months over the summer.

As much as he didn't want to admit it, Eli was right about girls. To have a chance with Lina, he needed to be where she was. He had to be at Washburn. Without control over the direction of his life, he would never have a girl like her. But he didn't want a girl *like* her, he only wanted her.

He had her attention for now. There had to be a way to keep it beyond the summer.

He scrolled through her contacts until he found himself listed as Cody the Cowboy Duke. Raising an eyebrow in her direction, he added a purple flower emoji, a heart, and a silly smile face to his details. Then he set his contact at the top of her favorites. He accidentally dialed his phone from hers. "Need You Now" began playing from his phone in her hand.

The sudden music startled her. She turned his phone to show him the screen. Her contact was labeled as The Most Beautiful Girl. It shouldn't have been a surprise.

"Oh no, that's too much pressure," she teased and began tapping at his screen again. She showed him when she was finished. Now it simply read *My Lina*. "Better?"

"Better." Better than anything he had dared.

"Okay." She held out her hand. "Ready to trade back?" Once she had her phone, she rested her head on his shoulder and took a selfie of them. "To remember today." She texted him the photo and sighed. "I should be going. My dad will be home from work soon."

Cody checked the time—almost four o'clock. The bench was in full shade. The afternoon had flown by while they'd lazed around in the town square. They strolled to his truck, reluctant to part. "Can I give you a lift?" he asked.

"No, I have my bike and a few errands."

"I could come with you on your errands. It feels weird to just leave you here."

She stood close, close enough to wrap her in his arms and kiss her. *Not here.* Not with kids getting dropped off at the karate studio across the street and a car honking at a pedestrian. The perfect girl required the perfect setting for the perfect kiss.

"I promise, I'm fine." She backed away and the moment was lost. "Thank you for today."

"I'll call you later."

Cody drove away, and she waved and watched until he turned out of sight.

His phone rang with the default ringtone. It was Eli. Lina hadn't changed the ringtone for all of his contacts, only for her calls.

"Cody, are you on your way back? We could use a hand baling the hay before it gets dark. Tay had to go—his wife went into labor—and Spence isn't back from the feed supplier yet."

"Where's Chancer?"

"Not sure. Haven't seen him since he burned popcorn in the bunk room."

"On my way."

CHAPTER 24

Cody

WHEN CODY GOT to the garage, the stench of burnt popcorn still lingered. He knocked on the bunk room door. Chancer answered, barefoot and bare chested, his doughy midsection out of character for a ranch hand. In Cody's experience, real cowboys worked too long and hard to be soft.

"Hey, man, it's a workday," Cody said.

"Yeah, I know. I finished mucking out the stalls."

"Around here, we work until the jobs are done, not until *our* job is done."

"Sorry, man. I wasn't sure what to do next."

"Okay, get dressed. We need help with the haying." Cody turned, giving Chancer a minute to pull himself together while he checked the whiteboard.

So, Chancer had been lounging around, eating popcorn and goofing off on his laptop. Cody wanted to be mad about that, but he'd done no better. He had spent the entire afternoon with Lina. He could've been setting a better example for the new guy.

Chancer emerged, properly dressed for ranch work.

Before they left the garage, Cody explained, "If you ever finish early, you can check the board for other chores that need doing. Or you could always ask Wayne."

"I couldn't find Wayne."

Cody pointed to the board. "He's out at the north pasture. You could've ridden out there to find him or used one of the radios." It was so weird to talk to Chancer this way. He was a grown man, not a child.

"Sorry, it was just a rough morning. I woke up late, and I had Eli in my face, and—"

"I get it." It wasn't hard to feel second rate next to Eli, and if he was acting like a know-it-all … Well, Cody might have wished he were somewhere else too. Somewhere eating popcorn and watching Netflix. "Come on. Eli already has the equipment out there."

When they arrived at the hay field, Cody drove his truck over to where Eli had paused the tractor. Eli jumped down to meet them.

"I've brought you some help," Cody said, looking over the field where cut grass lay all over the ground.

Eli pulled his hands from his gloves and gave them a shake. "Chancer, what sort of tractor do you have experience with?"

"I've driven a compact John Deere."

"Okay, you take the newer one." He pointed to the tractor he had just come from. "I'll drive the hunk o'junk."

"I wish I could stay—" Cody started.

"Never mind that." Eli slapped a hand on Chancer's shoulder and steered him toward the work. "This field has been drying all day. We'll get it baled up before dark," he assured Cody.

"You're not going to help?" Chancer leveled a challenging glare over his shoulder.

"I've got my own work to do," Cody called back, even though his work was none of Chancer's business.

When he got home, Mrs. Bauer was tidying up the kitchen and Mom was sorting a basket of socks from her rocking chair.

"There you are." Mrs. Bauer clapped her hands excitedly. "I didn't want to leave until you got home."

"How was she today?" Cody set aside his ball cap and came to wash up in the kitchen that smelled of chilies and broiled cheese.

"Fine. She was just fine. I see you got a haircut. It's about time." Mrs. Bauer set a green salad on the table. "Now, how's Lina?"

"She's fine." He might have shared more, but the embarrassment about not having done any work this afternoon lingered to dampen his mood.

"Nonsense. You don't get a haircut for 'fine,' now do you?" She wasn't backing down.

"No, ma'am." He peered into the fridge and helped himself to a pitcher of lemonade. "After the haircut, we had a picnic in the town square. We talked awhile, until she had to go. It was a nice time."

She gave him an impatient stare. When he didn't offer any further details, she gave up. "That's all I'm getting out of you, isn't it?"

"Yes, ma'am."

"Well, invite me to the wedding." She slung her purse over her shoulder. "Dinner's in the oven. It'll be ready in about ten minutes." She stopped to give Mom a side hug on her way out. "See you Wednesday."

"Bye, and thank you." Cody called.

After Mrs. Bauer had left, Cody helped his mom finish

matching up socks. "Does Lavender Vanilla ice cream sound good to you?"

She made a face. "No, but chocolate syrup fixes a lot of problems."

"Yeah, I guess it does," he chuckled.

"Your hair looks nice." She shook her head at two mismatched socks, yet still paired them together. "You look like your father."

"Hmm … I've always thought I looked more like you than him."

"Well today, you look like him." She shoved the basket away, the job unfinished but having reached her limit. "Are you hungry?"

"Yeah, dinner should almost be ready." He seated her at the table and dished up a pile of salad onto her plate just as the kitchen timer buzzed. The enchiladas bubbled as he took the casserole dish from the oven. He brought it to the table and took his seat.

As he filled his own plate, his mom stopped him. "Save some for Dad."

He looked at the heaping serving dishes. The pan of enchiladas would be enough for three meals, at least. "There's plenty here, and I don't think Dad will be eating very much." The dead don't eat much at all.

When the kitchen was cleaned up and his mom was tucked into bed, Cody had a choice to worry about Mom some more or to remember his day with Lina. He chose Lina. He chose to picture her, hair wet with the salon drape around her neck, stealing his sandwich when she thought she was being sneaky, wrangling him into her lap with her kryptonite lips teasing just out of reach, and the photo of her with the Halloween devil. *Damn. How did he get in there?*

Be where the girls are. Eli's motto.

If Cody was going to be Lina's next Halloween date, he had to get to Washburn. He opened his laptop and logged in to his email. An automated reminder of his appointment at the school district offices waited for him. He clicked the green button to confirm the appointment. He was going, but not alone. If he could tag along to Lina's haircut, she could tag along to this.

"Hello, handsome," she answered the phone with a sultry voice. As if he didn't have enough trouble sleeping, now he'd lie awake with her voice on his mind.

"Hey, beautiful," he returned. "Are you busy Wednesday?"

"No. I have the library tomorrow, but Wednesday is free. Do you want to get together? There's a new Defender movie at the cinema …?"

"Actually," Why was he so nervous? "I have to go to the school district offices to see about getting my diploma. Would you like to come with me?"

"Eek," she squeaked. "Yes! I would love to come!"

He closed his eyes and exhaled. She didn't think this was a dumb outing. "Can I pick you up around one?"

"Yes, from my house this time."

"Because your dad will be at work?" Cody asked. It didn't sit right that he was spending time with a girl when her father hadn't met him.

"Yeah … please don't take it personally."

"I'll try not to." And he hoped she wouldn't take it personally that he hadn't introduced her to his mom. "Good night."

"Good night, and Cody? Thank you for inviting me."

He stayed on the phone until she disconnected. Then he browsed through the diploma program website again to pick out every detail that pertained to his situation. If he did his ranch jobs in the mornings and school assignments in the afternoons, this might work. And once he had a diploma, what then?

He pushed off his bed and opened a drawer at his desk. A long white envelope with the Washburn University seal topped a haphazard stack of papers. Cody removed the letter inside, held it up to the wall next to his bed, and pushed a tack through it.

Congratulations, it read. *You have been accepted to begin your studies ...*

He lay back against his pillow and read that first line out loud. Could his future really be better than his past? Could he really write his own ending? He borrowed a portion of Lina's hope and shoved over his own inadequacy to make room for it in his heart. The pulsing optimism, foreign to him, roared in his chest as though he were climbing to the peak of a roller coaster drop. He could do this. He *would* do this.

He fell asleep with big dreams but was awakened in the night to harsh reality. Mom was screaming in her room. He leapt out of bed to go to her aid, realizing he wouldn't be able to take care of her *and* go to college. He had to pick one.

CHAPTER 25

Cody

CODY ARRIVED at Lina's house early. He'd left the ranch as soon as Mrs. Bauer had shown up. Now, he sat in the truck, unsure how early was too early to knock on the door. Checking the time, he wasn't even self-conscious about his eagerness to see her again. He made his way up the driveway and knocked on the door. After a difficult night with Mom, today's outing was more about seeing Lina than finishing his education. What good was a diploma if he couldn't ever leave the ranch?

Lina answered the door with a dish towel in her hand. She wore a lavender dress with small white polka-dots and low boots. A wave of relief washed over him. There she was, warm and beautiful.

"I'm not quite ready," she said. "Come in for a minute?"

Cody stepped into the house that smelled like maple syrup, but he may as well have stepped into a magazine. The living room was fashionably furnished, and every-thing matched. There was no clutter anywhere, and vases of wildflowers created splashes of color throughout the room.

A large family portrait hung on the wall. He took a good look at the image of a young Lina next to Ruby and their mom. His blood cooled when he recognized her dad. Her father was the banker. The very same man who had reminded him how powerless he was over decisions about the ranch.

Cody was suddenly very glad Lina hadn't introduced them the other night. He needed time to get over the surprise before coming face to face with him.

"Follow me to the kitchen," Lina said. "I have to finish the dishes before I can go. You can keep me company." An open laptop on the island played a video. "I was just watching some rescue videos. You can close it if you want."

Cody sat on a stool at the island. "What kind of rescue video?" He expected a rescue of sea creatures from debris in the ocean, or any of the million other animal rescues that filled the internet. This looked like a documentary. The camera zoomed in on men with blurred faces and weapons drawn.

"There's a non-profit organization called Abolitionist-Ops. They work with national and local law enforcement to bust up human trafficking rings and sex slavery crimes. They rescue exploited kids and return them to their families if they can."

"That's awesome," Cody said. "I kind of thought you'd watch *Friends* reruns or *Grey's Anatomy*, but I suppose I should've known better."

"I watch those too, but I also like to follow Abolitionist-Ops's work. It might be Ruby they find one day, and if not, at least somebody is getting their sibling back."

Cody divided his attention between the video and Lina's back as she scrubbed a skillet in the sink. He was drawn into the drama of the undercover operation and rescue, and his heart ached for the terrified children with blurred faces. Lina saw her sister in these clips, and now he did too.

She dried the last dish and put it away, then closed her laptop and presented herself in front of Cody. "I'm ready now."

"You look really pretty." He took her hand, strengthened by her presence. "Thanks for coming with me to do this."

"It's my pleasure." Lina's smile still radiated from his compliment when she turned to lead him through the living room on their way out. Mr. Grant's inscrutable glare from the family portrait followed him as he walked through the room.

On their way to his truck, Cody confessed. "I've met your father already, at the bank. I don't think he liked me."

"Really?" She raised her eyebrows. "What happened?"

"Nothing much. He couldn't help me—my name ain't on any of the accounts. He was just doing his job, I guess." He opened the door for her to climb in.

She perched at the edge of the seat, half in and half out. "When was this? Was it before we went out?"

"Yeah." He braced an arm against the side of the truck. "I was kinda surprised to see him in your family picture. But I'm glad to know ahead of time that he's your dad, so when you do introduce us, I'm not blindsided."

She straightened in the seat, and he closed the door. By the time he came around the truck to the driver's side, she had slid over to the center seat again. The contact with

Cody's thigh distracted him as much as ever, but this time, he was ready for it.

"My dad's going to like you. He's going to ask you about a bunch of things that are none of his business, but then he's going to like you, I promise."

She rested her head on his shoulder as he drove and listened while he told her about the new ranch hands. She giggled against him when he told the story about Eli's roommates short-sheeting his bed.

The offices for the school district were in a red brick building on the edge of town. Cody dragged his feet as they walked up to the entrance. He had just barely gotten the idea to do this, and he was already here.

"You nervous?" Lina asked.

"Yeah." Cody ran a hand through his hair, only remembering his haircut when his fingers didn't have as much to push back off his forehead. He steeled his heart, unwilling to let Lina's optimism run away with him, and opening the door for Lina, followed her in.

The receptionist was speaking to a middle-aged woman in a green pantsuit at the front desk, so Cody had a few seconds to get more nervous. He shifted uncomfortably under the pantsuit woman's appraisal.

"Cody Schafer?"

"Yes, ma'am."

"I'm Ms. Jeffries, assistant superintendent." She shook his hand and then Lina's. "Please follow me." She led them down a short hallway to a glassed-in office where they sat in upholstered chairs in front of a massive desk.

"Cody, you are here about earning your diploma, is that right?" She double-checked some information on her computer.

"Yes, I am." Not sure where to put his hands, he sat stiffly, clasping and unclasping them. Finally, he settled them on the armrests of his chair.

"I have your transcript. You are very close." She looked up at Cody. "Your GPA is three point eight. And you did very well on your SAT exam."

Cody nodded. "Yes, ma'am."

Ms. Jeffries pushed back from her computer and tapped a pen against her other hand.

"May I ask what happened? Most of our students who come back later to finish are those who struggled all through high school."

"My father passed away a few weeks before final exams. My mom and I took it real hard. I just couldn't do it. But I'm ready now."

"My sympathies to you and your mom. I'm glad you're back—education is something one never regrets pursuing."

"No, ma'am." Cody reached for Lina's hand, gave it a squeeze, and didn't let go.

Ms. Jeffries returned to her computer. "You are eligible for our Come Back Kids Program as long as you finish before age twenty-one." She glanced at him over the top of her eyeglasses. "But you won't have a lot of time. Your birthday is soon, right?"

"Yes, ma'am. October. I will finish by then."

"Very well. The Come Back Kids route only requires you to complete the elements you are missing rather than starting from the beginning of an equivalency program." She clicked with her tongue as she checked the list of requirements on her computer monitor. "All you need are the second semesters of statistics, writing, and civics. Our program is online, and each class has a twenty-dollar fee that you'll pay through the website. You'll work at your own pace, and when you're ready, the final exams are administered here, by appointment."

She set Cody up with a student account and turned her monitor around to show them. She explained how the site worked and where to find the course syllabi and lessons.

The weight on his shoulders lightened now that he had a clear path to right some wrongs. He glanced at Lina. She glowed, and he hadn't even accomplished anything yet.

"Do you have access to a computer and internet?"

"Yes, ma'am." The first question and he had the right answer.

"Good, I suggest that you start with some practice tests. Those will show you where you're rusty and you can focus your study efforts on those areas. Perhaps you won't need to relearn everything, hmm?" She wrote down Cody's username and temporary password on a piece of paper.

"Is college in your plans?" Ms. Jeffries asked.

Lina's grip on his hand tightened.

When he looked at her earnest face, he had no other plan but college. He needed to be where she was. "It is, at Washburn. Someday."

"Would you like me to send your updated transcripts to Washburn admissions as soon as you pass?"

Cody lowered his head and pursed his lips. It was one thing for him to finish high school—he could do that from home—but Washburn was over an hour away. He needed time to get more help on the ranch and figure out what to do about Mom.

Lina answered for him in his hesitation. "Yes, please do."

Cody looked up at her encouraging gaze. She held his hand between hers. It was her. It was all about her. He turned to Ms. Jeffries. "Yes, thank you."

"We have a financial aid specialist in the office on Tuesdays. As soon as you are ready, even before you graduate, you should stop in and see what help is available for you at Washburn."

"Yes, I will. Thank you, Ms. Jeffries," Cody said.

The assistant superintendent rose to usher them out of her office. Back at reception, she shook Cody's hand again.

"I hope to hear from you soon. Best of luck," she said.

As they left the building, Cody exhaled in a rush and grabbed at the back of his head where his hair used to be. He stopped walking midway down the path to the parking lot and took Lina's arm, bringing her to a halt.

"Thank you for being here with me," he said as he pulled her closer.

"You've got this," she said. "You're a really good student, remember?" Lina held her phone out at arm's length and tilted her head toward him for a selfie of the two of them in front of the school district office.

"You always need a photo of the first day of school." She checked the photo before she showed him. "You're so handsome, and you look happy."

He wiped any trace of humor from his features. "Lina, I gotta ask you something …"

Her brow furrowed and she lowered the phone.

He couldn't keep a straight face any longer. "Would you like some ice cream?" Lina smiled her relief and playfully swatted his shoulder.

"Yes, and just a heads-up, I'm getting the Peanut Buster Parfait this time, so I hope you like peanut breath."

Cody tugged gently on one of her curls as he opened

the passenger door of the truck. There wasn't any kind of breath that would turn him away from her.

CHAPTER 26

Lina

THE SUN HID behind high clouds and a breeze lifted a shortened lock of Cody's hair off his forehead and let it fall again, only to do it all over a moment later. Grateful the lock had been spared by the stylist, Lina watched, mesmerized as the light glinted off his sun-bleached streaks.

"You're staring."

No, I'm falling. Lina smiled. "I'm wondering if you have any peanuts left."

Cody passed her what was left of his Peanut Buster Parfait and she spooned the drippy, chocolatey peanuts into her own cup.

They were sitting on a park bench again, this time under an oak tree at the park across the street from the Dairy Queen. It was a mild day, which allowed them to enjoy their ice cream at a slower pace than last time. Cody stretched an arm over the back of the bench around Lina's shoulders, seemingly content to let the hour pass.

A spongy football hit Cody in the shin. He picked it up

and looked around for the owner. "Did you see where this came from?"

"Right there." She pointed to a small boy with a puckered, quivering face. "Throw it back before he cries. He's afraid to ask you for it."

"Whoops." Cody tossed the ball to the boy. "I was looking for someone taller. Didn't see him there."

The boy watched Cody lean back and waited for him to stretch out his legs and return his arm to Lina's shoulders before he threw the ball again at Cody's legs. Amused, Cody shook his head, and again tossed the ball back to the boy. The boy ran to his mother, so Cody relaxed again next to Lina.

The ball hit him a third time.

"You think your dad hired him to keep me from getting too close?"

"That's the only reasonable explanation," Lina said.

Instead of tossing the ball, he walked over to the boy's mother. "Pardon me, ma'am. Is it okay if I play catch with your son for a while?"

"Thank you." She bounced a fussy infant on her hip. "He would like that. His name is Archer."

Cody and the boy played a clumsy game of catch as Lina finished her ice cream. She glanced at Cody's unfinished dessert. *Blasphemy*. She would never waste ice cream on purpose. It worked to her advantage, though. She fished out all the bits of hot fudge and peanuts until there was nothing exciting left in his cup.

She leaned forward in rapt attention when Cody crouched down to show the boy where to put his fingers on the ball.

Falling.

She didn't want to make any of her previous relationship mistakes with Cody. *Love doesn't happen this fast. Does it?* It was good he hadn't kissed her yet. She would've been a goner. But while watching him with the little boy, she yearned to see him as a father, to be the woman to help him become a father.

Later, after Archer's mom bundled her children into a double stroller and left the park, Cody checked the time. "I should be headed home."

"And you want to get started on your homework?" She was only teasing, but she hoped she was right. The sooner he passed those tests, the sooner he could be with her in Topeka.

He drew his keys from his pocket as they walked toward his truck. "Something like that."

As they drove through the outskirts of town, Lina spotted a flash of color on the side of the road. "Stop! Cody, can you stop?"

He slowed and pulled over onto the shoulder. "What's wrong? Was something there?"

"Yeah." She hopped out of the truck before he could ask any more questions and ran into the grasses next to the road. She found the purple flowers that always meant summer to her and stroked the delicate petals. When she broke the stem near the ground, it tore away ragged.

Cody caught up with her. "What did you find?" He raised an eyebrow and smiled down at her with his thumbs tucked into his front pockets, his hands hanging loose.

She stood to give him the flower. "Tansy aster. They're in the sunflower family." She showed him the ragged break in the stem. "I need clippers. They stay fresh longer if it's a clean cut."

He rubbed the back of his neck as he thought, then he pulled a pocketknife from his jeans pocket.

"Will this work?" he asked.

She took his knife and bent to cut flowers. She handed them to him one by one until he held half a dozen. To a passerby, Cody would have appeared alone near the side of the road with purple flowers in his hand, because no one could have noticed the girl kneeling on the ground, surrounded by high grasses.

"Do you want me to do that for you?" he asked.

"I know using a knife is more manly than holding flowers, but trust me, you have never been sexier." She squinted up at him to verify to herself that what she'd just said was true. It was.

"I only meant that you're kneeling in the dirt with your dress."

Lina paused and looked at her dress. There were dirty spots the size and shape of her knees on the skirt. "Okay." She rose to her feet and traded the knife for the flowers.

She was wrong about him being at his sexiest before, because this was better. His back and shoulder muscles flexed and stretched as he knelt low, reached for the flowers, and cut them free. The rhythm of reach, cut, reach, cut, became too much for her to take. She ran her fingers through his hair and turned his head toward her. He smiled up at her.

"You have enough?" he asked.

"Mm-hmm," she nodded. Her heart raced.

He stood, folded his knife, and returned it to his pocket. His hands were dirty—he wiped them on his jeans the best he could.

"Cody, I ... I mean ..." *I want you.* She gulped. "Thank you."

"Come on." With the flowers in one hand and her hand in the other, he brought her through the tall grasses back to the truck.

Her dad's car was in the driveway when Cody dropped her off, so once again, Lina said goodbye at the truck.

"Will you call me later?" she asked.

Cody smoothed a silky lock of her hair behind her ear. "Yes, ma'am."

She walked up to the porch and turned to wave before she slipped through the front door. Inside the house, she leaned against the closed door with her bouquet and sighed.

CHAPTER 27

Cody

AS CODY NEARED THE RANCH, he spied Spence out in the field cutting more hay with the tractor. His heart sank as the guilt set in. Once again, he hadn't been helping. He had been eating ice cream and picking flowers when there was work to be done. Haying was a big job and took a long time. Depending on how long he had been out there, Spence may be ready for a break. But Cody couldn't offer to help until he'd checked on Mom, and if she wasn't doing well, he wouldn't be able to help at all.

Going back to school wasn't going to be easy. Not just the schoolwork itself, but balancing the demands on his time. His mom, the ranch, Lina, and school—he wasn't sure which took priority between the last two. He *was* sure that if he didn't finish school, he'd never have much to offer a girl like Lina.

Mrs. Bauer's truck was still there, so Cody sought out Wayne before going in the house. He found him and Eli repairing an outer perimeter fence. They both scowled at the gap in the barbed wire and spoke in low tones.

"This isn't normal wear and tear," Wayne said. "I drove

out here yesterday and this hole wasn't here."

"Somebody cut the wire?" Cody asked.

"Cattle thieves," Eli said.

"Who would steal cows?" Cody puzzled. "I mean, in my lifetime, I've never heard of rustlers around here."

"Anybody wanting to make a couple grand the easy way." Eli stretched a new wire across the gap. "We'll have to inventory the herd to see who's missing."

Wayne removed his hat and scratched his head. "Let's rotate them back into the north pasture and scan as they cross through."

"I'll round up the boys to help," Eli said as he headed for the UTV. "We've got to get right on this for the police report and the insurance claim."

"I'll ride back with you," Wayne said. They climbed into Cody's truck. "How's Rosie?"

"I ain't been to the house yet. Just got back."

"How'd it go at the school?"

"I have three classes I need to pass." Cody ran his idea past the older man. "If I give you the mornings, can I have the afternoons to study?"

Wayne took off his hat and fanned himself with it. "That'll be all right. I know you're hard on yourself about pulling your weight around here, but your mom first, then school, ranch comes last. Especially now that we got some new hires. Eli is worth two men; not sure how much Chancer is worth yet."

When they pulled up to the barn, Wayne got out. He leaned back into the cab to say one last thing. "It's time to do the bills again. You and me, tomorrow morning."

Ugh. Bills again. Nothing was more discouraging than watching a bank account already on life support dwindle even more.

CHAPTER 28

Cody

AS CODY ENTERED the front door, bubbly, animated voices echoed from the kitchen. He rounded the corner to find Mom kneading a pile of dough on the countertop and Mrs. Bauer drying some dishes at the sink. The air was filled with the smell of baking bread and something hearty —beef, perhaps.

"He needs a head." Mom chuckled, twisting off a piece of dough and rolling it into a ball.

"Save enough to make another full loaf."

"But what kind of boy doesn't have a head?"

"Well, how can I argue with that?" Mrs. Bauer used the dish towel to protect her hands as she pulled a tray of loaf pans from the oven. A fresh wave of the yeasty aroma emanated from three hot, golden-brown loaves of bread and wrapped Cody up in cozy safety.

"Uh, hi." Cody raised an eyebrow at the pair in the kitchen. "Are you gals Lucy and Ethel today?" He hadn't seen *I Love Lucy* since he was a little boy, but the pair of ladies in the kitchen gave a spot-on impersonation.

"Oh, Cody, don't start that," Mrs. Bauer said. "We're

baking some bread today, and Rosie wanted to get artistic." She pulled back a towel to uncover balls of dough on a baking sheet. They were arranged to form a torso with arms and legs.

"Is it a teddy bear?"

"It's a boy," Mom insisted, placing the final ball of dough into the space reserved for his head. "He's your new brother." She patted the dough belly. "And you can name him."

"Can I eat him?"

"Not before we show him to your dad."

Cody met Mrs. Bauer's worried frown.

"What did Dr. Pace say?" she asked, tipping a hot loaf from its pan onto a cutting board.

He shook his head. "He retired. She has an appointment with Dr. Hilderbran next week. The hard part will be getting her there."

Mom stuck two raisins for eyes on the dough boy's face.

"Rosie?" Mrs. Bauer moved into her space and got her attention. "Would you come with me and Cody into town next week?"

"I don't know." Mom covered the bread boy with the towel and left it to rise. She wiped her hands on her apron. "I can't say, but Cody needs to eat."

"Well, think about it." Cody guided his mom to the kitchen sink to wash. Maybe was better than no. "It's important."

Mrs. Bauer filled a bowl with beef stew and set it on the table next to thick slices of freshly baked bread. "Have a seat and tell me how things went at the school."

Cody watched steam rise from the bowl and curl in the air. "Went okay. I think I can do it if I make time to study." He tore a slice of bread in half and spread it with butter.

"Did you see Lina while you were in town?"

His mom joined him at the table. "Your dad used to kiss me every day." Her hands trembled. She frowned at her trembling hands and clasped them in her lap. "Cody, little Cody …"

He glanced at Mom, half in and half out of reality, upset again by the mention of Lina. "I'll have to tell you about it later."

Mrs. Bauer poured a glass of milk and brought it to him. "Goodness gracious, a thumbs up or thumbs down will do!"

A grin forced its way across his face, and he raised a thumb. "Have you ladies eaten yet?"

"Yes, I was about to put Rosie in the shower and send her to bed. She's been a bit high-strung and is tired out."

Cody pushed his chair back. "I can help."

Mrs. Bauer waved him away. "You may as well let me help while I can. I'm getting old, you know. One day it will be all you." She patted Mom on the arm and led her out of the chair and to the bathroom.

Cody helped himself to another bowl of stew and opened his laptop on the kitchen table. He searched the internet for the AbolitionistOps website and read every page and sidebar. He hadn't been able to forget his unresolved feelings from when Lina showed him the video earlier, like a story half told. He watched another video. Undercover agents posed as dirtbags looking to buy children. They arrested the traffickers and rescued the children.

Cody's heart raced as he watched the operation go down. When the video ended, he had so many questions.

They hadn't shown what happened after the rescue or how much damage had been done to those kids. How could they live a normal life after what they'd been through? Ruby might be suffering just like the kids in the video. And the bad guys? They deserved prison without parole. But the video ended with no mention of their consequences. He went down the rabbit hole of the internet to read anything he could find.

His stew had gone cold by the time he landed on a page that described the qualifications necessary for the various positions on the team. Aside from the undercover agents, there were analysts, profilers, researchers, psychiatrists, social workers, and the list went on. The pounding in his chest reached his ears and pulsed there while he scanned the page. One thing was common for most of the positions—a degree in criminal justice. He opened a new browser window and did a search for Washburn's degree programs. As he scrolled the list, his heart calmed, the pounding in his ears quieted, and everything became clear. He would pursue a criminal justice degree at Washburn University.

He thought of little Archer at the park today. Kids like him went missing sometimes, like Ruby. They needed a new ending, even more than he did. He closed down his laptop and let it all sink in. He finally had a calling, a purpose that both motivated and terrified him. Instead of trading ranching for *anything* else, the only thing he *could* trade it for was rescuing children from human trafficking.

"Rosie's tucked in," Mrs. Bauer said, interrupting his thoughts. "I'm off. Now stand up, hon, so you can hug me proper."

After the hug, she grabbed his chin to look at his face.

"You look like you're hiding a hundred secrets," she

said under her breath. She released his chin and shrugged. "Can't come tomorrow, so you're on your own until Friday."

"Thanks, Mrs. B," he called after her as she left.

Daylight had faded outside. Any work that was still going on would be wrapped up soon. He wasn't up to Chancer's glare if he were to show up at quitting time. He tidied the kitchen and went to his room. The two-year-old acceptance letter from Washburn dangled from the tack. It beckoned him to dream of a different life.

He stretched out on his bed and opened the floodgate that had been keeping his dreams under tight control. There could be a life, with a job that mattered, with a girl that likes flowers. He closed his eyes and saw Lina twirling in a roadside meadow, her purple dress the same color as the flowers in her hand. Dark hair fell over her eyes and he brushed it from her face. The last thing he remembered before drifting off to sleep was her calling him sexy.

CHAPTER 29

Cody

MOM SLEPT LATE. Cody had to wake her so he could get her set up for the day before he met with Wayne. After he'd fed her, cleaned her up, and settled her in her chair, Skippy jumped up for his morning rock on her lap. She stroked the little dog's ears.

"Is Lina here yet?" she asked.

She caught him off guard. He remembered how she'd trembled last night when Mrs. Bauer asked him about Lina.

"What? No … I … Mom," he stammered. "I've got chores."

"She better hurry, before the wind comes."

"I'll tell her to hurry. Take care of Skippy. I'll check on you in a bit." He narrowed his gaze at his mom. This was not her usual kind of disorientation. Sort of, but different. He decided to come back as soon as the bills were done rather than working until lunch.

In the garage, a stack of invoices was piled high on the workbench and two stools were pulled up, but Wayne was nowhere in sight. Cody checked out in front of the barn and found him and Eli speaking to a police officer. The trunk of the patrol car served as a table where Eli's tablet was propped up and the officer took notes.

"Three cows are confirmed missing," Eli said. "I have their ID tag information here, and a photo of each animal."

The officer gave him a tolerant look. "Photos?"

"What? I finished cataloging all the animals a few days ago." Eli tucked his tablet under his arm. "It was fun."

"So, you're claiming a broken fence that you've already repaired and three missing cows. And nobody saw anything suspicious?" the officer asked.

Wayne stepped in to help Eli out. "No, but we'll be more alert now. If you find anyone selling these stolen cows, we'd appreciate hearing about it."

The officer snapped his notebook shut. "I'll be in touch." He got in the patrol car and drove off.

"We ain't never seeing those cows again." Wayne kicked at the dust.

The pressure of the situation weighed between the men. "Damn, I named them …" Cody said, his humor a poor attempt at lightening the loss of the cattle.

"Oh man! What a loser." Eli punched Cody in the arm, and they scuffled a minute.

Wayne had had enough. He stalked off to the garage, scolding them. "Ain't neither one of you got a brain in your blasted skulls."

The boys stilled their wrestling, Cody's ball cap in the dirt and his head locked in the crook of Eli's arm. As soon as Eli released him, Cody straightened out his shirt. Eli may have been taller and stronger, but he was out of breath. At least it hadn't been easy for him to lock Cody.

"Are the missing cows ours or Chancer's?" Cody asked, dropping the playfulness of their wrestle.

Eli hitched up his pants. "They're yours. Thank goodness—wouldn't want to lose the contract with Frank Chancer."

"Yeah, we need the income." Cody picked up Eli's tablet from the ground where it had toppled. "Sorry for making jokes. I think I was trying to show Wayne I ain't mad at him and it's not his fault."

"I get it. All this stuff can get heavy, and as foreman, I'm sure it weighs on him."

"Yeah, that and the finances." He dusted off his ball cap. "Hey, Eli, will you sit in while Wayne and I go over the books? I've a feeling we've been making it harder than it needs to be. Maybe you can check us?"

"Sure, happy to help," Eli said as they made their way to the garage. "Sorry about the missing cows, seriously. I hope they turn up and the cops catch the rustlers."

For the next hour, Wayne selected invoices that could not be put off, Eli filtered out those that could be paid online and took care of those payments with the ranch bank card, and Cody wrote checks for the rest and forged a reasonable version of his mom's signature. The next checks were payroll, and those were trickier because of tax withholdings. Cody had no idea how to calculate those. He had always let Wayne figure it out. Cody just signed them.

At last, they were finished until the next billing cycle.

"How much is left from the yearlings we sold?" Cody asked.

Eli showed him the new account balance on the computer. It wasn't huge, but with the incoming payments from Frank Chancer, they'd get by until the fall sale. That was if no emergencies popped up.

"Okay, boys, I'm gonna go check on the hay making." Wayne left without giving Cody and Eli instructions.

"He's really upset about the rustlers." Cody said. "He's not usually so short-tempered."

"I'm upset about it too. You want to ride the perimeter with me?" Eli asked. He was a self-motivated employee.

"My mom's out of sorts. I need to stay close." Cody walked with Eli to the barn. "You know anything about getting power of attorney?"

"Not much, but when my grandpa had surgery last year, he and I signed a document that said I could make his medical decisions in case he was incapable. That was a medical power of attorney. You're probably thinking of something so you can sign your own name on the checks?"

"Yeah. The banker won't even talk to me about the account without one," Cody said.

"Good thing you do your mom's signature so well. You had a lot of absence slips in high school?"

Eli got a punch in the arm.

"Hey," Eli said. "I met a guy at my church who's a lawyer. Want me to ask him some questions?"

"Maybe. I dunno." Cody glanced at the house. How on earth did one get power of attorney for someone like Mom? She was already incapable of making decisions. "I'll see you later."

He was about to come around the corner of the house to the front door when Skippy bounded toward him, tail wagging.

"Hey, Skippy, you didn't leave Mom, did you?" He picked up his pace, leaving the dog to follow him on his little dog legs.

Mom stood, petrified, in the open doorway, her robe gaping open over her nightgown. White-knuckled fingers clutched the doorjamb on both sides like talons. She squinted in the sunlight and from across the porch, it looked almost as though she was smiling.

Cody ran to her. "Mom, what's wrong? You feel okay?" He inspected her for signs of injury. "Can I take you inside?"

He pried her fingers loose, but he couldn't nudge her from the doorway. Cody scooped her up with an arm under her knees and carried her back inside. He set her on the couch next to him and cradled her head against his shoulder. Skippy hopped up too, and the three of them nestled into a family cuddle.

"Little Cody … Did I ruin it?" Mom asked. "You need a brother." He couldn't make sense of her ramblings.

"What can I do for you, Mom?" Cody whispered.

Her adventure to the front door had exhausted her; she dozed off against him. When Cody was sure she was asleep, he eased out from under her and slid a pillow under her head. He paced, following the same route his mom had scored into the floor. Skippy stared at him.

"How could you let this happen?" he asked the dog. Skippy turned a circle and lay back down.

Cody fetched his laptop and brought it to the family room to be near his mom. He found an email address for Washburn's admissions office. How did one ask for a second chance? He decided to keep it simple. After a brief introduction, he just asked for what he wanted: *Are you willing to reinstate my acceptance upon receipt of my updated transcripts?* He sent it before he could change his mind.

When his mom woke at lunchtime, she was quiet. She

ate a sandwich and rocked in her chair without incident. Cody made her drink a tall glass of water so dehydration wouldn't lead to more behavior shifts. They sat together all afternoon. She rocked and looked out the window, and Cody took practice tests online for his classes.

Just before sundown, he tucked his exhausted mother into bed. Then, his mind wandered, preventing his own rest. Needing a diversion, he called Lina.

"Hi." She was breathless when she answered.

"Hey, what's going on?"

"I'm playing *Just Dance* on the Wii with my dad. But I can take a break. I'm glad you called."

"I can't picture your dad doing *Just Dance*."

"Well, I win, if that tells you anything," she said. "How was your day?"

Stolen cattle and being cooped up with Mom's rough day were two details he'd keep to himself for now. "Uh, all right, I guess. I've been studying—kinda boring." He wandered into the kitchen and peered into the fridge. Chocolate milk. Mrs. Bauer was the best.

"You should come study at the library tomorrow. I'll be working … we could see each other?"

"Yeah, maybe I will," he said. Mom would have Mrs. Bauer tomorrow, so Cody could get away. Unless Wayne needed him to catch up on things he hadn't done today. He drank straight from the carton.

"Hey, Cody? What are you wearing?"

Silence. Cody froze, then coughed. *What?* He looked down at his boxers, what he normally wore to sleep in, but there was no respectable way to respond to that question.

"Don't worry, I'm kidding." Lina laughed.

Damn … Cody breathed again. "Can your dad hear

you? He'll never like me if he hears you say things like that."

"Okay, I'll stop. But I'll see you tomorrow, right?" she asked.

"Yeah, tomorrow. Good night."

CHAPTER 30
Cody

HE FIRST SAW her from behind. She stood tiptoe on a footstool, reaching to dust the top of a bookshelf. The hem of her red blouse rode up and exposed a strip of creamy skin above the belt of her skinny jeans. Cody's heart pounded, and he turned away. But then, there was nothing indecent about that strip of flesh. He looked again at Lina and let his heart race.

"Mm-hmm." Miss Fayla moved in between him and the view. "You looking at her rearview, young man?"

Cody sputtered as his face heated. He'd been caught. "Yes, ma'am."

"Enough of that now. I know that's not the reason you're here."

"No, Miss Fayla, sorry."

"Lina, your man's here," Fayla called across the room.

"Miss Fayla! Shh … This is a library." Lina stepped down and came to save Cody from her bodyguard.

"If you say so." Fayla waddled to her chair and opened a book on her lap. "More like a meat market today."

Lina sighed and smiled at Cody. "Hi." She touched his

arm. "I'm going to let Mrs. Paul know I'm taking a break, and then I can sit with you and help you study, okay?" She left him to select a table.

"Yeah, okay," Cody muttered and looked around the room. This was not getting off to a great start. He wasn't in the mood to study with Lina, he was in the mood to lay her back on a picnic blanket. Fayla gave him the evil eye over the top of her book as though she could read his thoughts.

He chose a table in the corner near a sunny window and logged in to his classes on his laptop. When Lina joined him, she positioned her chair close to his and passed him two brownies on a napkin under the table.

"Mrs. Paul brought these to work today. I've already eaten a bunch in the break room. I can't stop." She broke off a small bit and sneaked it into her mouth. "But we can't let her see us have them out here."

Cody did the same sneaky taste. The chocolatey goodness melted in his mouth.

"Good, right?" Lina asked.

They kept watch for Mrs. Paul as they shared the secret brownies under the table. Cody ignored the practice test on the computer screen. It may as well have not even been there, not when Lina's mouth was so fascinating as she brought bite-sized pieces up to her lips.

He cleared his throat in an effort to stay focused on why he was there. The computer had logged him out; he entered his password again. He rubbed his stubbled jaw and raised an eyebrow at Lina. He didn't want to send her away, but he wouldn't be able to concentrate with her so close at hand, not unless he put her to work.

She quizzed him from the statistics test. His careless

answers earned him a forty percent. He groaned and wiped a hand down his face.

"Don't worry, you'll get it," she said. They tried again with a small improvement.

"Nobody even uses statistics anyway," Lina said after he bumbled a tricky question.

His decision to study criminal justice was so new, and she was so adorably optimistic about his wrong answer, he just couldn't ruin it for her. But she was mistaken. He would be using concepts learned in statistics all the time.

Twenty minutes later, Lina pushed back from the table. "My break is over. I guess I better leave you alone so you can learn." Her hand was on his arm again, spreading warmth through him.

She returned to her work. She shelved books and straightened chairs. She dusted cabinets and removed outdated announcements from a bulletin board.

Cody was aware of every single thing she did while he was supposed to be studying. Every move she made on the far side of the room called to him. He only got more frustrated as the afternoon wore on. Eventually, he grabbed the laptop and strode across the room. As he passed Fayla, she closed her book and folded her hands on top of it.

"How's the study coming?" she asked.

He glimpsed Lina from the corner of his eye. She was straightening a stack of papers at the circulation desk. "I can't remember my own name with her around."

Fayla let out a gurgle that grew into a full laugh. She heaved to her feet.

"I'm gonna help you." She pointed at his chest and accompanied him to the circulation desk where Lina stapled the stack of papers.

"Lina, you've tortured this boy enough. Have mercy and clock out so he can take you home."

Heat rushed to the tips of Cody's ears. "Oh, that's okay, I'm just gonna go."

"*Humph* ..." Fayla said as she walked away. "You can lead a horse to water ..."

"You're leaving?" Lina asked. "Did you get a lot done?"

"Not really." Cody tipped his head toward Fayla. "Is she right? Can you clock out now?"

Lina checked her watch. "Yeah, it's close enough. Do you want to do something?"

He nodded. "Yeah, I wanna take you outta here."

"There's a farmers' market this afternoon out by the community center. Want to go there? I just need to put my bike in the back of your truck."

Cody had something more private in mind, but anything she wanted to do would be okay with him. He produced his keys from his pocket with a smile. "Yes, ma'am."

CHAPTER 31

Cody

LINA SHOVED a bite of stinky cheese into Cody's mouth. She wasn't very gentle, and most of it smeared across his chin. Their game of getting each other to try samples from the vendors at the farmers' market had gotten out of hand.

"Easy, or I'll make you try the Honey Jalapeño ice cream." His threat was weak and ill-planned because the ice cream shop didn't even have a booth at the farmers' market.

They strolled past the stalls and stopped to look at a selection of hand-made jewelry. Lina admired a pendant made of polished stone in a flower-shaped setting. The violet color of the stone was the same shade as the flecks in her eyes when they flashed with anger or desire.

Cody had first seen that color in her eyes when she had demanded to know why he was in possession of *Romeo and Juliet*. Then again when he had frightened her by the side of the road. It had been there on the dance floor of The Bad Bronco, and in the patch of wildflowers. Her eyes, when they blazed like that, held him captive.

She held the pendant up to her neck and checked her reflection in a small tabletop mirror. "What do you think of this?" It dangled from her fingertips, the purple stone winking in the sunlight just like her eyes when they sparkled with humor.

"It was made for you." Cody took the chain from her and reached around her to clasp it behind her neck. He took his time lifting her hair free, then he straightened the pendant at the base of her throat. While he was there, he trailed his finger along the portion of her collarbone that peeked from the neckline of her blouse. He raised his gaze to hers and met his undoing.

"I like it on you," he whispered.

"That there's one of a kind," the vendor butted in. "I'll give it to you at half off. Today only."

The spell Cody was under cracked at the vendor's disruption. He pulled out his wallet. "Yeah, she'll take it."

"Cody, are you sure?" Lina asked.

"We can't leave it here." He swiped his card. "It's too precious." He would have given her the world if he'd been able to. He couldn't even give her *his* world. But he could give her a trinket that might, one day, represent his heart.

Lina accepted his gift with a smile. They walked away hand in hand, no longer interested in the rest of the vendor booths.

Later, after Cody unloaded her bike in front of her house, a wave of uncertainty kept his hands shoved in his pockets. All afternoon, kissing her had been on his mind, and this was the last chance of the day. A deep breath didn't do anything to calm the erratic heartbeat that pulsed in his extremities. He looked everywhere but at her, afraid of the clear, unspoken invitation on her face. If he kissed her now, he might never stop. A car drove through the neighborhood, and a curtain twitched in the neighbor's window. It was just the two of them there on the sidewalk, but they weren't truly alone.

Lina held onto the handlebars of her bike and waited. Her eyebrows pulled together, and she tilted her head. "You okay?"

"Yeah, you're just so pretty." Cody rubbed the back of his neck, pleased at the blush rising in her cheeks. "When can I see you again?"

Lina grinned at him. "Wednesday next week?" She touched his elbow, reached a kiss to his cheek, and lingered there. He had plenty of time to react if he chose to. But he closed his eyes and used the time to inhale her scent before he mourned its loss when she pulled away.

"Wednesday," he said, then watched her roll the bike to the porch and enter the house. The things he had wanted to say and do but hadn't tormented him all the way home. If he couldn't take advantage of those uncomfortable opportunities, he would have to create a comfortable one.

CHAPTER 32

Lina

LINA BRUSHED dust off her jeans but had little hope for the smudge across her white blouse. She'd only been at the ranch for five minutes and she was already dirty. She couldn't be sorry about her wardrobe choice though. The wide neckline pulled low off one shoulder showed off her new pendant against the backdrop of her skin.

"You ever ridden before?" Cody smiled up at where Lina sat on the fence rail as he cinched a saddle on Delilah.

"Yes and no."

"How can it be yes *and* no?"

"At the county fair. They plop you onto a horse and walk it slowly around the corral. You're riding it, but not really." She twirled Mrs. Schafer's cowgirl hat around her index finger, hers to borrow for today.

"Come on over here. I'll help you up." Cody adjusted the bill of his baseball cap.

Lina came close. He showed her where to grab the smoky-gray horse's mane and the back of the saddle. She lifted her knee, reaching her boot to the stirrup, and Cody guided her toes into place.

"Ready?"

At her nod, he boosted her up with a hand on her rear until she landed in the saddle. She couldn't read his expression as he checked the stirrup lengths.

"You just touched my butt," she said.

"It was an accident." Cody winked at her.

"I'm pretty sure there's another way to help me up without getting handsy."

"Yeah, you caught me. I just wanted to touch you." Cody stroked the horse's nose. He was being very open, and his ears weren't even turning red. "Are you mad?"

"Not even a little bit." Lina's cheeks were beginning to ache from smiling.

Passing her the reins, he said, "Hold them in your left hand," then he gave her a few instructions on directing Delilah.

He mounted Big Red and led the way from the barn. After they passed the house and the garage, Cody brought Big Red alongside Delilah.

"So, *this* is your ranch." She looked around, taking it all in. "What's your favorite part of this place?"

"There's a creek that runs along the north edge of the property. Lots of trees. It's cooler there, and quiet."

"Is that where we're going?"

"We'll pass through, but there's somewhere else I want to show you today." He smiled. "It's a surprise."

Lina hadn't known what she was in for when she woke up this morning. Cody had said to wear jeans and boots, so she should've guessed something like this. After the farmers' market, the only thing she was sure about was the label on her feelings. The label she would bite off her tongue to keep from a man who may not be ready to hear it. She still wasn't sure how Cody felt. He acted like he cared, but he'd been slow to make a move until he'd touched her butt just now, and that didn't count since he was just helping her into the saddle … Unless there really *was* a less touchy way to do it.

A few cows lifted their heads to watch them go by. A pair of calves mooed at them.

"It's hard to believe that these will all be food one day," she said.

Cody shook his head in a stern warning. "Don't think about that if you ever want to eat a cheeseburger again."

"Okay. I trust you to be right about that." Lina adjusted the hat further back on her head to see Cody better. "How is school going?"

"It's all right. I'm scoring better at the statistics practice tests. I have some good news—at least I hope it's good."

Curious, Lina gave him her undivided attention.

"I went to the district office yesterday and took the writing final."

"That's awesome! I didn't realize you were so far along in the coursework."

"I wanted to give it a shot. I just need to pass, right? I never used to settle for just passing before, but I want this done with."

"What was it like?'

"A couple of paragraphs and an essay. It was a literature prompt." He held Lina's gaze as he spoke.

"Well …?"

"I wrote an alternate ending to *Romeo and Juliet*." Amusement pulled at the corner of his mouth and revealed his dimple.

Lina gasped. "You copied me?"

"Nope. Mine is better than yours."

"Really?" She raised her eyebrows and set her chin in defiance, fully expecting him to prove his claim.

"I wrote it in iambic pentameter." He looked out at the horizon, as though the essay was no big deal.

"No way! Really?" She raised a hand to high-five him, but the distance between the horses was too great. She gave it up with a shrug. "Well, you're good at just about everything, so you probably aced it. When will you get your score?"

"Monday."

"I'm happy for you and proud of you and amazed."

"Wait ... *just* about everything?"

Lina flashed him a cheeky grin. "I still don't know if you're a good kisser." Teasing him backfired because now she was embarrassed. She pushed Delilah ahead so he couldn't see her mad blush.

Her cheeks were still hot when he caught up a second later.

"I promise you I won't make you wait a moment longer than is necessary."

"Necessary for what?" She kept her focus straight ahead, fearing how badly she wanted to be kissed was written all over her face.

"To know that I mean it when I kiss you."

Lina gulped hard against the butterflies that made their way up her throat. Wasn't that what she wanted? A guy who wouldn't toy with her, who wouldn't let her believe he cared unless it was true? The three guys in the photos that used to be on her mirror—Todd, Brandon, and Gary— hadn't been anything like Cody. At least Cody didn't want to kiss her unless he meant it. So, since he hadn't made a move, did he have any feelings?

She shouldn't joke about kissing, or tease him, or put

any pressure on him. Not if she wanted him to be sincere. Easing up was not her natural inclination. She usually went after what she wanted, even though that left her heartbroken, disappointed, and alone.

Her new approach to romance had been a rocky effort at the start, but she'd been getting better at waiting for Cody to make the first move. She didn't *want* to wait any longer, but he'd basically just promised that he *would* kiss her when he was ready.

She watched him sway in his saddle. His shirt clung to his biceps and lats as he moved. Ranching had made him strong. For a guy who didn't enjoy the cowboy life, he looked the part.

He entertained her with a story about his dad teaching him to ride, then he moved on to a time when a cousin from Arizona had come to spend the summer with him and they camped out overnight on the property. He made her laugh again and again until they reached a grove of trees along a creek.

A reverent hush descended around them as they entered the trees. Lina tipped her head back in the welcome shade to view the underside of the treetops. Leaves ruffled in the breeze and allowed spots of sunshine to dance on her face.

"I used to read the alternate ending of *Romeo and Juliet* here. It's a good place to think," Cody said. "You saved my life, Adeline Grant. Right there." Cody pointed to a large rock under a giant sycamore.

Lina found him looking at her. His vulnerable brown eyes offered his soul to her with an intensity from which she didn't want to break free. If she weren't astride a horse, she would have gone to him, taken him into her arms, and gotten as close as possible while still being in her own skin. "Cody." Her voice broke and trembled.

"That's why I had to find you." He removed his hat from his head. There was nothing between him and herself but space. "Only, I didn't know you were you, or that you weren't done with me yet." He brought Big Red closer.

Her heart pounded. She wished their feet were on the ground with no horses in sight.

"We have to cross the creek." He passed her as though he hadn't just bared his heart. "Keep Delilah's head up. Don't be nervous."

If she was nervous about anything, it wasn't crossing the creek.

Big Red stepped into the water and picked his way across the rocky bottom. Cody clucked to Delilah, who followed. Once on the other side, Cody led the way up the embankment, and as they left the trees behind them, he threw a smile back at Lina.

"We're on my neighbor Mrs. Bauer's land now." He pointed ahead. "That's where we're going. Almost there."

A few wildflowers mixed in with the grass caught her eye. The farther they traveled to the high meadow, the thicker the flowers became.

Cody dismounted and helped Lina down from Delilah.

Flowers—large, vibrant blooms in all colors—spread out in every direction. "You brought me to the flowers …?" Her hands flew to her cheeks. She'd never seen such a thick patch of wildflowers or such variety in one place. Tansy asters, daisies, and Queen Anne's lace grew as a natural mixed bouquet with rose verbena, prairie clover and bluehearts.

"Yeah, when I saw you go nuts over those purple ones on the roadside, I knew I had to show you this."

Lina stood in their midst. She slowly rotated to take it all in. She'd never experienced such a beautiful place. Gratitude welled up in her chest, but when she opened her mouth to speak, there were no words. All she could do was spin around, head tipped back and arms outstretched under the cloudless blue sky.

Dizzy, she sank to the ground and sat cross-legged, surrounded by the delicate petals. Some of the flowers were high enough to reach her shoulders. Her delighted laugh came out shaky and unsure. She looked around for Cody. He needed to be a part of this.

He was at the edge of the meadow tethering the horses in a cluster of trees. Then, he came toward her with his phone out, snapping photos of her bathed in the sea of wildflowers. She gathered in armfuls of flowers and posed for him. Turning her back, she smiled over her shoulder at the camera. Cody edged closer, taking photo after photo until he towered over her as she lay back on a blanket of flowers, their petals crushed beneath her.

"Do you have a favorite?" He snapped another photo.

She reached for him. "You. You're my favorite."

"Favorite *flower*." Cody sat by her side.

Lina sat up and reached across him to pick a bloom. "This one."

"A daisy?" he asked. "That's a simple flower, and you're such a complicated girl."

"This *is* a complicated flower."

Cody raised a dubious eyebrow.

Lina plucked a petal from the daisy to teach him the backstory. "He loves me." She let the petal fall to her lap and tore off another. "He loves me not." And another. "He loves me. He loves me not," She leaned closer to Cody with each petal, until she was close enough to feel his sharp intake of air.

He interrupted her child's game and took her face in his hands. "Do you want him to love you?"

"Yes." Her answer was a breathless whisper, but the message carried the echo of an impatient shout.

"Then stop after the next petal." His gaze rested on her mouth.

Barely able to breathe, she broke off one more petal. "He loves me."

Cody lowered his mouth to hers and placed a tender kiss on her lips.

The remnant of the daisy fell to the earth as Lina clasped her hands behind his head. She held him to her with undeniable hunger and deepened the kiss.

Cody took a nervous breath against her mouth. His hands trembled as he gathered her hair behind her and placed a kiss just below her ear, then another.

A shiver rattled through her. Lina pressed herself tight to his chest as he held her close, his arm supporting her back as he lowered her into the flowers. She returned kiss for kiss while they lost track of time in the meadow of wildflowers that was surely enchanted.

Only when Delilah whinnied did Lina regain her awareness of time and space. Big Red had tugged loose and wandered into the flowers.

Cody rolled his eyes toward the sky. "Curse that horse. He has the worst timing." He pushed to his feet and left Lina's side to deal with his animal.

She inhaled deeply to calm her racing heart. If Big Red hadn't interrupted, she would have melted into Cody with no hope of recovery, no desire for it either. She licked her lips for any lingering taste of him.

While Cody retied Big Red, she searched for the daisy with the missing petals. It ought to be pressed between the pages of *Romeo and Juliet*. How could she find one particular damaged flower when they had crushed dozens underneath them? As she sifted through the crater they had shaped with their bodies, Cody returned and dropped to his knees beside her.

"Thank you for coming on a ride with me today," he said, his touch wandering, tracing her face as though she was made of fragile petals herself.

Her eyes fluttered closed, and she sighed, content to live in this moment forever.

"We can't stay here much longer. We'll lose the light."

"Aww ..."

"Come on." He helped her to her feet. "I have another surprise." From his back pocket, he produced a pair of gardening clippers and placed them into her hands.

With wide eyes and a joyful smile, Lina surveyed her choices. She started with a big, perfect daisy and added other flowers to it. The choices whirled with colors, shapes, and sizes. All the while, she remained hyper-aware of where Cody was in her orbit.

He took a few more photos of her, then he helped her by holding the flowers. When the bunch of stems became too wide for his hands, Cody brought twine from his saddlebag and lashed them together. While he tied the bouquet behind the saddle, Lina clipped a few more flowers and braided their stems together. She formed a wreath and placed it on her head as she joined him by the horses. "How do I look?"

His gaze caressed the features of her face before lowering to her necklace. "Beautiful." He lifted the chain and slid the clasp to its rightful place behind her neck.

Continuing to set her aright, he raised the fallen sleeve of her blouse and set it higher on her shoulder.

Then, he turned her toward the lowering sun and wrapped his arms around her from behind. She rested her head against his chest and sighed. She took a last look at the meadow with pure contentment and absorbed the fragrance in the air.

"I think you need to meet my dad," she said, allowing reality to intrude on their reverie.

"I know."

She tipped her face back and Cody kissed her mouth one more time.

Before he boosted her up onto Delilah, he gave her a warning. "I'm gonna touch your butt. On purpose."

Lina gasped in mock outrage.

"Don't worry," Cody said. "It shocks me as much as you." He laughed and threw her into the saddle as though she were weightless.

CHAPTER 33

Cody

CODY DROVE SLOWER and slower the nearer they got to Lina's house. He had just barely gotten her into his arms the way he'd yearned to, and he wasn't ready to let her go tonight. He had expected she would be happy to see the wildflowers. He hadn't expected her to be overcome. As he'd watched her revel in the blossoms, he realized that the flowers hadn't overwhelmed her. It had been him. His desire to show her he cared had come across loud and clear. To him, it was louder and clearer. He more than cared. He loved her.

She had the flowers in an old paint can full of water, braced between her knees so it didn't spill in the truck. Because of the size of her bouquet, she sat in the passenger seat and they held hands, arms outstretched across the empty center seat.

They pulled up to the house in the evening twilight. He opened her door and took the bouquet as she slid down from the truck. Handing the flowers back to her, he kissed her while her hands were full. "In case your dad won't let me kiss you good night later."

"Don't worry about my dad. I'll be with you," she said as they made their way up to the porch. "We're a team."

Lina pushed open the door and Cody stepped into the entryway.

"Dad?" No answer. "Wait here in the living room, okay?" She showed Cody to a girly chair that might not have even handled his weight and took the flowers with her to look for her father.

He ignored the chair. The portrait of the Grant family drew him close. He studied Mr. Grant's eyes, looking for a trace of good humor. He hadn't noticed any that day at the bank, but it was there in the ten-year-old image. The faint lines on his face were the shape of laughter as he gathered his wife and daughters in close for the photo. At the bank, those same lines, deeper with the passage of time, had been the shape of worry and hardship.

Cody had misunderstood that day. He had taken the lowered eyebrows and downturned mouth as disapproval and disinterest in helping him with the ranch accounts; his countenance could have been simply heartbreak.

Lina returned without the flowers but with Mr. Grant. He still wore his dress shirt but the knot in his tie was loose and the top button hung open at his neck.

Cody offered his hand. Her father eyed him like a predator, circled around a big recliner, and left Cody's hand in midair a few seconds longer than was courteous. It gave Cody time to measure the expression on Mr. Grant's face against the one in the portrait.

He clasped Cody's hand and gave it two solid pumps while Lina made the introductions.

"Have a seat, please." Mr. Grant watched him take a seat on the couch until he felt sure he had chosen the wrong place.

Lina perched on the arm of the couch next to Cody. They both waited for Mr. Grant to speak.

There was a glimmer of humor in his eyes when he looked at his daughter, but it disappeared when he turned his gaze to Cody. "You haven't brought your mother in to the bank. Did you change your mind about your questions?"

"No sir, I haven't changed my mind. I've been busy, but I still plan to do as you suggested."

"Lina mentioned that you're a high school dropout—"

"Daddy, I didn't say it like that." She turned to Cody. "I didn't say it like that."

"She's right, unfortunately," Cody said. "I'm a few credits shy of my diploma. I'm working on it—expect to have it finished in the next few weeks."

"And what then? What are your goals?"

Cody shifted on the couch. He cleared his throat and looked at his hands clasped together in his lap.

"I have an interest in criminal justice."

"Are you looking to be an officer? A lawyer?"

"No, sir, I'm thinking more of a behind-the-scenes role —a profiler or investigator."

Mr. Grant finally relaxed into his chair. He crossed one leg over the other. He had a hole in his sock and his bare toe glowed like a beacon in the room. Mr. Grant didn't seem to notice it, but it put Cody at ease, despite the effort not to look at it. Even a man as successful and together as Lina's father had a flaw. A minor flaw, far less consequential than his own, but Cody's socks were intact.

"You don't plan on being a rancher, then?"

"No, sir. I've never loved it. Sort of fell into it as an occupation when my dad died."

"Is that why you were at the bank? To find a way out of it, maybe sell the ranch?"

"I just try to help my mom pay the bills. Thought if I had more information, I could make more sense of it."

"Things are tight?"

"We're afloat for now."

Mr. Grant pressed two fingertips into each of his temples and closed his eyes for a moment. When he opened them and returned his hands to the armrests, he looked at Lina but spoke to Cody.

"I'm not thrilled about my daughter dating drop-outs." Now he looked at Cody. "I expect you'll have earned your diploma before you take her out again." Mr. Grant stood, the signal that the meeting was over. "And I'd like to meet your mother, so I can get a sense of what kind of family you come from."

Cody set his jaw and squared his shoulders. He had expected Mr. Grant to be tough. If Cody had a daughter, he would be the same. He rose from the couch to meet him at eye level. Lina's hand on his elbow offered him support. They were in this together.

Cody held out his hand once more. "Glad to meet you, Mr. Grant." A half smile lifted the corner of his mouth. "I'll bring my diploma over to show you as soon as possible."

"You do that, young man." Mr. Grant went to the door and held it open for Cody to leave.

"Yes, sir. Have a good evening." Cody winked at Lina as he stepped outside. The door closed on him. It wouldn't do to let on to her how uncomfortable that meeting was for him. With a great sigh, he relaxed the tension in his shoulders but not in his mind. He *wasn't* good enough for Lina. He had already known that. Even if he'd finished school on schedule and had been halfway through a college degree, he wouldn't have been good enough for her. But she was worth aiming high for.

He was about to get in his truck when the front door opened again, and Lina ran out to him. She threw herself against his chest and his arms went around her naturally.

"I'm sorry," she said. "He knew I went with you to the district offices, but I said you were taking classes. I never said dropout."

"It's okay; I *am* a dropout. It's okay to call it what it is."

He hugged her tight, breathing in the fragrance of her hair until Mr. Grant flashed the porch light off and on, over and over.

"I want to fall asleep tonight with the taste of your kiss on my lips," Lina said against his shoulder.

He tilted her face up. Her eyes were a dark abyss in the starlight, but he imagined their violet flecks as he stroked his thumb across her lower lip. Kryptonite. The porch light still flashed.

"Yes, ma'am." He kissed her parted lips as long as he dared with her dad watching them through the window.

He got in the truck, but she remained in the street. "I can't drive away until you are safe in the house," he said through the open window.

"Okay, but I'm going in under protest," she said, blowing him another kiss. She returned to the porch and entered the house. The porch light went off and stayed off.

CHAPTER 34

Lina

CONDENSATION DRIPPED from the ice-cold root beer bottle. Lina hadn't taken a single sip yet. The coaster wouldn't hold much more moisture before it became useless. With a sigh, she raised the bottle from its puddle and rolled it across her forehead. The cool glass eased her agitation with Dr. Bowman.

"You're my therapist. Aren't you supposed to take my side?"

"I'm your father's therapist too," Dr. Bowman said. "I can't take sides. I can only help you see the best way to sort yourselves out."

"It's just that … I've never minded how overprotective he is. I get it. The world can be a dangerous place. But Cody would never hurt me. In fact, I'm safer with Cody than I am without him."

"How would you describe your feelings about Cody?"

Lina peeled the corner of the label off the bottle. It tore and nearly disintegrated with the moisture, so she started again on a different corner.

Dr. Bowman tried again. "You believe these feelings are real? More than infatuation?"

Lina nodded.

"When did you first notice a change in these feelings?"

"It started like a crush," Lina said with a sigh, "like it always does. And now it's bigger and encompasses so much more. I'm not sure when it switched, but I can envision a life with him."

"You seem sure that he would never hurt you, but are you willing to let your guard down to him?"

"What guard? I've told him about Mom. And Ruby. He knows what scares me. He didn't back off. He didn't assume that I'm damaged or messed up." Lina finally drank from the bottle of root beer. The bubbles danced down her throat like spiky prickles that mirrored the sting of being "damaged." She went on. "And he didn't push on the wound, either. It's more like he wants to shield me from it."

Dr. Bowman removed her glasses and hung them from the neckline of her blouse. Her eyes were laughing on her normally straight face.

"You should tell your dad this," she said. "It might help if he knew that he's not the only one in the world who wants to protect you. Because that's how he feels." She shifted and crossed her legs. "Going forward, and before you marry this guy …" She raised a teasing eyebrow. "I'd advise you to see how he interacts in a social situation, when it's not just the two of you. Invite him to the house for a family dinner. If not that, then a double date or a group activity."

"And what will this show me?"

"Lina, you are a social person, but you've been in this love bubble of only the two of you. It might be sustainable for a little while, but you thrive on associations with people. You need a partner who can keep up."

"You've never told me this before."

"You've never reached this point in a relationship before."

Dr. Bowman stood and walked Lina out of the office. "Your assignment this time is to tell your dad how Cody supports you. Not about *your* feelings, but about Cody's actions."

LATER THAT AFTERNOON, Lina loaded chocolate cake batter into a Bundt pan and slid it into the oven. It was Dad's favorite of Mom's recipes. If she was going to complete Dr. Bowman's assignment, it might be easier for him to swallow if he washed it down with cake.

She admired the flowers from the meadow while she cleaned the kitchen. A daisy towered over the others, an invitation to play. With her heart aflutter, she pulled it from the vase and took it into the backyard patio.

She separated a petal for a game of "he loves me," but she hesitated. There were an even number of petals. The game would end on "he loves me not."

Her phone buzzed with the ringtone of "Need You Now." She tucked the daisy behind her ear where it couldn't taunt her with the unhappy outcome and answered the call.

"Hi, Cody. I was just thinking about you."

"That's fair, I haven't stopped thinking about you."

"Did you get your writing score?"

"Ninety-two percent. I passed."

Lina heard the smile in his voice, but she wanted to see

it. They switched to a video call and there he was, standing next to his truck with a broad grin and that adorable dimple decorating his proud face.

"Congratulations, smarty-pants! I bet it was the iambic pentameter that clinched it."

He yanked his cap off his head. "Maybe. It could also have been the content."

"Will I be able to read it?"

"Yeah, I'll show it to you sometime." He looked down, giving her a glimpse of his thick lashes. Before she could call him out for being shy about sharing his work when he had already read hers a hundred times, he opened his eyes and met her gaze. "When can I see you?"

Lina chewed on a fingernail as she thought. "Are you willing to go against my dad?" She was, but Cody was more respectful than her.

"I don't want to cause problems, I just want to see you, and kiss you. I don't know what you thought of me, but you are a fantastic kisser."

Lina flushed. "You were terrible. We need more practice."

Cody rubbed the back of his neck and looked down from the camera hiding his own reddening face. "Yes, ma'am."

To spare themselves further embarrassment, Lina changed the subject. "Hey, you never told me about wanting to study criminal justice. When I asked you before, you said you weren't sure what to major in."

"It's kind of a new decision."

"Well, I think it's cool. You're cool."

Cody was distracted by someone speaking to him. He turned away from the camera to respond, and she had a view of the gravel drive as he walked away from his truck. It took him a few seconds to return.

"That's my mom's friend. She's just leaving."

"Speaking of friends, would you be okay with a double date? My roommate, Izzy, might come visit this weekend, and I thought maybe your friend Eli wouldn't mind meeting a pretty girl …?"

"Are you going to tell your dad that I'll be there?"

"I haven't decided yet. Does that bother you?"

"A little. I want to get on his good side if that's possible."

"Well, I have a few days to convince him then, right? You ask Eli, okay?"

"Okay. Send me a picture of Izzy. Eli might need persuasion." A woman's voice called his name in the background. "I gotta go. Text me the details. I miss you." Cody winked into the camera and disconnected.

They weren't one of those sickening couples who argued about who was going to hang up first. Still, the goodbye was a bit abrupt.

Lina went inside, put the daisy back in the vase, and checked on the cake. The rosy glow of new love was all she could see as she hummed around the kitchen. She texted Izzy.

Come visit this weekend. I know a hottie eager to meet you.

CHAPTER 35

Cody

A FEW STARS lingered in the sky as the sun prepared to emerge. Cody stepped out onto the front porch, hoping the exertion of chopping firewood would release the steam that throbbed inside his head. Mom had just nodded off after a night in hysterics.

Hurry, before the wind, and *Lay flat in the wind*—it made no sense. She was obsessed and getting worse. He had to figure out a way to get her into town for her doctor's appointment. Before town, he had to get her into the car. Before that, he had to get her to leave the house.

Cody went to the woodpile around back, set a cut log on the old stump, and swung the ax. It split easily, the bit sinking into the stump. He only needed to do that a hundred more times to get out all the frustration.

The wood had come from an oak down by the creek bottom. A windstorm had brought some of its branches down last year, so he had used the tractor to drag them to the house. He swung again and split another section into firewood.

He hadn't done much ranch work the past few days.

Wayne and Eli were always so nice about excusing him. They'd been down a hand with Tay taking time off for his wife and their new baby. He hadn't seen much of Spence, since he hadn't made it to the hay field or the pastures. As for Chancer, he gave Cody dirty looks when they saw each other around the barn or the garage. They didn't like each other much anyway, but the little man's resentment about Cody not working had been getting on his nerves.

The exercise of chopping wood was a welcome change after tending to Mom and being on the laptop. Cody had built up a respectable pile of firewood by the time Eli pulled in. He balanced the ax on the stump and waved Eli over.

The ranch hand parked his truck and came to greet him.

"How's your apartment in town working out?" Cody asked.

"Great! I got two more phone numbers since I moved, but I'm wasting away without Mrs. B's egg sandwiches."

"I think Chancer misses you in the bunk room. He's been a ray of sunshine," Cody said.

"Never mind Chancer. He hasn't got any people skills. Maybe not any cattle skills either. Don't know if you've heard yet, but four more were stolen night before last. From that same stretch along the highway."

"This is bad." Cody rubbed his brow. "Seven cows are a small fortune—or a large one, if you ask me." Equal to half a year of Eli's wages. "Have the police been notified?"

"Yeah, I filed a report yesterday, but the insurance might not renew your coverage if this keeps happening."

Cody stacked the last of the cut wood. He just couldn't catch a break. "Have they even paid the last claim yet?"

Eli shook his head.

"So, we're out the cows, don't have the insurance money, the cops have no idea where to look, and the rest of the herd are just sitting ducks? Not to mention Frank Chancer's herd. If we lose any of his, he could sue us."

"We'll catch these guys, even if I have to patrol the perimeter all night long." Eli pulled out his phone and looked something up. He showed Cody an advertisement for security cameras.

"If we had some surveillance," Eli said, "we would see who's doing this, maybe get a license plate number. At the least, we'd pinpoint what time they're coming so we can catch 'em in the act."

"How much would it cost to get a setup like that?"

"Would you like me to get an estimate?" Eli asked.

"Please. Even if it's out of our price range right now, there may come a time when the cost is better than the losses."

"I agree."

"Are you still cool with the double date Saturday?" Cody couldn't imagine he wouldn't be. Eli had been really excited to get invited. He had said he was looking forward to hanging out with Cody off the ranch. But come on— the man was on the prowl.

"Yeah, I'm up for it. I haven't been to Granny's Barbecue yet, but I've heard it's good."

"I like it, haven't been there in a long time." Cody shaded his eyes from the sunrise. The fatigue hurt more when the sun was up. "I've gotta go in. Eli, if you get the eggs from the coop, you can take 'em home with you."

"You sure? I don't mind bringing them into the house for you." Of course. Eli was always helpful and selfless. But Mom would probably freak out if Eli tried to bring eggs in.

"They're yours. I'll see you later, man." He fist-bumped Eli, then made his way into the house. Now that wood-chopping had exhausted him, he would be able to sleep. He showered in a hurry to lie down in his bed. He needed all the rest he could get so if Mom flipped out again, he wouldn't be too tired to be useful.

His sleep was fitful, busy with dreams of trying to keep Mom happy while Lina beckoned him from a distance. A noise at the front door woke him up. He sat up in bed in a panic that Mom was in the doorway again, until he heard Mrs. Bauer in the kitchen.

He found her making sandwiches and talking, mostly to herself, while Mom rummaged in the fridge.

"How's she doing?" Cody entered the kitchen in his pajama pants, rubbing an eye with his fist. "She had a really hard night."

Mom closed the fridge, having found an apple, and took a bite.

"From the looks of you, I suppose she must have, but she seems all right now. You're just getting up?"

"Yeah."

"Still planning to take that test this afternoon?"

"Yeah, but Mom's doctor appointment is in an hour. Want to see if we can get her into the car?"

"Sure, I'll help. Eat a sandwich and get ready."

He ate bites of his sandwich as he changed clothes, tied his shoes, and combed his hair.

"We're ready," Mrs. Bauer said in a cheery voice when he came into the family room. Mom was sitting on the couch, wearing a striped dress and sneakers.

"Okay." Cody took his mom's hand and led her to the door.

She followed until he crossed the threshold to the

porch, and there she stopped. Terror disfigured her features. She screwed her eyes shut, her mouth twisting into an uneven frown. She clamped a hand on the doorframe and clung with surprising strength.

"Mom. It's okay, I'm right here. I won't let anything hurt you."

She sobbed, shaking her head and pulling at his grasp.

"The doctor is waiting for you," Cody explained.

"Rosie, Rosie …" Mrs. Bauer tried to calm her. "We just want to help."

"No!" Mom shouted. "No, no, no!" She escaped Cody's hold on her hand and ran deeper into the house.

"What am I supposed to do?" he asked Mrs. Bauer, who flustered about. "Should I just pick her up and throw her in the truck?"

"I don't know. I just don't know." She followed after Mom.

Cody kicked at the porch railing, at his wit's end with her, her illness, and his complete lack of control.

SATURDAY CAME, and Cody kept checking his watch. The hours of the day passed too swiftly. He needed more time to calm his mom before Mrs. Bauer arrived to relieve him for the double date. Mom's impatient pacing back and forth past the family room window had erupted into violent thrashing and yelling several times already. She refused the applesauce and the pudding and the lemonade —everything he'd tried to hide her medicine in. He hadn't gotten her to eat at all.

Finally, when there was no help for it, he called Mrs. Bauer. "I'm not going out tonight after all. Thanks anyway for being willing to come over." He couldn't leave his mom like this for Mrs. Bauer to deal with.

There was no telling how Lina would take it. He'd been looking forward to this double date more than Eli had, and it was killing him that he needed to cancel, but without much choice, he dialed her number.

"Hi, Cody, can't wait to see you." She was in a noisy place. The background sounds made it hard to hear her.

"I can't come tonight ..." He waited through a long silent pause. "Lina?"

"What do you mean, you can't come?"

"My mom is having a hard time. I need to stay with her. I'm sorry."

"She can't spare you for a couple of hours? I really wanted to see you."

"No, I'm really sorry." He couldn't stand the disappointment in her voice, but there was nothing he could do to change the situation.

"Well, call me tomorrow, okay?"

"Yeah, I will." He hung up feeling like the biggest jerk she could possibly date.

CHAPTER 36

Cody

IT WAS after midnight when Cody closed his laptop and rubbed his eyes. He needed more study, and it wasn't going very well. He had spent the last two hours in his truck, parked out on the highway by the pasture the cows had disappeared from, looking up answers for the statistics questions he had missed. He hadn't seen any sign of cattle rustlers. Certainly no trailers that could haul away a few cows. The two vehicles that had passed by hadn't even slowed down.

He gave up the stakeout and returned home. Hopefully, Mom had been asleep this whole time. Eli's truck was out front and the light was on in the garage, right on time for his turn at the fence line.

Eli looked up from the workbench when Cody pushed open the door. A user manual lay open in front of him, and he held a few wires in his hand.

"Hey, man, what's going on?" Cody rubbed at his tired eyes.

"It's costly to put out enough cameras to cover the fences, but I wanted to test one out to know if it might be worth it at some point." Eli aimed the camera at the garage door and showed Cody the footage on his phone. "It works with an app and holds twenty-four hours of surveillance."

"Cool." Cody's exhaustion prevented him from being too impressed. "You gonna take a turn out on the road?"

"Yeah." Eli tweaked something on the camera and set it on the workbench. "You okay? You seem off."

"Tired."

"You don't have any hard feelings about the date, right?"

"What do you mean? I was the one who canceled. Do *you* have any hard feelings?"

"No, because I went on the date … Sorry, I thought Lina would have told you."

Cody leaned against the workbench and folded his arms across his chest. "What are you talking about?"

Eli took a deep breath and made a neat stack of the camera instructions. "Hey, man, I didn't get the message that the date was canceled. I showed up at Granny's and Lina and Izzy were already there. So I had dinner with them."

"I'm bummed that I missed it, but you thought I'd be mad about that?"

"Not really. I thought you'd be mad about the bowling alley."

Cody's hackles rose. There was more?

"We went bowling after dinner. Izzy wasn't into me, but she met somebody at the bar in the bowling alley and left me alone with Lina. We bowled, and we talked. Hey, man, if it matters, she is all about you."

"It's my own fault for not going." Lowering his head, Cody stared at a spot on the floor.

"I feel really bad about spending time with your girl-friend without you. I could've just left, but then she would've joined Izzy, and I thought maybe you'd rather have her hang out with me than with Bubba and his friends. I'm sorry if I'm wrong about that."

Cody wasn't going to thank Eli for spending the evening with Lina, not when he wanted to see her so badly himself. Especially because Eli was so many things that Cody was not. Any girl would be crazy to choose him over Eli.

"Not gonna lie … I don't like it," Cody said. He clenched his fists, unable to look at Eli. He blew out a breath and turned to walk away, needing some time to sort this out in his head.

Eli called after him. "Lina's really great. You're a lucky man."

Cody let the door shut on Eli and his appeasements as he pictured his beautiful Lina laughing at Eli's jokes.

CHAPTER 37

Cody

CODY INTENDED to apologize to Lina again right away, but he figured he'd just end up begging her to not fall in love with Eli. He called her the next evening, having taken that long to stop kicking himself about missing their date, stop being mad at Eli, and stop blaming Mom.

Watching her on the video call, it only took a moment to realize she had already gotten the wrong idea about why he had canceled.

"Well, my dad is pretty happy that you've been staying away." Lina kept her voice low, but the irritation resonated through. "He thinks he's winning, but I'm not a child and he can't decide if I see you."

"I'm sorry, Lina. This ain't how I want it."

She chewed a fingernail, her dubious gaze flicking to his before darting away. "I guess I just don't understand. Have you changed your mind about me?"

"No. Never. It's just that my mom has some health problems. She's been needing extra help."

Lina's expression softened. "I'm sorry. I know this must be hard for you too. I just missed you."

"What are you doing tomorrow? I'll be taking a test in the afternoon, but I want to see you afterward."

"I'll be at the library. Please, *please* come by when you're finished. We can celebrate together."

"Yes, ma'am."

Lina blew kisses into the camera before hanging up.

THE NEXT MORNING, Mom rocked in her chair and half hummed, half sang along to Carrie Underwood. She was medicated and content with Skippy on her lap. She craned her neck until she saw Cody at the kitchen table.

"Sing with me, little Cody."

Cody left the laptop and sat near her on the ottoman. "Okay, Mom." After a few days of unpredictable behavior, a complete sentence that made sense deserved his undivided attention.

She smiled and sang louder, not caring about getting the lyrics right.

Cody squeezed her hand and breathed a shaky sigh of relief. He joined in to sing "Church Bells."

Mom laid a hand on his cheek and stroked his stubble back and forth. She continued humming when the song was over and carried it over to the next song on the playlist. Cody sang that one with her too.

He pinched the bridge of his nose as he mourned the mom he used to know, the one who had sung while she cooked and loved to two-step around the house.

Her hand on his cheek discovered his tears. She stopped her song and turned her hand to examine the wetness. Her brow furrowed and she mouthed silent words.

"Mom, you okay?" Cody asked.

"Did Lina make you cry?" Mom was gone again.

A strangled cry ripped from his chest. This was too much. He laid his head in her lap next to Skippy and shed all the tears of a motherless son.

CHAPTER 38

Lina

LINA SAT cross-legged leaning back against a library bookshelf with a pile of books at her side. She should have put them away by now, but since her phone pinged with a new message, her job had become a low priority.

"You better stop looking at that phone before Mrs. Paul catches you." Comfy in her favorite chair, Fayla hadn't even looked up from her book, but somehow knew Lina was checking her text messages again.

"He canceled again."

"Now that surprises me with the way he was sniffing around your skirts. Thought he'd stick around. Not like other boys who take off as soon as they get what they want."

"What are you talking about?" Lina snapped. She had little patience for riddles.

Fayla turned the book around and showed her the impossibly handsome open-shirted man on the cover. "Oh, you know. The rake who's in it for the chase."

Lina stood, needing her full height against Fayla's assumptions. "Cody is not a rake."

"Who is he then? If he was a prince charming, he would be here."

"He's something in between." She chewed a fingernail as she searched for a way to defend Cody's behavior.

"I know." Fayla shook her finger at Lina. "He's a Romeo. As sincere as he can be, but just can't make it work."

Lina froze at the comparison. There was no way Fayla could know about her and Cody's connection to that story. "So that would make me Juliet," she said in a small voice. Juliet, the girl whose lover was dead by the time she woke up.

"Makes sense. Didn't Juliet's father have a problem with the Montagues, kind of like your dad has a problem with Cody?"

Lina huffed and flounced down into a chair opposite Fayla.

"If you were in love with someone but your parents forbade it, what would you do? Obey the parent or follow your heart?" Lina spoke faster and her voice rose. "Because no matter which choice you make, you'll hurt someone you love."

"Lina, just ask the boy why he canceled. You'll make yourself sick carrying on like this." Fayla turned a page in the book, appearing to listen with only one ear.

Lina typed a text on her phone. *Are you avoiding me because of my dad?*

He responded right away. *Nah, it's my mom. She isn't feeling well. I've gotta stay with her tonight. Miss you.*

"He says that his mom is sick and he needs to stay with her," Lina said to Fayla.

"Seems like the right thing to do," Fayla said. "Sounds

like the kind of thing *you* would do, caring for the sick and all."

"Yeah, I would. I can't fault him for that." She had often visited the retirement home near the Washburn campus. If she hadn't brought treats or flowers, at least the company had usually been appreciated. Loneliness could be difficult for the infirm. Lina's eyes grew wide with an idea. "But maybe I can help him."

CHAPTER 39

Lina

ON HER WAY home from work, armed with a pair of scissors borrowed from Mrs. Paul's desk, Lina stopped on the roadside and collected tansy asters for Cody's mom. She took them home to arrange in a vase, added a few sunflowers, and deemed it a cheery bouquet to lift any sick person's spirits.

"Those are pretty," Dad said as he wandered into the kitchen. He pulled a few vegetables out of the refrigerator to chop for dinner.

"I'm going to visit a friend after dinner. She's not feeling well."

Dad kissed Lina on the forehead. Guilt crept into her heart with her sin of omission, but her father had already moved on from the topic to discuss the meal preparations.

After the dinner dishes were washed and put away, Lina drove out to Cody's ranch. She started out later than she'd planned, and she missed a turn and had to backtrack. The evening light was diminishing fast. A tiny voice in her head told her it was too late at night for a visit, but she was already there, and the desire to see Cody was irre-sistible.

She parked the car and got the vase from the floor of the back seat where it was held steady by a cardboard box. Looking around, she decided it wasn't so late—there were lights on in the house. She returned Eli's wave from the open garage door across the wide gravel drive.

Lina cleared her throat and practiced how she would greet Mrs. Schafer as she walked up to the house. "Hello … Hi … Pleased to meet you …" Maybe she would see Cody first and he would introduce her. Maybe his mom was already in bed and she wouldn't meet her at all.

Lina rang the bell.

From inside the house, three bangs and a crash preceded a bloodcurdling scream.

Cody ripped the door open in a fury. When he saw Lina on the porch, he closed his mouth, drowning what-ever angry outburst had been forming.

A woman barreled through the entryway. Her night-gown billowed out from her body and took up all the space in the small area. She was illuminated by the light behind her, leaving her face in shadow, and her hair stuck up in tufts all over her head like the Statue of Liberty. She screamed.

Lina stumbled back with a gasp as a chill settled into the pit of her belly. What on earth had she walked in to? Her racing pulse urged her to run but blinded her as to which direction. She bumped into an old wooden chair and the vase crashed to the porch, shattering. Feeling around for something stable to hold onto, her hands grasped only air.

The woman rushed toward her. Lina shrieked and collided with a handrail behind her, then she turned and ran to the driveway. Eli met her halfway to her car and caught her, intercepting her terrified retreat. "Let me go!" She tugged, whipping her head around to see Cody throw the woman over his shoulder and carry her back inside.

Bursting into tears, she yielded, letting Eli bear her weight. He held her head tight to his shoulder.

"Shh … shh … shh …" Eli soothed her as he turned his worried face toward the house.

She raised her head and stayed upright by clenching fistfuls of Eli's shirt. "What … *was* that?"

"I'm not sure," he said. "Come on." Eli guided Lina into the garage where he sat her on a stool at the workbench before draping his jacket over her shivering shoulders.

She took a few cleansing breaths in the safety of the garage. "Was that his mom? Have you ever seen her behave like that before?"

"I've never seen her before *at all*, but I get the idea she has some mental health issues."

"I should never have come here." If Cody hadn't been having second thoughts about her before, he would be now. Her face screwed up tight, gearing up for an ugly cry.

Eli sat on another stool as she shuddered through a heavy sigh. "Most likely, this has nothing to do with you."

She nodded. Whatever was going on in that house had already been in motion. She had heard the crash and the shout before Cody answered the door.

Eli set a hand on her shoulder. "You gonna be okay?" His touch was comforting, like that of her father.

"Yeah, I think so." But not by dwelling on what had just happened. Another deep breath.

As her nerves calmed, she took in her surroundings. At first glance, it seemed like a cluttered garage, but now that she took a closer look, she realized everything was ordered and well-kept. A row of four-wheelers and utility vehicles were lined up at the ready, the wall above the workbench where she sat displayed tools in order of purpose and size, and there appeared to be a rhyme and reason to what seemed a random assortment of items on a wall of shelves, like a library.

"What do you like best about working here?" she asked.

"Oh, there's a lot I like about the job—being outside, working with the animals. I like hanging out with Cody."

"Yeah, me too. The Cody part," Lina said. *Cody.* She hadn't even gotten a good look at him before running for her life. "Do you think he's been acting strange?"

"I haven't seen him much lately. He's been under a lot of pressure with his mom and school. But yeah, he's been weird the past few days."

"I haven't seen him since he and I kissed." She glanced up at Eli in time to see him wipe a glimmer of a smile off his face. "Could he have changed his mind about me?"

"Ah ..." He shrugged and shook his head. "I don't think so. But who knows?"

"Then my dad had to go and frighten him away ..." She covered her mouth to stifle a hiccup.

"Hey, now." He rubbed her upper arm. "I've only known him a short time, but I'm pretty sure the only one he's afraid of is himself."

Eli made no sense, but she was too emotionally drained to figure out what he meant. "Thanks." She stood, her legs having found their strength once again. "I think I better be going. My dad is going to worry." She shrugged out of the jacket and gave it back to him. "I'm okay now."

"I'll walk you to your car."

All was quiet as they passed the house. So quiet, the only sound was the crunch of their feet on the gravel driveway.

The front door opened, and Cody was there. He shut it behind him and jogged over to Lina, where he thumped Eli in the shoulder like a tag team wrestler.

Eli took the hint. "Good night, Lina. I'm glad you're okay." He went back to the garage.

"What are you doing here, Lina?" Cody asked as he walked her the rest of the way to her car.

"I missed you. I wanted to see you."

"I wanted to see you too, but this …?"

"I know you've been busy. I just want to help."

"Help? What help?"

"I … I brought some flowers … for your mom. You said she wasn't feeling well."

"That doesn't help. At all." Cody shoved his hands deep into his pockets and kept his focus on the ground.

"I'm sorry. I guess I don't understand." Lina put her hand on his arm and stepped close.

He stood there detached and silent. He didn't even look at her. She was about to give up and get in the car when he covered her hand with his. She lifted her eyebrows and her face tipped up toward his.

"You should go. I've got a mess to clean up," he said.

"Can I hel—"

"No, you can't help." He raked his hair with both hands and growled under his breath. "I don't need your help!"

Lina flinched. "But—"

"I just need you to leave me alone while I … figure this out." His voice had softened but his exasperation remained.

After all her efforts to create a genuine connection with him, he was shutting her out. He didn't need her the way she needed him. What if he was just like all the others? Her lower lip trembled. She didn't have much time before she lost it, and she didn't want to lose it in front of him. She spun around and got in the car.

"Lina," he called out.

She revved the engine and peeled out. As she raced down the highway, his outburst rang in her ears over and over again.

By the time she arrived home, her tears had dried but she was a wreck. The initial hurt of being yelled at had fermented into a bubbling mess of doubt and resentment. Lina didn't even know him at all. Cody had lied about his mother this whole time. He had made it seem like she just wasn't feeling well. The fact that he had hid the truth about her proved that he didn't trust Lina with the details of his life. How could he love her if he didn't trust her? She had told him everything, every last detail about Ruby and her mom, and even her own issues in the aftermath that sent her to therapy. She had held nothing back, but he had.

She stormed into the house and threw herself across the couch with a groan.

With the mantel clock ticking in the background, Dad, in his recliner, looked up from his laptop. "You were gone a while. Is your friend feeling better?"

"Just a heads-up, Dad—we aren't going to be meeting Cody's mom anytime soon."

Her dad closed the computer. He took in her tear-stained face and red-rimmed eyes. It seemed a long moment before he finally asked, "Did you have a fight?"

"You could say that."

"Do you want to talk?"

Lina buried her face in a couch pillow. "This is so embarrassing."

"What did he do? Are you hurt?"

"Only on the inside."

Dad moved to the couch and brought her in to lean back against his shoulder. Lina sighed. He used to read to her and Ruby like this when they were little, a girl on each shoulder. Lina ignored his vacant shoulder on the other side.

"What can I do?" he asked.

"I don't know. I thought it was going to be me and him, you know?" She sniffed and wiped her nose on his sleeve. "I thought he cared for me, but he doesn't trust me."

"You should tell me what happened."

"Well, he's been blowing me off and I thought it was me or … that he wasn't daring enough to go against you." Lina looked down at her fingers where she plucked and twisted a pillow tassel. It was hard to admit to her father that she'd had every intention of disobeying him.

"He told me that his mom needed him because she didn't feel well. But Dad, she screamed at me and chased me away."

"She objects to you kids dating too?" He squeezed her shoulder, his dad-humor missing the mark.

"No, I mean there's something wrong. Like, she needs medication and a padded room."

"Hold on now—you're not a doctor. But I guess that explains why she didn't come with him to the bank. It's possible he's embarrassed by the situation. You know, it can be hard for men to show their vulnerabilities, especially to a pretty girl." Dad rubbed her shoulder and kissed the top of her head. "You like him a lot, don't you?"

"Yeah."

"You're young. There's plenty of time for things to turn around for you two."

Lina sat up and stared at her father. *He* was the one who had said Cody needed to finish school before dating his daughter. *He* was the one who had made Cody feel so uncomfortable in their home. *He* was the one who had flashed the porch light when they were saying good night. "What, you're rooting for us now? I thought he wasn't good enough for me."

"No one will ever be good enough, you know that. But I was just trying to give him a push. You're headed back to school, and if it's right between you two, wouldn't you want him to go with you?"

"*If* it's right. But I've been hopeful about so many guys before. I may have finally learned my lesson." Lina lay back down. She braved a glance at Ruby's vacant spot, and despite the presence of her father, she felt very alone.

CHAPTER 40

Cody

WHILE HIS MOM slept off last night's rampage, Cody spent the morning hours putting the disheveled house back together.

As he washed the dried blood smears from the shower tiles, he blamed himself for not trying harder to get her to the doctor. He had never seen his mom this bad. She had become a burden too big for him. He wanted to take care of his family—he'd been trying his best. But he was nothing more than a kid fumbling around in a grown-up world.

He remembered Lina's vase still in shatters on the porch and headed out there with a broom.

Eli was already there, sweeping up the mess and dumping the shards of glass and wilted flowers into a small trash can.

"Good morning," Eli said without looking up.

Cody grunted. He stepped farther outside and attempted to relive the events of the previous evening through Lina's eyes.

"You okay?"

Another grunt.

"What happened here?" Eli asked.

"Her mind ain't right," Cody said with a deep breath. He lowered himself into a wooden chair. "It started with depression when my dad died. They gave her some medication for it, but she's gotten worse and worse, and now she speaks mostly nonsense and looks out the window."

Eli finished the job and sat opposite Cody.

"Last night was the first time she's stepped foot outside the house in two years. And she won't even remember it." Cody rubbed his eyes and hung his head. "And she scared away my girlfriend."

"No, man, I think you did that part yourself."

"No, I was trying to keep my mom away from her. I was protecting her!" Or had he been trying to protect Mom from Lina? Trying to keep anyone from realizing how bad she'd gotten.

"To Lina, it might have seemed like you were telling her to go away." Eli looked away. "Yeah, I heard every-thing. Sorry."

"Do you think Chancer heard?"

"I didn't see him at all after quitting time."

The front door opened. Dread entered Cody's heart. *Not another episode.* Both men turned to look at the woman in the doorway. Gone was the banshee of the night before. Mom's robe was tied, her hair combed smooth, and she wore a calm smile. Skippy circled her bandaged feet at the threshold.

"Little Cody, bring your brother inside," she said.

Cody and Eli looked at each other.

"You have a brother?" Eli mouthed.

Cody shook his head. "Only child, remember?"

Mom stretched out an arm and summoned them with her fingers.

"Do you dare?" Cody asked Eli.

They both stepped into the house. Even though she could barely reach, Mom tried to ruffle their hair as they passed her. Once inside, she sat in her rocker and ignored them.

Cody wasn't sure what to think. His mom had always been so predictable, but lately, he didn't know what to expect. Without the predictability, he was as housebound as she was.

Eli waited just inside the kitchen, clearly uneasy until Cody put a bowl of eggs on the end of the counter. He lined up a spatula, bacon, and butter next to it.

"You do the eggs. I'll make some toast." Cody kept an eye on his mom while they prepared breakfast.

"I have some bad news," Eli said as he cracked eggs into a bowl. "When I went to watch the fence line last night, I found another damaged section. I'm afraid it may have happened while your mom … caused a distraction. I'll be figuring out who's missing today."

"Have we lost any of Frank Chancer's herd?" Cody pushed four slices of bread into the toaster.

"Not yet." Eli whisked the eggs with a bit more zeal than necessary.

Mom started watching them from across the room when the eggs hit the hot skillet with a sizzle.

Cody pressed his lips into a tight line. Only *his* cattle. "Any other ranches around here getting thieved?"

"Cops say no. Also, no leads. They're probably taking the cows pretty far out of the area to sell."

"Shouldn't be that hard to track down a few cows,

especially with the electronic ID system you've got us using."

"There's always a way. They either rebrand over the top of an old mark, or they cut off the ear with the tag. A crook will always find a way."

"Well then we gotta outsmart them."

"I feel like we could, if we knew *who* to outsmart."

The toaster finished with a loud pop. Cody thought of the AbolitionistOps team. They knew who they were up against. Not the individual, maybe, but the type of person. "What sort of profile fits a rustler?"

"Someone who knows where to sell a cow, knows how far away to transport the animal to avoid the authorities looking for it. They might have time to wait until a good market, or maybe they know a crooked auction house who doesn't mind if there are no papers."

"Let's ask Wayne what he thinks." Cody set plates of toast and bacon on the table just as Eli transferred the eggs from the pan to a bowl.

Mom came to the table and took her medicine, and the three of them ate their breakfast.

"Your presence here isn't upsetting her." Cody inclined his head toward Mom. "It's usually just me and Mrs. Bauer she can stand to have around."

"Ladies love me," Eli said with the smile Cody had only seen in the presence of females.

With a cautious glance at his mom, Cody asked, "Even Lina?" He had seen her in Eli's arms last night as he had bundled Mom back indoors.

Eli held his fork in midair and looked up. He cleared his throat before answering. "She was scared. It was you she wanted. You should call her, sooner rather than later. Or go see her."

Cody hung his head and wouldn't meet Eli's eyes. He may have already blown it. He shoved his plate away. It might not matter anyway if he'd never be able to leave Mom alone again.

"Call her right now," Eli urged. "Let your voice be the first thing she hears this morning. I'll clean this up." He began clearing the dishes and bringing them to the sink.

Cody stepped out on to the porch and dialed Lina. She didn't answer—it went to voice mail after several rings. He redialed rather than leave a message. She answered after the fourth ring.

"Hi, Cody." Her voice sounded weary.

"Hi." He choked on the greeting. Breathing deeply, he shook it off and started again. "I'm sorry … You're the last person I ever want to yell at." He pinched the bridge of his nose.

"You misled me," she said.

"I told you she wasn't feeling well."

"That's not 'not feeling well.' That's some kind of psychosis and she needs professional help."

"Lina … I'm sorry."

"It's okay. This is my fault. All of this is because I pushed you too hard."

"What?" How could what *he* had done ever be Lina's fault?

"I pressured you to take me to The Bad Bronco. I pushed you into everything because I wanted you. And I pushed myself on you last night too. I'm sorry I never let you decide if I'm really what you want."

"Aw, Lina. It ain't like that."

"No? Because that's how it seems."

Cody struggled for words. If she hadn't pushed him, he would never have done anything these past few weeks.

So, yeah, she'd pushed him into it. But he let her. He let her invade his dreams and made him dare to imagine a different life. He allowed her to reach inside his chest and scribble her name all over his heart. The thoughts were slow to form and even slower to verbalize.

Lina was done waiting. "We don't have to drag this out. It's okay."

"Lina, no …"

"Goodbye, Cody."

Cody looked at the phone. She had it all wrong. He dialed again, but it went to voice mail. *Damn!* He dialed Mrs. Bauer, a cold sweat prickling at his hairline as he paced back and forth until she answered.

"G'morning, hon."

There was no time for her cheery greeting. "Can you come over? I have an emergency with Lina."

"She okay? Something wrong?"

There was no wind in his chest. "Other than her leaving me?" He barely eked out the words.

"I'll be there in ten, hon."

He went back inside, his gaze darting from Mom in her rocker to Eli washing dishes in the kitchen.

"She let me take her to her chair. I hope that's okay. And she called me your brother again."

Cody joined him in the kitchen. "Don't make this weird, but thanks for being here." He picked up a dish towel and started drying plates.

"Yeah, man, no problem."

Cody's shoulders slumped. The towel was too heavy for him. Everything was too heavy for him.

"Hey, you okay?" Eli asked.

"I've gotta go get my girl back."

"Then go, man, just go."

CHAPTER 41

Lina

SITTING AT THE KITCHEN ISLAND, Lina stared into a soggy bowl of cereal flakes. Her eyes had been slowly leaking all night and would probably continue throughout the day. She'd barely had time to breathe a sigh of disappointment and dab at the tears after talking with Cody when Dad's phone rang inside his briefcase. Pulling it from the case, she held it out to him.

He set down a bag of coffee beans and took the call. "Hello, Xander Grant here." His face paled to an ashen color. "Yes … yes … Of course." His limbs collapsed awkwardly into a dining chair. "Where? … I'm on my way." The phone clattered to the table and he covered his face with his hands.

"Dad, what's happened?" Lina asked. "Who was that?"

He raised his face to look at her and pulled her down into the chair beside him. "It was the FBI."

Lina gulped. The last time the FBI called, they had told them about the body they'd found. She couldn't hear her dad speaking past the pounding in her ears. His lips moved, but there was only the pounding. The tears on deck for Cody gushed now for Ruby. Her limbs weak, Lina's forehead fell to the tabletop and great, excruciating shudders racked through her.

Dad shook her hard. "Lina! Lina!"

Her head wobbled on her neck.

He grabbed her face. "They've busted a sex trafficking ring. We have to go to Miami. Right now."

Her whole body trembled. She grabbed whatever handfuls of her father she could reach and gripped hard to steady herself.

"Go pack some things." He disconnected himself from her clutches and opened his laptop. "I'm getting us some plane tickets."

Lina stood there in her unsteady, unfocused shivers.

"Go! Pack!"

CHAPTER 42

Cody

CODY REHEARSED his apology as he sped toward town. She wouldn't be able to cut him off or hang up on him if he was standing right in front of her. She would have to listen. And he would tell her everything, from how he'd felt when he first laid eyes on her and made her drop that romance novel in the library, to how he had realized his feelings for her in the wildflowers. She hadn't pressured him into anything he hadn't already wanted to do except the karaoke. And as far as last night went, he was the only one in the wrong.

He skidded to a halt in front of her house. Mr. Grant was closing the trunk of his car in the driveway. *Good. He might as well hear this too.*

Cody vaulted himself from the truck and strode up the drive. "Sir, is Lina here?"

"It's not a good time. We're on our way out."

"I only need a few minutes, if I could just—"

Lina burst from the house. Her face was splotchy from crying, her eyes red and puffy. Her mouth was set in a grim, determined line on her haggard face.

Cody faltered when he saw her, his own heart wrecked at the sight of what he'd done to her.

She hurried past him on her way to the car. "I can't talk to you right now, Cody."

He grabbed for her elbow, but Mr. Grant blocked his way as he helped his daughter into the car. Cody pressed forward. "Lina, please—"

"She can't talk right now, son." Mr. Grant pushed Cody away from the car. "Let her go." He got in, and the engine rumbled to life.

Cody, alone and rejected on the driveway, watched as the girl he loved drove out of sight.

He had only wanted to make his future better than his past, but now everything looked worse than ever. Cody sat with his head in his hands on the front steps of Lina's house. Was ranching really that bad of a life?

A man took care of his family. Lina would never be someone he could care for. Mom took everything and left little to nothing for anyone else. Perhaps it was foolish to try to add Lina into his circle of family.

The morning sun was shaded by cloud cover. Humidity hung heavy in the air. A pair of birds, chirping too happily for a morning as tortured as this, flitted about in the maple tree that graced the front lawn. A little kid scooted his tricycle by on the sidewalk. He had a red popsicle that dripped down his elbow. The kid slowed down when he noticed Cody watching him. He stared, sucked on the popsicle, and continued on his way in his uncomplicated life.

Cody checked the time on his phone and wondered how long he'd have to wait before Lina came home.

There was a voice mail from Ms. Jeffries: "Hey, Cody, just checking in. I thought we'd see you yesterday for the statistics test. Let me know if you'd like to come by today."

Cody sighed and scratched his head. It wasn't doing any good to sit on Lina's porch. When he drove off, he slowed down as he passed the tricycle boy and returned his stare. While the boy's stare was borne of curiosity, Cody's was steeped with resentment for the simplicity of the kid's life.

At the district office, Ms. Jeffries greeted him with a cheery smile as though she had a personal stake in him graduating. He slogged through the test. He looked at the questions, but he saw Lina's tear-stained face. If she hadn't inspired him with all that talk of a future better than the past, he wouldn't have even tried to go back to school.

"Your last exam!" Ms. Jeffries said when she collected his test papers. "Are you pleased to be a graduate?"

Not today. The only thing that could please him was a chance to fix things with Lina. "Yes, ma'am."

"I'll get this graded for you this afternoon. Check your email for your score. Shall I arrange to mail your diploma, or would you rather pick it up?"

"The mail is fine, thank you." Cody left the building. He should've asked Mrs. Jeffries to mail it directly to Mr. Grant. If Lina forgave him, dating her was about all it was good for. Then again, a man with half a future was not worthy of her, and that's what he was. It wasn't likely he'd be able to leave Mom for college.

He drove by Lina's house on the way home. Mr. Grant's car hadn't returned yet. Only her little Subaru was parked in the driveway.

Thick, gray clouds had rolled in while he was taking the test. Summer thunderstorms didn't typically last long, and they kept the grass growing green—usually not a big deal. But Cody needed to get home. With how volatile Mom had been, no telling how she would react to the storm.

The police were at the barn when he arrived home. Eli and Wayne were again filing a report. Chancer was there as well.

"No, I didn't see anything strange. I was in town last night," Chancer said.

"We're missing four more." Eli filled Cody in.

"They're pulling up with a trailer, cutting the wires, and loading up a couple cows. Probably any that graze close to the fences," Wayne told him.

Cody stood in the group but only half listened. He had no solution. It was too large of an area to patrol effectively. More importantly, he didn't care. Not about the cows, the ranch, or anything else.

When the group dispersed. Wayne pulled Cody aside. "How's Rosie?" he asked.

"She's been having a hard time," Cody said. "She cut her feet up last night running on broken glass like she didn't even feel it."

"How're you holding up?"

"It ain't easy. I'm glad we have Eli and Chancer, since I haven't been able to give you much."

"Like I said before, Eli is worth two men, but Chancer's only worth half a man. Sure glad he's only here for the summer. I'll look for his replacement, don't worry."

"Thanks, Wayne, you're a big help."

"See here, I want to talk to you about that, Cody." Wayne pulled off his hat and wiped his forehead. "All this cattle rustling is going on under my watch. I'm sorry to be failing you."

"You're not to blame. We just got to catch 'em. And we

will. For whatever reason, someone's targeting us. They *are* going to slip up."

"It's not just that," he said. "I've known you since you were a munchkin, and when Boyd died, I just couldn't leave you on your own. But I was fixin' to retire back then. I'm an old man."

"What are you saying?" Cody squinted at Wayne.

"Eli is more qualified to run this place than I ever was. The ranch will be in good hands with him."

"That sounds like a goodbye," he said with a heavy sigh.

Wayne nodded, his focus off in the distance. "I need to bow out. Talk to Eli. See if he wants the job."

Some of Cody's earliest memories involved Wayne. This place would be strange without him, but Cody understood a desire to leave the ranch. "I'll miss you around here." He pulled his shoulders back and stood straighter, like a man.

"I'll keep showing up until you've got someone else in place." Wayne's hands shook as he used both to place his hat back on his head, pulling the brim low over his eyes. "Better see to your mom. We got a line of thunderstorms coming in the next day or so. There's a tornado watch on. I'm gonna see to things out here in case the wind picks up."

"All right. Hey, Wayne? I finished high school today."

"Proud of you." Wayne put a hand on Cody's shoulder. "Real proud of you."

LATER IN THE EVENING, Cody fed his mom a sandwich and tucked her in for the night. The storm hadn't materialized yet; it was only cloudy and windy outside. The evening light had a green tinge to the clouds, and the air was heavy. Cody was restless as he checked his grades. He scored a sixty-eight on the statistics final. He could probably have done better if his mistakes with Lina hadn't been playing on repeat in his mind. He'd never gotten a D before, but he'd passed. He was finished.

His mom snored softly in her room. He had given her an extra pill with her dinner. It wasn't recommended to exceed her dosage, but he suspected her dosage needed adjustment anyway.

He scrolled through photos of Lina on his phone. He zoomed in on one he'd taken the day of their horseback ride to the wildflowers. Looking up at the sky, she laughed and threw flowers into the air. She was so bright and happy, completely different from the girl with a splotchy face who wouldn't talk to him. When he closed his eyes, he could feel the sun and smell her perfume.

Cody peeked at his mom. She was sleeping soundly. He left the house and saddled Big Red out in the barn.

"You in the mood for a night ride?" He rubbed the horse's muzzle. "Okay, watch your step."

Once in the saddle, he turned the horse toward the creek bottom. Big Red stretched his legs and carried Cody through the dark. They were both breathing heavy from the exertion by the time they reached the creek. Big Red stopped and waited.

Cody's chest tightened as he glanced at his thinking rock where he had sat so many times before. He hadn't even known Lina then, but she'd had the power to affect his life. And now that he loved her, she had even more power. She had given him a purpose worth fighting for.

The trick now would be to keep the purpose even if he lost the woman. The tightness twisted.

He urged the horse onward through the water and up the embankment. They picked their way to the center of the wildflower meadow. It was different now, but not just because of the dark. It was haunted by what might have been.

"I don't know what I was expecting ..." Cody said aloud. Feeling foolish, he brought Big Red around to return to the ranch, walking leisurely along the beaten path.

Cody passed by Chancer's herd in the north pasture. None of these animals had gone missing, only his own. The cows were quietly huddled together against the wind. He turned off the path to ride by the south pasture where the other cattle were grouped in a huddle as well. As Cody neared, there was a disturbance on the far end. He peered through the dark.

The cows moved out of the way of a figure on horseback that rode near them. Cody urged Big Red faster. He pulled up to find Chancer. "Hey, what's going on?"

"I came to check out the herd, keep an eye open for trouble," Chancer said.

"You think the rustlers might come again tonight?"

"Better to be safe, right?" Chancer looked over the pasture with an assumed air of authority. "Everything seems fine here."

Cody nodded. "All right. I'll stay out here a bit and keep an eye out."

Chancer hovered by for a while. He passed some time on his phone. "Gonna storm tomorrow," he said after a lengthy, awkward silence.

"Yeah, probably." Cody picked up a weird vibe from

Chancer, but then, they had never really clicked. "Did you and Spence get all the hay baled?"

"Yep."

More silence.

Finally, Chancer circled about. "I guess there ain't gonna be trouble tonight. I'm headed back."

"See ya." Cody rode along the fence one more time before heading back himself. Something was off about Chancer. Cody had never understood the guy, and this chance meeting in the dark gnawed at him. He texted Eli.

Come by the house in the morning, I need to talk to you about something.

Mom was still sleeping when he checked on her after his night ride. He watched for a minute from the doorway.

It ain't right for a parent to ruin their kid's life.

His stomach turned. Ashamed of the unkind thought, he punched a wall in the hallway on his way to his own room, leaving a fist-sized hole in his wake.

CHAPTER 43

Cody

THE NEXT MORNING, Mom smiled and laughed like the old days. She sat at the breakfast table, calm and pleasant, following the conversation back and forth between Cody and Eli while she munched on slices of bacon.

"Chancer was out in the south pasture pretty late last night." Cody spread jam on a slice of toast made from Mrs. Bauer's most recent batch of homemade bread. "Said he was keeping an eye on things, but something was off."

Eli's eyes widened as he sipped from a glass of orange juice. "That surprises me. He's not the type to volunteer to do anything after quitting time … or during working hours, for that matter."

"Right? And something else—I got the feeling I was interrupting something, you know?"

"I'll keep an eye on him," Eli said. "I think I better stay over until the rustlers are caught. But if Chancer has anything to do with it, he can't know I'm here. He has to feel unguarded."

Mom reached over and placed a hand on Cody's forearm, her brows furrowed with worry. "Rustlers? You need to tell Dad."

"We're gonna take care of it, Mom. Please don't worry." Easy to say, harder to do. Eli couldn't stay in the bunkhouse, or Chancer—if he was involved—wouldn't try anything.

Cody patted his mom's hand and looked to Eli.

"My mom lets you in the house. You can stay here," Cody said. "Can you set up the security camera so we'll see if he leaves the bunk room in the night?"

"Yeah. We'll figure this out."

The boys finished off their eggs, each lost in his own thoughts. Cody had more to figure out than just a fishy ranch hand. Lina hadn't been willing to talk to him, and he was also about to lose his foreman.

"Hey, Eli, would you be interested in taking Wayne's job?" Cody asked. "He wants to retire."

"Are you sure? I just barely graduated."

"You've been doing this your whole life." Cody counted off the reasons on his fingers. "And you love it. And you already treat the ranch as well as if it were your own." He turned to his mother. "Mom, you like Eli, right?"

"Yes, I like your brother," she chimed in.

Eli laughed and wiped his brow as though relieved to have her approval.

"She likes my brother." Cody said. "Do you need another reason?"

AFTER CODY SET his mom up in her chair with Skippy, and before joining Eli for some ranch work, he dialed Lina's number. When he got her voice mail, he sent a text instead.

I'm sorry that I hurt you. Please let me explain.

The rest of the morning passed with no response from her. He and Eli weighed a few calves that would be sold in the fall. Cody entered the numbers into the tablet with angry jabs of his fingers. It was his own fault she was distancing herself from him. When he checked on Frank Chancer's cows with the UTV, he floored the pedal and took corners fast. Why couldn't she at least let him explain? As he cleared manure from the horses' corral, he pitched it hard and kept overshooting the waste cart. How long was she going to torture him?

He had put his heart into the hands of this woman, and now he relied on her forgiveness to make or break him. He'd never been a control freak, but this was one thing he would have liked some power over.

By afternoon, the storm had moved in closer. The wind picked up and thunder boomed in the distance. Wayne called it an early day. Chancer didn't argue. Cody and Eli gave each other a knowing nod. It was time to set their trap.

Cody stopped at the house to check on his mom. She was humming to Carrie Underwood from her rocking chair. "Mom, I'm going on an errand with my brother. Will you be okay for a few more minutes?"

She pointed out the window and smiled. "The wind is here. Lie flat in the wind." She returned to her humming.

Gone was the woman he had enjoyed breakfast with just a few hours ago. "Okay, then. I'll be back soon."

Back at the garage, Eli wiped down a UTV, making a show of being finished with work for the day in front of Chancer. "Gotta make some calls, see if any of my honeys are free tonight. What about you, Chancer? Any plans tonight?"

"I'm gonna just watch a movie on my laptop in the bunk room. What are you doing, Cody?"

"I've got to study."

"Figures." Chancer rolled his eyes.

"Well, I'm headed back into town. See you tomorrow," Eli said as he left the garage.

"You want anything from the Gas 'n' Sip?" Cody asked Chancer. "I'm going out to get some study snacks."

"Yeah, potato chips." Chancer didn't even look up from his cellphone.

The last thing Cody wanted to spend money on was a snack for Chancer, but he had to look like he was leaving the ranch for a good reason.

Eli got in his truck and drove off down the highway. Cody took his own truck to the Gas 'n' Sip and met Eli in the chip aisle. He stopped at the fridge and grabbed two Mountain Dews as well. The caffeine and sugar would come in handy if this turned out to be a long night.

Eli gave the pretty blonde clerk his most dazzling smile. "Is it okay with you if I leave my truck here tonight? I'll move it in the morning."

The clerk had the giggle of a little girl, not the thirty-something woman she was. "Sure, park it around back."

As they finished paying, she told Eli, "I'm not here until ten tomorrow."

He winked at her as they left.

Cody shoved him in the arm as they walked out to their trucks. "How is it so easy for you?"

"You don't need it to be easy. You have Lina."

Cody wasn't so sure about that. He had felt so alone since she started avoiding him.

They rode back to the ranch together in Cody's truck.

Chancer was nowhere in sight when Eli slipped from the truck and into the house. Cody went to the bunk room.

"Wind's picking up," he said, tossing the potato chips to Chancer, who reclined on his bunk with his laptop open.

"See you tomorrow," Chancer said. Not even a thank you.

Gusts of wind blew hard against Cody's back as he jogged to the house. Thunder cracked and rain began to fall.

CHAPTER 44

Cody

WHEN CODY WALKED into the kitchen, Eli and Mom were dancing to Carrie Underwood's "Dirty Laundry." Mom sang the lyrics as she turned under Eli's arm. Cody was taken aback. This was the weirdest thing he'd seen in a long time—his mom in her nightgown and robe, dancing with his brother-friend. While she was occupied, he put Mrs. Bauer's leftovers to heat in the microwave.

"It's my turn." Cody cut in to rotate Mom around the dining table and into the family room. "You set the table," he told Eli.

"You've gotten better at this. Have you been practicing?" Mom asked. It had been a while since she had acknowledged something he did well.

"Yeah, a little." He guided her through a reverse turn—something he had learned from Lina at The Bad Bronco.

The microwave beeped.

"Dinner's ready." Cody brought his mom to the table. Eli stood behind Mom's chair and only sat after she was seated.

"With your permission, Rosie …?" Eli set his tablet on the table.

"Yes, of course," she said. "I don't mind."

Cody used to get scolded for having his phone at the dinner table.

While they ate, Eli used the app on the tablet to view the surveillance feed. The camera was pointed at the bunk room door. If Chancer left the room, they would know.

"Do you think he'll realize he's on camera?" Cody asked.

"Not likely. I hid it under a pile of wadded up papers and shop rags."

Cody and Eli took turns watching it—the most boring television ever.

They sat up, alert, when they saw movement. Chancer crossed the hall to the bathroom. He returned to the bunk room a short while later. Both men sat back, disappointed.

Eli started stacking dirty plates to clear the table. "Thank you for the meal, Mama Rosie."

"You're welcome. Hardworking boys need to eat." She rubbed her eye with a fist. "Cody, it's getting late."

"I'd better get you tucked in." Cody pulled out his mom's chair and said to Eli, "Holler if anything happens."

She did most of her bedtime routine by herself. Cody only needed to adjust the thermostat and switch off the light. As he left her room, she spoke.

"Cody … little Cody. I think you grew up sad." Mom rolled over and pulled her blanket to her chin.

He waited a moment, but she didn't say anything more.

He left the door open a crack and returned to the family room. He and Eli lounged on the couch with their pop, staring at the unmoving view of the bunk room door.

"Have you given any thought to being in charge around here?" Cody asked.

"Sure. I'd like to take you up on the offer, but I always thought I'd have my own place someday. I'm not sure how long-term I'd be before I set out on my own."

Cody rubbed his head. The idea that had been turning around in his mind solidified enough that he could see what form it took. "You want a ranching life, but I never did. I've been looking for a way off the ranch since I was fourteen, and thought I had it. But then my dad was gone, and my mom … Well, I'm still here."

"Any idea what you'd want to do instead?"

"Yeah." He cued up an AbolitionistOps video on his laptop. "I want to be involved in something like this." While Eli watched, Cody monitored the surveillance feed.

When the video ended, Eli closed the laptop. "Wow, that's a noble ambition." He sat back and studied Cody. "I bet you'd be really good doing that kind of thing."

Cody nodded his thanks for the vote of confidence. "If you want your own ranch, what do you think of this one?" Eli was new around here, but Wayne trusted him, and Cody trusted Wayne. Eli had proven himself on the job. Even now, he was working through the night trying to protect the ranch. And for some reason, Mom liked him.

"You have a great spread here, with a lot of potential. Are you thinking of selling? I know I'm not in a position to buy anything yet."

"Actually, I've been thinking. If I ever get power of attorney, I could cut you in as a partner." Cody had known Eli about as long as he'd known Lina, and he *loved* her. He would commit his future to her if she'd let him. Why couldn't he have found a business partner in the same amount of time?

He pointed down the hallway. "And if I ever figure out what to do with my mom …" He pointed at himself. "I'll go to school …" Finally, he pointed at Eli. "And you can run the place."

Eli chuckled, shaking his head as he leaned forward. "How long have you been planning this?"

"About five minutes." He waved away the question. "When, or if, I graduate and start my career, you can buy me and Mom out cheap. We'll back out, and it's all yours."

"How is that a good deal for you, Cody? It sounds like you're trying to just hand it over."

"It's a good deal for me because I'll need some income to get through college. If you'd be willing to have me as a silent partner until I graduate, it's worth it to me."

"So you're saying, if I put my kid brother through college, I get the ranch?"

"Yeah, that's what I was thinking." Cody rubbed the back of his neck. It was one thing for Mom to call Eli his brother, another for Eli to call himself such. Cody might need another minute to fully agree. "We got two wild cards though—my mom and the power of attorney."

"Oh yeah, that reminds me. I spoke with the lawyer I met at church. He does contracts at a corporate firm in Topeka. He gave me his number, and he's willing to meet with you about how to get access to the ranch accounts." Eli opened his phone and forwarded the contact information to Cody. "His name is Peter Mallory."

"Thanks, man." Cody took a sip of his pop. As he set it back down next to the tablet, Chancer came out of the bunk room, typed something on his phone, then left the garage.

"Time to go," Eli said.

Cody peeked in at Mom. She was facing away from him, motionless on her bed. He sent Skippy into the bedroom, then he and Eli went to find out what Chancer was up to.

CHAPTER 45

Lina

LINA SQUEEZED her dad's hand as they waited in the foyer of a Florida aftercare clinic. A social worker named Jennifer—a pert redhead with a thousand freckles—was signing them in. Lina craned her neck to see into a larger room beyond the woman.

"If you'll wait right here, I'll take you to her in a moment." The redhead checked Dad's driver's license against information on her clipboard. After all this time, the last few minutes of waiting were unbearable. Perspiration gathered in Lina's armpits and dripped down her ribs under her shirt. She fidgeted and squeezed Dad's hand again as her thoughts and questions vanished only half-formed in her mind.

At last, Jennifer led them through the large room, which was divided into several sitting areas. In one, a mother cradled a small boy to her chest and sobbed into his hair. Hope and sorrow were tangible, and Lina waded neck-deep in the mix of the two. The woman looked up, meeting her gaze as she and Dad walked past. The woman wasn't wading—she had surrendered to the whirling current. Her expression seemed to say "Just wait, you'll see." Lina clutched at her throat to soothe the ache that had settled there and followed her father and Jennifer down a wide hallway.

"It usually goes better if you wait to ask a lot of questions," Jennifer coached in a low voice. "Today is just about love." She stopped at a door halfway down the hallway. Her hand was on the doorknob.

Turn it, turn it! Lina restrained herself from pushing the social worker aside and busting through the door.

"I'll be in the main reception area if you need me." Jennifer opened the door to a private sitting room. A coffee table, a couch, and two chairs filled the room. Two women sat across from each other. One, a nurse in pink scrubs. The other, Ruby. A taller, paler and hollow-cheeked Ruby. She was pursing her lips and giving the nurse a cold, hard glare. Lina and Dad had interrupted something.

As the door opened wider, Lina brushed past Jennifer. Ruby's face lost the hardness. Her eyes grew wide and misty. Their arms reached toward each other before even one step was taken across the room. In an instant, they were wrapped around each other, their dark hair mingling and their chests heaving in sync with great breaths. Lina was vaguely aware that their father had his arms around them both, creating a Ruby sandwich.

When they finally dared to release one another, they were alone in the room with wet faces and shy smiles. Lina couldn't take her eyes off Ruby. Nothing was like she remembered.

Ruby's hair was cut short in a shaggy A-line bob. A lopsided lump bulged from the bridge of her nose and a small scar broke the line of her upper lip. Dark circles shaded the skin under her eyes, and a series of piercings followed the curve of her left ear. She smiled as she looked between her father and sister. Her front tooth was chipped.

The broken tooth made a whistling sound when she asked, "Where's Mom?"

CHAPTER 46

Cody

THE WIND GUSTED around Cody and Eli as they ran across the yard and ducked behind the side of the barn. Chancer was saddling Gunner, a Paint, in the corral. The horse was antsy and gave him a hard time of it. Chancer fumbled in the rain to get the girth cinched.

Cody and Eli were pelted with fat raindrops while they waited, peering around the corner. As soon as Chancer rode off, they tacked their own horses. Thunder clapped overhead and the lightning flashed high up in the clouds.

"Easy, boy," Cody said to keep Big Red calm. "We're gonna go bust the bad guys that stole your friends."

"AbolitionistOps for animals?" Eli asked.

"Damn right."

From the shelter of the barn, Eli called the police with his cell phone. "There's an intruder. We believe he's the one responsible for the cattle thefts. Yes, right now," he said. "We're gonna go track them down."

They rode out in the direction Chancer had gone. Rain beat down on Cody's ball cap and the wind pushed them from behind. If it weren't for Chancer's betrayal, they wouldn't have to be out on a miserable night like this.

As they got closer to the highway, Gunner's light-colored patches stood out in the darkness up ahead. Eli circled wide around so he and Cody could close in from opposite sides.

Chancer approached the herd huddled together in a mass. He roped a cow around the neck and drove it toward the fence. Another cow bellowed and followed, swishing her tail. Chancer jumped off his horse, tied the animal to a post, and approached the herd again. He was going for another.

A set of headlights appeared through the rain in the distance, and a truck with a trailer pulled over to the side of the road near the two cows. A man stepped out of the truck into the rain, opened the back of the trailer, and lowered the ramp. Exactly like Wayne had supposed. Cody searched in the night for Eli. With the dark, rain, and wind, Cody couldn't see him. With any luck, he was waiting just on the other side of Chancer's stash. If not, it was up to Cody to keep Chancer and that truck here until the police showed up. *AbolitionistOps for animals!* His own pre-game pep-talk.

The man shook a bucket of feed as he neared the cows. He used fence pliers to snap the wires and pulled the section open. Chancer and his horse chased a third cow toward the breach in the fence where the man lured them in with the feed bucket. As the cow neared, it veered to the side. Chancer cut it off and again directed it toward the waiting trailer. He had never worked this hard for the ranch.

A flash of lightning illuminated the pasture.

"Easy now." The lightning worried Big Red, but also

showed where Eli was waiting opposite him. If Cody could see Eli, then the rustlers could have seen him. Thankfully, they seemed occupied. The man chased a cow up the ramp into the trailer and tried to lure the other with the bucket of feed. Chancer dismounted to help the man bring the cattle to the trailer.

Cody's whole body was wound tight, ready to spring into action. He listened for a signal from Eli but only heard the roaring wind. He crept Big Red closer.

Out on the road, an unlit vehicle emerged from the dark and traded its stealth for headlights. The man at the trailer startled from the cows. He threw up the ramp and was in the process of closing the back of the trailer when sirens flashed. Chancer ran on foot back into the darkness of the pasture.

Cody nudged Big Red. "Go."

As the rain beat down, Chancer slid and tripped through the dung-strewn pasture, and Big Red easily outpaced him. When he was close enough, Cody leapt from the saddle and tumbled Chancer to the ground. They rolled and scuffled on the wet earth.

Cody's face smashed against the ground. Pain burned across his cheek, blinding him to the rain, the wind, the fact that if he didn't move, he'd get hit again. Chancer pushed harder, grinding his face into the mud. Cody rolled, desperate for space between him and his enemy. Chancer came at him again, but this time Cody was ready. He hooked his foot around Chancer's leg and brought him crashing down.

Cody pinned him down and punched Chancer's face. His wet clothing stuck to him and shortened his range of movement, only further enraging him. He hit him again.

He hit him for the cows, for the betrayal, and for the sticky, wet clothes.

He raised his arm back to strike again. But even with all his strength, he couldn't throw the punch. A guttural growl rumbled in his chest when he learned what held his fist.

Eli had caught his arm.

He pulled him off Chancer. Cody caught his breath as Eli yanked Chancer to his feet and twisted his arm behind him to walk him back to the scene of the crime.

Cody, bombarded with stinging raindrops, searched for his ball cap. It was gone in the dark. He would have to do without. As he gathered Big Red's reins and those of Eli's horse to lead them to the fence line, his fingers protested. He flexed his fingers and shook out his hand. Hopefully Chancer's face hurt worse.

Raindrops blew sideways in the wind. They reflected the flashing red and blue lights like a kaleidoscope. By the time Cody reached the roadside, one officer had cuffed Chancer's partner and put him into the back of the police SUV and the other was speaking into the radio.

Cody tethered the horses at the fence and climbed into the trailer to collect his cows.

Chancer shot a glare at Cody when he got his own set of cuffs. He had a split lip and a swollen eye. "You think you're something? Hiding out in the house while everyone else does all the work. You don't deserve this place."

Eli paused his report to the officer and raised a threatening finger to Chancer. "You shut up! You don't know what you're talking about."

"You don't deserve this place!" Chancer shouted again. The officer deposited him in the SUV next to his accomplice and closed the door, muffling his shouts.

Cody was glad to see him go, even if they were down by half a ranch hand now. He and Eli stepped into the trailer with the officers to speak out of the rain. The officer with the radio called for impound to come collect the truck and trailer.

"Any idea who that other guy is?" Cody asked.

"He hasn't got ID on him, and he's not talking," one of the officers answered. "The truck is registered to a Chester Selte. Does that name ring a bell?"

"No, I don't know him," Cody said.

"We'll see what we can piece together and contact you in the morning."

When the police left with Chancer and his partner in crime, Cody breathed a sigh of relief.

"Phew! That was awesome!" Eli appeared a little too happy about what had gone down. "You flew off your horse like some kind of avenging demon. I wasn't sure I could keep you from killing him."

"I just wanted him to stop." Cody raised his voice to be heard above the wind.

Eli clapped him on the back. "Let's get out of the rain."

HIS WEARINESS LIFTING, Cody joined Eli in a spirited recounting of the arrest as they took the horses back to the barn. Eli draped the horses in wool coolers while Cody started wiping down the tack. He shook droplets of water from his head as he worked, looking forward to changing into sweats and being warm again.

A snapping noise made him stop and listen, but the wind took the sound before it could reach him again. He listened harder. Nothing. It must have been his imagination.

Then Skippy ran into the barn with his yappy bark and circled Cody's feet. His tail wagged like a propellor.

"What's wrong with your dog?" Eli asked.

Cody was already halfway across the barn.

"It's my mom," he called back.

The front door was open, the wind clapping it back and forth on its hinges. Cody quickly checked the family room on his way to Mom's bedroom. Her bed was empty.

A cold lump formed in his throat. His face throbbed and he brought his hand to his head to stop the spinning. He ran back out into the rain. There was no sign of her. He threw open the garage door. No one there.

"She's not in the house?" Eli asked.

"No."

Eli hurried to a UTV. "Call you if I find her." He took off to the south.

Cody climbed onto another UTV and headed north.

The tires slid in the mud as Cody raced along what were normally dirt roads. He searched close to the house first, then widened the circle.

The headlights were weak—he strained his eyes as he hunted for his mom in the dark. Cody could not begin to guess where she would have gone. She never left the house! Her favorite place was indoors.

He scoured the property. His worry pressed the crease between his eyebrows until it hurt as bad as his cheek. He turned down a dirt road between pastures.

"Mom! Mom!" Only the sound of the storm answered back. He was consumed with disgust over his earlier thoughts, of daring to wish to be free of her, and now she was nowhere to be found. He had wanted this. He ignored his own shivering and pushed the UTV faster into the wind.

"This is all my fault," he repeated over and over as he turned down another dirt road. Gripping the steering wheel through the pain of his swollen fingers, Cody shivered in the wind and rain.

He reached the farthest edge of the property. He could go farther out, or circle back and make another pass, but the going was slow— the mud kept bogging down the tires. He couldn't imagine she had ventured this far from the house. But then, until she had chased Lina, he hadn't expected her to make it as far as the front porch.

"Where? Where?" he called into the night. *Left.* But his arms turned the wheel to the right. He was headed closer to home, revving through puddles and sending up giant sprays of water.

"This is useless!" He pulled a U-turn. As if in slow motion, the grass blew to the side, revealing a bit of pale fabric in the dim beam of the headlights. Sick dread coiled around his spine. He wasn't ready for what he suspected he would find.

Turning the UTV off the track, he raced to the spot. A foot appeared in the dark, then another. He positioned the UTV so that its meager headlights shone on Mom. She lay face down in the mud and grass, her fingers interlocked behind her head.

Cody hurried to her, crouching as he searched for a pulse. The side of her neck was cold and still, as were her wrists. Panicking, he gave his mom a little shake. He called Eli, and giving him their location, he realized the significance of the field they were in. The same one where his father's accident had occurred.

Hadn't he lost enough?

He fumbled with the slippery phone to call for an ambulance.

Eli must have been close, because he arrived and added the light of the second UTV to the spot while Cody was still trying to find a pulse. The emergency operator talked him through it, but Cody could barely hear anything.

Eli turned her onto her back and placed two fingers to the side of her throat, leaning very close and concentrating. He looked up at Cody and nodded. "She's alive!"

Relieved beyond words, Cody squeezed his eyes shut and pressed the heels of his palms to them. Pain in his cheekbone from his fight with Chancer lurched him into action. There would be time to cry later.

He lifted his mom from the mud and climbed into the passenger seat of Eli's UTV. He held her in his lap with his arm about her shoulders as they sped to the house. She was so cold and wet, and she didn't respond when he tapped her cheek. "Stay with me, Mom." His foot pressed hard against an imaginary gas pedal.

At the house, Eli took her from him and carried her into the family room.

"Put her on the couch." Cody's jaw chattered, but not Mom's. She lay pale and still, with a blue-ish cast to her fingers and toes. "We have to get her warm."

Eli took charge. "Get some blankets."

Cody returned with the blankets from her bed and spread one over her lifeless body. "This is my fault." He should've been home, not playing hero to a couple of cows. With clumsy fingers on his injured right hand, he floundered with the second blanket.

Eli took it from him and unfurled it with a snap. "Now

is not the time." He wrapped her with the second layer, tucking in the edges. "Talk to her."

Cody knelt at her side and toweled off her face. "Mom, wake up. Wake up, Mom." *I need you more than Dad does.* His shivers became convulsions until he could no longer speak.

Eli crouched on the floor opposite him. He'd been to Cody's room—he shoved a pair of sweats and a hoodie at him. "Change," he said. "You're gonna have a long night ahead of you. You don't want to spend it wet."

Cody wrestled out of his wet clothes.

"Is it okay if I pray for her?" Eli asked as they waited for the ambulance.

Cody nodded through his sob-like shivers and bowed his head. If divine help was a real thing, now was the time to ask for it.

Eli offered his prayer in a practiced and reverent tone. Cody couldn't focus on particular words, only the urgent need. He didn't know enough about God to know how He worked, so Cody relied on Eli to know what he was doing.

When the ambulance arrived, the paramedics asked so many questions: How long had she been outside? Was she feeling okay before she went outside? Did she have pre-existing conditions?

While Eli found her prescription bottle and gave it to them, Cody answered the best he could.

He climbed into the ambulance alongside her. Before the doors closed, he met Eli's gaze through the rain. Was this what it was like to have a brother? Someone to chase through the rain at his side, and to pick up the slack when he fell short? Eli had proven himself to be all that and more.

CHAPTER 47

Cody

A MACHINE BEEPED SOMEWHERE down the hall. Nurses hurried back and forth between rooms. An elderly lady across the waiting room twisted her handkerchief while her husband dozed next to her. Cody closed his eyes and concentrated on the meadow and Lina twirling in the sunshine, until he saw where his mom lay face down in the grass. He recited the alternate ending in his head, and then thought about the meadow again.

A nurse nudged his shoulder.

"How's that paperwork coming along?" she asked. His fingers were cramped around the pen. His knuckles were cracked and scabbed, making it hard to bend them. He had barely started with the clipboard balanced on his lap. Name, date of birth, address—he'd filled those in. Her medical history was more challenging. He knew the name of her medication, so he'd written that.

"Can you at least give us her health insurance card?" the nurse asked.

"Not without my wallet." His throat was hoarse from raising his voice over the wind all night.

"Can you have someone bring your wallet?"

"Not without my phone."

The nurse walked away and returned a short time later with a Styrofoam cup of coffee.

He gratefully accepted the cup. The warmth soothed his fingers. "What does the doctor say?"

"I'll go get an update for you."

At that moment, Eli walked in and went straight to the nurse's desk. "Rosie Schafer?"

The nurse pointed at Cody.

Eli had changed into fresh clothes and combed his hair. He dropped a backpack into an empty seat between them as he sat. "How is she?"

"I ain't got any news yet."

"I had to drive your truck, mine's at the Gas 'n' Sip," Eli said. "I brought a few other things too." He opened the backpack to show him.

"Your wallet, laptop, and charger in case you're here a long time. And I stopped on the way and picked up a breakfast burrito for you."

"Breakfast?" Cody fished the insurance card from his wallet.

"Yeah, it's six o'clock. You need help with that?" Eli took the insurance card and the clipboard from Cody.

Cody wearily let Eli take over. "Did you see my phone anywhere?"

"Nope. It's probably still out in the field."

The nurse came back, and she brought a doctor with her.

"We treated your mother for hypothermia," the doctor said. "But we need to run some tests to rule out other possible reasons for the loss of consciousness."

Cody let out a sigh of relief.

"We also gave her a light sedative. She woke up and was very confused. She didn't understand where she is or why. She can't tell us how she ended up in the mud during a thunderstorm."

Because she thinks you have to lie flat in the wind. "Can I see her?"

Cody followed the nurse down the hall to a patient room. Mom was clean and asleep, buried under blankets. He took her hand, reassured by its warmth.

"She has some wounds on the soles of her feet," the nurse said. "They don't look fresh though …"

"She stepped on broken glass two nights ago."

"Okay, mystery solved," she said. "I'll be outside. Use her call button if you need anything."

Cody went back out to Eli. "Thanks for bringing my stuff. I'm gonna hang out here in case she wakes up."

"Good idea. I think I'll go home and sleep for a couple hours. I already explained what happened to Wayne and told him I wouldn't be at work until later. He's going to get the full story about Chancer from the police." Eli put a hand on Cody's shoulder. "You did really well last night."

"Only because you were there." Cody had gaps. He wasn't the best cowboy, or businessman, or son. But Eli was, and he filled in those gaps. Instead of a rival, Eli had become Cody's ally.

He turned, about to go back to Mom's room, when Eli grabbed his shoulder and pulled him in for a hug. Not a one-armed, casual bro hug, but a two-armed brother hug.

"She'll be okay," Eli said.

Choked up, Cody nodded. "Thanks. I'll see you later."

He went back to his mom, sitting next to her and staring at her shallow breathing and the numbers displayed on the monitor. "I'm sorry I wasn't taking very good care of you. But the truth is, I don't know if I can do any better." Mom was only forty-two. The prospect of a lifetime of worrying over her and babysitting her overwhelmed him, but he had no choice but to try.

"I never should've left you alone for a minute." A hiccup wrenched from his chest. He shook his head clear to set his mind on a more productive path. *At least she's out of the house.* That was the best he could come up with?

Cody looked in the backpack for the burrito. It was cold. He went out to the nurse's station.

"How are you doing?" It was the same nurse who had asked about Mom's feet.

"Better now that my mom's safe," he said. "Do you have a microwave?" He held up the burrito.

"Sure, I'll take care of that." She took the burrito and disappeared down a hallway only to return two minutes later with his warmed breakfast. "There you go, need anything else?"

"No, thank you, ma'am. How long do you expect she'll sleep?"

"Hard to say with the sedative. If you need to leave for a bit but don't want to miss anything, we're taking her for a CT scan around ten. That'll be a good time to slip out."

Back in his mom's room, Cody propped his socked feet on the edge of the bed while he checked his email and ate the burrito. There was something from the Washburn admissions office.

We regret to inform you that we are unable to reinstate your previous acceptance. However, you are welcome to submit a new application. The application deadline for fall semester has passed. The application deadline for next year is ...

Cody didn't read anymore. It was probably for the best. Mom should've been his priority. *A man takes care of his family.* He was out of his mind to suppose there could've been more in his life.

He caught a couple of hours of uncomfortable sleep in a hospital recliner next to Mom and the occasional pinging of her monitor.

Cody woke with a jolt. Eli was sitting on the other side of his mom, flirting with the nurse who was measuring Mom's vital signs. It was almost ten.

Cody yawned and rubbed his aching head. Mom looked better. The pallor was gone. He touched her forehead to assure himself of the warmth of her skin. She was going to be okay.

"I'm about to take her for her CT scan," the nurse said. "This is a good time for you to regroup, get some food."

All Cody could think of was how badly he wanted Lina with him right now. His losses ached all the way to his bones. Washburn, his mom, Lina …

"We're going to take real good care of her," the nurse said.

Cody nodded, but he didn't believe it. No one could take real good care of her—she was erratic. He knew her best, and even he had failed.

"Come on, let's go get my truck," Eli said. "Desiree will call me when you're needed back here."

"Desiree?"

"Your mom's nurse …?"

The nurse smiled at him and waved as though they were just meeting rather than speaking for the fourth time. "Do you have Eli's number?" Cody asked her.

"Already gave it to her," Eli said.

Figures. Giving his number to a pretty girl was Eli's superpower.

As they left the hospital, Eli passed Cody the keys only to have them handed back.

"You drive," Cody said. He just didn't feel up to it.

Before they turned onto the highway back to the ranch, Cody's heart began to race. Adrenaline pumped through his veins as they neared Lina's neighborhood. He still needed to make things right with her. Even if all he could do was explain himself and let her decide if she wanted him back, he had to try.

"I need to make a stop before we leave town." Cody pointed out Lina's street. "Turn here."

Mr. Grant's car was not in the driveway, but hers was. Perhaps she would talk to him without her dad getting between them. Eli waited in the truck while Cody knocked on the door.

There was no answer.

He rang the bell and knocked again.

Pounding harder, he called her name through the door. There was no way she couldn't hear this.

"Lina! Lina, are you here?" His shout faded. "I need you …" he whispered, forehead against the door. Shoulders slumped in defeat, Cody returned to the truck.

Eli kept the conversation on ranch business, particularly Frank Chancer's herd and his nephew's treachery. Cody only half listened. They stopped at the Gas 'n' Sip, and Eli drove his own truck from there.

Back at the ranch, everything was quiet. Cody went to the garage first to check in with Wayne. He wasn't there, but the whiteboard told him where everybody was. Spence was repairing the fence, Wayne was touring the ranch in search of storm damage, and Tay was monitoring the herds for illness or injury. All the UTV's were gone, so he took Big Red out to the field to look for his phone.

Big Red picked his way around mud puddles, his hooves leaving deep imprints in the rain-softened road. Low clouds left big gaps for sunshine to break through. A hushed peace diffused the upheaval of the night before. The cattle were tranquil as he passed, hardly giving him notice.

His hand ached. He hadn't felt a thing when he used it to bang on Lina's door, but now it throbbed. He had punched someone last night, something he'd never done before. Fighting came at a cost, and if only his knuckles suffered, it was worth it. But the real price of last night's battle with Chancer had been his absence when Mom had needed him.

The ranch itself was none the worse for wear after the storm, and in the moment, Cody could appreciate his home as a paradise. A paradise for Eli, not him. No place would ever truly be a paradise unless Lina was there.

The UTV he had used last night had a dead battery. It was exactly how he had left it in the middle of the field. Grasses trampled flat to the ground marked the spot where he had found his mom. It didn't take him long to locate his phone. It had spent the night in the mud and rain and was useless—another casualty. He cursed under his breath and mounted his horse. There was so much damage to be tended to, but the most urgent was the damage inside of him.

He let Big Red gallop to the creek bottom, flinging clods of mud from his hooves and sending splashes wide across the road. He had hoped to be done with dark thoughts, but here he was again listening to them just as before. Back where he'd started, ranching and caring for Mom, only worse because he had dared to hope. He had let Lina down. The broken heart and shattered dreams lurked in the clouds overhead. If he had been hanging on by a thread before, now that thread was on fire.

Sitting down on his rock, he propped his elbows on his knees and rested his head in his hands. He recited the alternate ending to *Romeo and Juliet* in his head, but the dark thoughts lingered. He recited it again, aloud this time. His spoken voice gave him strength, and he lifted his head.

The water bubbled high against the embankment. It rushed by, its current rough and sinister. If he let it take him, how far would he go? It might take him from here, but unless it took him to Lina, there was no point.

The rocks at his feet, tumbled smooth by the river, had started from somewhere else. They were only here because the river had brought them. This point of the river may not have even been their final destinations. He picked up one of the rocks that was not yet smooth on all edges. This one hadn't journeyed far enough. He flexed his sore hand around it. How long had it been stuck here, waiting for the river to rise or a current strong enough to carry it onward?

Cody hefted the rock judging its weight. It needed a little help to get back on course. He shared a story—and a journey cut short and left stagnant—with this half-jagged, half-smooth rock. There had to be a way to take control of the rest of his mess, to make his future better than his past.

He chucked the rock into the river. It was swallowed by the churning water. He found another not yet polished. This one he gave a name before he threw it. "Inadequate." His aim was off, and Inadequate ricocheted off the bank before joining the boisterous flow of the water. He threw a dozen more rocks, each named for a dark thought that he was done with. Useless. Incapable. Alone …

Each throw was accompanied by the same vindication

as the punches he had thrown at Chancer. No longer a victim to a duplicitous employee, no longer watching his herd dwindle, no longer abandoned to his fate. Each punch had delivered him by degrees. And each rock thrown into the river did the same for the thoughts holding him captive.

Without the cloud of those thoughts, the thing he wanted most became clear through the dissipating mist. He had to find Lina. Nothing would be right until he saw her. She was all he could think about. Unsure if she could forgive him, he wasn't sure of much at all, but he *was* sure just hanging on wasn't good enough anymore. With fresh determination, he and Big Red galloped back to the barn.

CHAPTER 48
Lina

VISITS WITH RUBY were kept short. She was dealing with not only the ups and downs of addiction and the grief from learning their mom was dead, but also the disbelief that she was, indeed, finally safe.

While Dad was occupied with Jennifer, making arrangements for a rehab clinic closer to home, Lina wandered into Ruby's temporary bedroom where her sister lounged on the bed with a cold compress over her eyes.

As children, they had been known to jump test all mattresses. Their own, their parents', Grandma's, the one at the Disneyland hotel. Dad had never minded, but Mom would always scold them. "Get down, before you monkeys break something!"

For Lina, the best part of jumping on the bed had been holding hands with Ruby as they bounced and laughing as her sister's hair flipped around. They should be jumping right now, but she suspected those days were over. Ruby was here, right in front of her after all those years apart, but she no longer seemed to be the sort of girl who would jump on a mattress.

She climbed onto the bed next to Ruby, careful not to jostle too much, and lifted a corner of the compress. "Are you awake?"

"Yeah. I hardly sleep. Have you or Dad told anyone about me?"

"Dad called Grandma a little while ago."

"Please don't tell anyone else."

"Why not? There are a lot of people who've been worried ever since you disappeared. They'll be so happy you're back." *A heartbroken kind of happy.*

Ruby threw the compress across the room and sat up. Her face went green, and she froze, clutching Lina's arm until her world stopped spinning. Trina, Ruby's nurse, had warned about getting up too fast.

Lina rubbed her back in circles. "Okay?"

Eyes closed, Ruby nodded. "I'm not back. Not really."

"Well, you will be soon, won't you? As soon as you're healthy again—"

"Stop." Ruby turned away and looked out the window. "There's no coming back from where I've been. There's only going forward to somewhere else."

Lina laid her head on Ruby's shoulder. "Do you want to talk about it?"

"No." She covered her face with her hands as she shook her head. "The person I was, she was the old me. If I tell you about it, I would be bringing her into my new life."

"But, it's Grandma, and Aunt Marianne …" Lina glanced at Ruby's feverish pink face. There was a story behind the piercings and scars, a heartbreak behind each tear that fell onto her cheeks. They were Ruby's stories, and even if Lina knew the details, the stories would always belong to Ruby. She smoothed her sister's hair and cradled her head. "It's okay. Even if people knew what happened to you, they could never understand what it was like to be you."

"I'm afraid …" Ruby hiccuped as she attempted a deep breath. "I'm afraid that if anyone knows where I've been and what I've been doing, I'll never be able to live it down or leave it behind."

Ruby had survived so much. It wouldn't be fair to carry the consequences of a life she hadn't chosen.

"You don't want to wear a label."

"I want to choose how people see me, but no one could overlook a detail like that."

"I can."

"Really?" Ruby raised a challenging eyebrow.

"I want to." Easier said than done. How could she know enough to be supportive without knowing too much to ever forget? Lina tucked her feet under herself and faced Ruby. "I want to see you as my sister, as my best friend."

"You don't already have a best friend?"

She had Cody, maybe. She had seen the thing behind the curtain that made him vulnerable before he'd been ready to show her. Would it have made a difference to how she perceived him had she known from the beginning that he was occupied every day with caring for his ill mother? It was too late now to honestly answer that question.

She would never introduce Ruby as her trafficking victim sister, only as her sister. People would have their questions, but those would be for Ruby to answer or deflect. Just as Cody had chosen to deflect about his mom. He would have told her the truth when he was ready. She had to believe that. And she *needed* to apologize for pushing the issue.

"There is someone, and I need to tell him—not about you, but why I left town in such a hurry. My boyfriend, sort of. We're either broken up or in the middle of a fight …" There would be another time, a better time, to talk about her boyfriend. She put an arm around Ruby's shoulder and pressed back against the headboard. They cuddled together in silence until Trina knocked twice before pushing the door open.

"It's time for some medication. It'll help with how sick you're feeling." She offered Ruby two pills, a cup of water, and a fresh cold compress. "Give her a break for a while," she told Lina. "You can come back in an hour or so."

Lina nodded and reluctantly made her way out of the room. Before the door closed behind her, Ruby asked, "What's his name?"

Their eyes met, and it was as though they had never been apart. They were still just two little girls who shared everything.

"Cody."

"You can tell Cody, but only as much as you have to to make things right."

Lina nodded and left to give Ruby time to rest. She made her way to the main lobby. Dad was still in Jennifer's office. They were talking quietly over coffee. Dad's tie was loose, and his posture seemed at ease. Not to disturb them, she exited the building and sat on the curb by the parking lot.

She took her phone from her pocket. No new messages. She dialed Cody but got his voice mail again. The words wanted to come out. She brushed a few runaway tears off her face.

"Cody, so much has happened. I could use a friend …" There was more to say, but her crumpling composure did not allow it. She disconnected the call and searched out a private space to have a good cry.

CHAPTER 49

Cody

CODY SHOWERED AND CHANGED, then he drove back to town. He stopped at Lina's house again before looking elsewhere. Still only her car in the driveway, still no answer at the door.

At the library, he found Mrs. Paul at the circulation desk. "Is Lina here?"

"No, I'm sorry," Mrs. Paul said. "She didn't come to work yesterday. Said she was out of town for a few days."

Out of town? Had she gone back to school?

He deserved that.

Cody would drive anywhere to see her if he thought he'd be welcome, but he had to get Mom figured out first.

At the hospital, a doctor was checking on his mom in her room when Cody walked in.

"I'm Dr. Nelson," he said. "You must be Cody."

They shook hands. Cody took in Mom's tired face as she looked out the window from her bed. She didn't acknowledge him.

"Your mom is doing much better physically. Her CT

scan looks fine, and her labs are pretty good. She is still experiencing cognitive difficulties. She hasn't told us very much. Can you fill us in on what happened?"

He had questions himself, and not only concerning her gradual decline. What drove her out into the thunderstorm while he was fighting Chancer? And why would he have left her to her own devices. "I can try."

"How long has she been taking her current medication?"

"About a year and a half." Should he mention the part where he doubled her dose? "The pills always helped until the last few weeks."

The doctor nodded as though that was the answer he had expected. "What were her symptoms when she was first prescribed it?"

"It was like she was depressed, didn't get out of bed, didn't eat, never felt like talking, wouldn't go outside. It was right after my dad was killed."

Dr. Nelson referred to notes on his tablet. "His death was traumatic for her, right?"

"Yes, sir. She saw the whole thing happen."

"The medication helped at that point?"

Cody furrowed his brow as he searched his memory. "Yeah, she started getting out of bed, eating. Started talking a little, but over time the things she would say became nonsense. Still never went outside until a few days ago."

"Describe the recent symptoms."

He lowered his voice. Mom appeared to be sleeping, but just in case… "She's been screaming more and more, throwing things. I found her in the doorway, like she was afraid to go out but unable to come back in either. Then couple days later, she chased my girlfriend off the porch, screaming." He leaned toward the doctor and whispered, "Scared us to death." Cody shook his head. "And then this, running out into a storm." She had picked the worst possible time to venture outside.

The doctor tucked his tablet under his arm. "Cody, she needs a psychiatric consultation before we discharge her. I suspect her symptoms are related to PTSD from your father's accident. It's not unheard of for severe cases of PTSD to develop psychosis symptoms that get worse if left untreated."

Cody rubbed his jaw and let out a long breath. "And if she is able to get treatment?"

"There's every reason to be hopeful. It's not going to be an easy road for her, but I believe it's worth trying."

"What is the treatment?"

"That will be determined by the psychiatrist, but it involves both medication and any of several therapy methods."

Lina had a therapist who helped her. Maybe it would work for Mom.

"Can I be here when the psychiatrist comes?"

"Yes, but here's where it gets tricky. You're the next of kin, so we can share information with you about her condition. But do you have medical power of attorney?"

"No, sir."

"You'll need it to have input into medical decisions on her behalf. Otherwise, plan of care decisions will be made by a court-appointed guardian."

Cody dropped into the chair by his mom's bed, and resting his elbows on his knees, lowered his face to his hands. He needed Dad. On his own, he wasn't equipped to deal with this.

"We can help you get a court order for power of attorney. Do you have a lawyer?"

He had Peter Mallory's phone number. Cody put his hand to his pocket. His phone wasn't there. "I'll get one."

With a brusque nod, the doctor left.

Cody found Desiree at the nurses' station. "Can you please give me Eli's phone number?"

"Yes, it's right here. Everything okay?" she asked, jotting the number on a slip of paper.

"Yes, thank you, ma'am."

He called Eli from the phone in Mom's room. The call went to voice mail. "Hey, Eli. I need a lawyer for power of attorney. Call me back at the hospital."

He needed a new phone too.

"Cody … little Cody." At Mom's faint whisper, he hung up the phone.

"Hey, Mom, how're you feeling?"

"Hungry."

"You're hungry?" He smiled at her and laughed. "What would you like to eat?"

"Fries."

Cody sat on the side of her bed. They were having a real conversation. "Anything else?" He took her hand, wanting to encourage the discussion as long as possible.

"Cheeseburger."

"What do you want to drink?"

"Chocolate milk."

"How about a cookie too?"

"Lina will bring cookies."

He slumped into a chair. It had been a wonderful exchange, even though it was short. Almost like the mom he used to know. He pressed the call button and placed the food order with Desiree, then turned on the television to the country music channel. His mom began humming. The need for a new phone was pushed to the back of his mind. He couldn't leave now in case Mom felt like talking again.

CHAPTER 50

Cody

CODY SIPPED coffee in the chair while his mom watched music videos, dipped her finger into ketchup, and licked it clean. There was a knock at the hospital room door—Cody rubbed his eyes before he identified the sound. A middle-aged man in golf pants and an open-collared, button down shirt hovered in the doorway.

"Are you Cody?" the man asked.

"Yes, sir." Cody went to the door to meet him.

"Peter Mallory," he said and shook his hand. "Eli told me you need some help. Power of attorney documents aren't where I specialize, but I'll be consulting with a colleague who does, so you'll have two of us on your team."

They left Mom's room and sat in a nearby lounge area. Half an hour later, a small coffee table was crowded with a legal pad full of notes and both of their open laptops.

Cody didn't even want to know how much this consultation would cost, but however much it was, it was worth the opportunity to learn what his next steps should be. Cody didn't feel so lost anymore.

"I'll let you know as soon as we have a court date," Peter said. "Shouldn't take long, given the time-sensitive nature of Rosie's condition. With the psychiatrist's recommendation and the fact that you're her only family, I'm sure there won't be any problems."

Cody planned to quickly check on Mom and then go replace his phone, but when he got back to the hospital room, a woman with curly brown hair and wearing a white coat over street clothes was attempting to get information out of her. "Can I help you, ma'am?"

"I'm Dr. Bally. I'm a psychiatrist here to consult on your mom."

He had wanted to be present for the psychiatric consultation. Who knew what Mom might say, if anything. He could be helpful to clarify or explain, or maybe he would just get in the way. "Has she spoken to you?"

Dr. Bally motioned for him to join her in the hallway before answering. "Not much, she's waiting for Lina to bring her some cookies. Is that real?"

"No." But he could try to make it real if he had her phone number.

"I've spoken with Dr. Nelson and Dr. Hilderbran. I'd like to recommend moving her to a facility that specializes in PTSD in Topeka. She'll receive excellent care. The on-site psychiatric team will be able to manage her recovery."

Cody faltered. She would be so far away. "Can she be treated from home? I can take care of her."

"You've been caring for her? By yourself?" Dr. Bally's face flooded with concern.

"Our neighbor comes to help. We were managing."

"I'm sure you've done your best, but she really needs professional, targeted attention." She spoke in a compassionate tone, but it still cut deep. His best hadn't been enough.

"How much does it cost?"

"Insurance won't cover all of it, I'm afraid. But I've brought you some financial assistance applications, and you should apply for disability on her behalf. Do you have power of attorney?"

"I hope I will soon." Without it, he was powerless.

After Dr. Bally left, Cody sat next to his mom and laid his head on the edge of her bed. She'd been through such an ordeal, and he was at the center of it. If he had tried harder to push her out of her comfort zone, he might have gotten her the help she needed earlier, before she had gotten so bad. The difficulties of forcing her into the truck, or tricking her, or however he might have managed it, had to have been preferable to the hypothermia and the unconscious ride in the back of an ambulance.

She absently stroked his hair while his mind buzzed. Doctors, lawyers, paperwork—all he wanted to do was track down Lina.

"Hi, Rosie." Eli poked his head in the doorway. He was carrying a small duffel bag. "I've brought you something." He put a finger up to his lips. "Shh, it's a secret."

He unzipped the bag and a furry head popped through the opening.

"Skippy!" Mom beamed and cuddled the dog on her lap, stroking his ears.

"This is just a visit," Eli said. "He can't stay with you, or he might upset the nurses."

Mom nodded and snickered at Skippy's wet nose.

"How are you doing? Big day?" Eli asked Cody.

"You can say that. Thanks for sending Peter. Without

power of attorney, I don't have any input. A court-appointed guardian will approve whatever the doctors want to do."

"What are the doctors recommending?"

"A facility in Topeka to treat her for PTSD."

"Is there a reason you don't want her to go?"

"It's expensive." Cody buried his face in his hands. "PTSD! All this time, I thought it was a depression thing. So much of this is my fault." His face heated. Confessing his shortcomings to a man like Eli didn't come easy, but they were brothers now. "I was a scared kid, what did I know? I'm still a scared kid."

Eli took a seat. "We're all scared kids to some extent. You did your best with the information you had."

"She is my family, my responsibility. I'm supposed to take care of her. And now they want to put her in a home that I can't pay for." Cody lifted the financial aid documents and slapped them down on the foot of the bed. "A man takes care of his family," Cody said softly.

Eli picked up the brochure of the facility and the financial paperwork and flipped through them. "You think getting financial help is not taking care of your family?"

"It's letting the government take care of her."

"And if you don't let her go to the facility because of the expense, is that taking care of her?"

Cody looked away. He couldn't win.

"Cody, you're gonna take care of her." Eli set the papers down and leaned forward. "You always will. But that might not look how you expect it to look." With his elbows on his knees, he steepled his fingers together. "You're thinking you'll bring her home and tend her night and day, maybe drive her to doctor's appointments a few times a week. Which sounds reasonable right now." He lifted a hand and shrugged. "But you'll be trading your future family for that. You've got to put yourself in a position to take care of them one day too."

"My future family ...?" Cody raised an eyebrow. "I don't even think I have a girlfriend anymore."

"Sure you do—you just need to straighten things out. Point is, take care of Rosie now in the best, smartest way possible so that in the future you'll be able to take care of both her and a wife," Eli grinned, "maybe kids."

Cody shook off the beginnings of a smile. It wouldn't help anything to imagine having kids with Lina, not when so much was in shambles between them. His father had taught him his responsibility was to take care of his family — no matter the one he came from or the one he would make for himself—but he didn't say *how* to do it. Was Eli right? Maybe Mom would get better and the facility would be temporary. He wouldn't be dependent on assistance programs forever. He neatened the pile of paperwork. "Maybe ..."

"I spoke with Frank Chancer today."

Cody perked up. "Did he know what was going on? Was he involved?"

"No. He was surprised when Chancer called him for bail money. Refused to help, and then he called Wayne to apologize. He offered his own cattle to replace the ones his nephew made off with."

"That's a decent gesture. Does he know the other guy, Chester Selte?"

"Said he didn't. Said he didn't even know his own nephew like he thought he had."

"Well, I'm glad Chancer won't be causing any more trouble around here. I've got enough of my own right now."

"Any word from Lina?"

Cody looked down at his hands. "I need a phone."

"Go get one. I'll sit with Rosie, at least until they discover the dog." Eli propped his feet up on the end of Mom's bed and got comfortable. "We'll be fine."

CHAPTER 51

Lina

LINA RECLINED her seat and stretched her legs as far as she could reach. She wasn't a frequent flier, but she could still appreciate the ultimate luxury offered in first class— space. The roomier seats were better for Ruby, who was already physically and emotionally uncomfortable.

Jennifer had arranged a spot for Ruby at The Hope Project, a rehab center for human trafficking victims in the countryside outside Topeka. As Ruby's aftercare team, she and Trina sat in the row behind them, close enough to handle panic attacks, cold sweats, or any other emergencies.

"Distract me, Adeline." Ruby closed her eyes and rested her head. "What was high school like for you?"

"Pretty normal, I guess."

Ruby opened one eye. "Lina." She tested the nickname for the first time. "I don't know what normal is."

"Right. Sorry." Lina began again. "I had classes and friends. I ate in the cafeteria, at least until I had a driver's license, then my friends and I would leave campus for lunch. The mall was across the street, and we would go to the food court."

"Did you have a favorite class?"

"I liked literature a lot. I still really like to read, romance mostly."

"Aha … Did you go to all the dances with your many, many boyfriends?"

"A few dances, but no real boyfriends. Mostly just crushes." Lina could elaborate, but to what end? Ruby hadn't experienced any crushes, hadn't danced at prom. They didn't understand each other's lives.

Ruby kept her eyes closed as she listened. "How did you meet Cody? And why are you guys in a fight?"

"I pushed myself into a part of his life that he wasn't ready to share with me." Lina explained the events of the last evening she saw Cody, everything from the canceled date to showing up uninvited on his doorstep. She told Ruby about Eli keeping her in the garage until it was safe to come out. Then, she described how upset Cody was about her being there, and how she took off before she started crying in front of him. "I was in such a hurry to deepen our relationship that I ruined it. Like I always do."

"I know I'm not an expert or anything, but I'm sure there are advantages to letting things progress naturally. Take it from someone who's not likely to ever have the opportunity …" She opened her eyes and allowed Lina a concerned glance. "Enjoy the ride. It might be the best part."

"Wow. That's deep. And a lot to think about." She leaned over Ruby to speak to their dad. "Do you concur?"

"I do. Ruby is very smart." He patted Ruby's hand on the armrest, then returned to his open laptop.

"Can I ask *you* something now?"

Silence, but Ruby kept her eyes open, which was body language for permission.

"How did you break your nose?"

"*I* didn't break it." Ruby signaled the flight attendant. "Can I get a Coke, please?"

"Of course. Any snacks?" The attendant dug in her cart for the pop.

"Yes, please."

The flight attendant served the Coke with a bag of peanuts and a fresh, warm cookie. "Anything for you?" she asked Lina.

Stalling. Ruby was stalling. Either she didn't want to answer, which was okay, or she needed time to compose her answer.

"I'll have the same and also for my father, please." Might as well get all the beverage and snack needs over with now. When the flight attendant moved on, taking her distractions with her, Lina opened her mouth to pose the question again. There was no need.

"Some men liked to hit me."

On the other side of Ruby, Dad stiffened.

"Gil always charged them more for the damages. But he kept hiring me out to them."

Lina gasped. She reached for her sister's hand, but Ruby withdrew it to her lap. They used to do everything together, but Ruby had faced those monsters on her own while Lina had attended dances and swooned over cute boys. Pressing her lips together, she bit down until she tasted blood. When she imagined herself in Ruby's place, she blanched at the heart broken beyond repair.

Their dad clenched his fists. A vein bulged in his forehead and his lips pressed into a deadly grimace, yet he kept his voice calm and measured. "Would you like to get your nose fixed? Maybe after the rehab?"

"Yes, but …" Ruby pressed a finger to the bump on her nose and placed her other hand over her abdomen. "Not just my nose. I have the broken tooth and …" She lifted her shirt to expose her belly. A stretched-out navel piercing hung loose and droopy where a wide-gauge plug used to be. "It was a client request."

Lina swallowed down the urge to vomit. The ordeal Ruby had endured these past nine years was wretched, and the scars reminded her of every torment. How could she ever leave the past behind if she still wore the signs of it on her body? Lina couldn't erase the marks Ruby bore, but she could shield her from prying questions and well-intended nosiness. Then, maybe one day, once everything was buried in the past, Ruby would truly be herself again.

CHAPTER 52

Cody

AT THE CELL PHONE SHOP, the salesperson was able to salvage the SIM card from Cody's ruined phone. He swiped the ranch bank card with a wave of guilt that this was a personal purchase. He sat in his truck with the new phone plugged into the charger. It came to life. Messages and missed calls pinged through. He had two texts from Lina.

Are you still mad at me? and *Please call me.*

She had called three times and left messages. He listened to the voicemails: "I'm sorry we didn't get to talk the other day. My dad and I were on our way out. Please call me back."

He was so grateful to hear her voice, grateful that she had reached out to him, grateful that being pushed away as she had hurried into the car wasn't the last he would ever see of her. He wiped his face, wincing as the bruised area pulsed, and gulped down the knot in his throat.

The second voice mail: "Cody, so much has happened. I could use a friend." Lina's voice cracked during the breathy message she'd left last night.

What had been going on with her? Cody replayed the message and listened intently. All he heard through the phone were her soft tears. Cody pinched the bridge of his nose. He would give anything to hold her right now, to let her head rest on his shoulder while his strength absorbed her distress like a thirsty sponge. He would have taken it all from her if he could and borne it gladly.

He listened to the latest message, left just this morning: "There's a lot that went wrong between us. We need to talk. I'll be home tomorrow, please come over around five. If you don't, I guess I understand why."

He questioned everything. This last message sounded more like closure after a breakup. If so, there had to be a way he could change her mind.

His fingers hovered over the phone. Tomorrow at five was an eternity away, but what he needed to say was better said face to face rather than over the phone. He wanted to see her eyes blaze violet if she was still mad at him or gleam with desire if she still wanted him. He wanted to feel her skin under his fingertips and watch her melt at his touch. None of those things could happen by phone.

CHAPTER 53

Lina

WHEN THEY ARRIVED at the Kansas City airport, they piled into Dad's car for the hour-and-a-half drive to The Hope Project. Lina, Ruby, and Trina sat shoulder to shoulder in the back seat.

Dad offered Jennifer control of the radio. "Anything but rap, or classical, or heavy metal, or that garbage electric stuff," he said.

"So, I guess it's not really my choice at all."

"Sure it is, with boundaries." He used the same playful tone as when he and Lina played Wii. A pushover blustering about like an alpha male.

"But I *like* EDM." Jennifer tuned the dial and, finding music she enjoyed, bounced side to side in her seat.

"But I'm the driver, and to drive safely, I need music that doesn't enrage me."

Jennifer laughed brightly. "You? Enraged? I can't picture it."

Ruby nudged Lina's elbow. She mouthed the words, "Is Dad a player?"

"He hasn't dated since Mom—not that I know of."

Go Dad. He had been lonely since losing his wife. Still, so weird to witness his lame stab at flirtation. From the shocked expression on Ruby's face, she wasn't ready, having only begun to mourn the loss of their mother.

Dad attempted a joke with Jennifer. "Turn it up to an eleven." She laughed anyway.

"He's pretty terrible." Ruby didn't even bother to lower her voice.

For flirting, or for being bad at it?

Ruby tipped her head back against the headrest and closed her eyes again. Trina's medication schedule throughout the day had helped Ruby manage her withdrawal symptoms, but it left her drowsy.

Lina let Ruby melt into her side as her sister relaxed with sleep. She gazed out of the window at the countryside racing by. There was so much from the past few days —so much to cry about, so much to smile about. She was caught in the middle and could not begin to guess how her next appointment with Doctor Bowman might go with all these blended emotions.

Through it all, Cody had never been far from her thoughts. She pulled her phone from her pocket. He hadn't tried to contact her or returned any of her messages. He must still be so mad at her. If she texted Eli, maybe he could make Cody respond to her. But ... that would be pushing again. If he was still angry, pushing wouldn't help. Their budding relationship was doomed. Moving on from Cody would hurt more than previous false starts with guys. She had put a label on her feelings the day they had gone to the farmer's market and had only become more certain since then. He was too important. She had to patch things up with him as soon as Ruby was settled at the rehab center.

CHAPTER 54

Lina

BACK AT HOME, nearing five o'clock, Lina dressed carefully in case Cody decided to give her a chance to apologize. She couldn't use her womanly wiles to convince him to forgive her, but if this was going to be the last time he saw her, she would look her best. She wore the blue dress from their first date, the one that let him touch the skin of her shoulders. There was a lot to make up for, and if she could remind him of that night at The Bad Bronco, it would only help.

She would never forget the look on his face when he had opened his door and found her on his front porch. Her understanding was better now than a few days ago—the embarrassment, the shame of having someone know your secret pain. Vulnerability must be given, not taken. But she had taken it from him that night. She didn't blame him for his reaction.

Lina lifted the pendant from the farmers' market from her jewelry box and fastened the clasp behind her neck. Her skin tingled as she remembered his touch when she tried it on. After a swipe of lip gloss and spritz of perfume, she was ready—ready to wait and see if he would choose to come over and talk to her.

She tapped on Dad's bedroom door. He was lounging on his bed with his laptop open to the drug rehab website.

"Come on in, pumpkin. You look pretty."

Lina crossed her eyes and stuck out her tongue. Her dad was *supposed* to call her pretty.

"Even better," he teased.

She joined him and laid her head on his shoulder. His other shoulder didn't taunt her anymore—it had an owner now.

"Thanks for bringing me home so I can talk to Cody face to face. Hopefully, he will forgive me before we go back to Topeka."

"I think he'll forgive you."

"What makes you so sure?"

"He nearly pushed me over to get to you."

"Yeah, well maybe he just wanted to yell at me some more."

"If that's what he wanted, then he doesn't—"

"Deserve me, I know." She fiddled with the tail of his necktie. "Can I read the letter you sent?"

"Sure. I don't know if he even needs an updated letter of recommendation to go with his transcript, but it couldn't hurt." Her dad opened his email and let her read the letter he had written to the director of admissions at Washburn University, who was also a longtime financial client and friend from the old days when they lived in the city. She tracked her finger along the words as she read. The letter reminded the director of Cody's earlier accep-tance and explained the tragedy that had interrupted his life. It went on to praise his character for his sacrifices and the responsibilities he'd taken on, and recommended him as a candidate for the criminal justice program.

"Dad, thank you. Can I tell him you did this?"

"I'd rather he spent a little more time thinking he needs to earn my favor."

Lina gasped and shoved his shoulder.

"I'm kidding. Truthfully, I don't want him doubting his own worthiness. Let him be confident in all that he's done on his own. After all, he did get accepted all by himself. That's not an easy feat."

"Even if things don't happen for me and Cody"—she touched the pendant, the weight of it grounding her—"I'm still glad, about everything."

"You want me to make myself scarce?" He winked at her.

Her face heated. "Dad …" Rolling her eyes, she stood. Before she left the room, she stopped at the door. "Yeah, thanks."

Lina waited in the living room, first on the couch, then she moved to the chair. She looked out the window, then sat on the couch again. Five after. Maybe it really was over. With every tick of the clock, her heart sank a little further. She thought it might never return to its rightful place in her chest, and if that was the case, she needed to figure out how to be okay without him.

She wandered out to the front porch and sat on the step. Her neighbor Tommy rode his tricycle along the side-walk. He ignored the pedals and pushed with his feet on the pavement. He waved at Lina as he crept by on his short legs.

Her own bike was close at hand on the porch. Since Cody hadn't shown up, she'd go for a ride and feel the wind in her hair. A poor substitute for kisses, but she didn't want to cry about lost love in front of her dad.

She grabbed the handlebars and knocked the kickstand back. Her back tire was flat. She squatted down for a better look. Adding disappointment to disappointment—a ride was not an option today.

When she stood back up, Cody was just parking his truck in front of her house. Her sunken heart leapt higher, overshooting her chest and crowding her throat. He had come. There were so many reasons to love him, but just that was more than enough by itself. He had come!

He climbed out and strode toward her, holding a daisy down by his side.

She had hoped he would come, but until this moment, she'd fully expected that he wouldn't. Not after how badly she had overstepped into his family life. Her heart hammered against her ribcage with wild blows.

She wanted to run to him and tell him the news, to let him hold the pieces together as the emotions of the past few days spilled out unrestrained and threatening to pull her apart.

He wasn't smiling. He looked weary. Dark circles under his eyes stabbed her with guilt. She made her way to the edge of the porch and braced for the scolding she deserved.

He hesitated at the bottom step and blew out a deep breath. "I'm trying to think of the perfect thing to say to you." He gazed at her face. "All I can come up with is I'm sorry."

Lina stepped down, her pulse racing, then stepped down again until they were eye to eye. Up close, the darkness under his eyes looked more like bruises, not lack of sleep. The area of his upper left cheek appeared tender and painful.

"I should have told you a long time ago about my mom. And I yelled at you when I should've been yelling at myself."

"I'm not sure what you mean," she said. "I intruded on a part of your life that you weren't ready to share with me. I should have respected you better instead of just assuming I'd be welcome."

Cody took her hand, and like the first time at the Dairy Queen, she interlocked her fingers with his. Only, she wasn't rushing anything now. Gone was the infatuation, the insecurity, and the need for his pace to match hers. She could wait for him to be ready for all she wanted to give him to go along with her hand—her heart and her future.

"I don't know what will happen with us," he said. "You're going back to school, and I'm … staying here for now, for however long. I don't know. I know I'm not good enough for you. I can't blame you for leaving me behind. But you've shown me a future that's better than my past. And I choose that future." He held up the flower and gave it to her. "I will always choose you." He lowered his head toward her. "Always you," he whispered.

Lina's lower lip trembled anticipating his kiss, but in her periphery, there was something amiss about the daisy. She looked more closely. Every other petal was missing. She raised an eyebrow at him. "You took out all the love-me-not petals?"

"I can't risk you thinking I don't love you."

He loved her?

She met his gaze and saw everything she needed to know in his warm, earnest eyes. Yes, he loved her. Lifting both eyebrows, she teased him with a womanly wile. "Then you better show me how the game goes now."

Cody swallowed, smiled, and unleashed his secret weapon—his dimple. He removed a petal from the daisy.

"I love you." He let the petal fall and removed another. "I love you." Another petal landed on the steps. "I love you." Another. "I love you. I love you."

Lina reached behind his neck and pulled herself closer until his "I love you" whispered against her lips.

She looked into the deep, dark eyes of the man who loved her, and the world vanished.

CHAPTER 55
Cody

ON THE PORCH STEP, Cody held Lina across his lap, kissing her velvet-soft lips again and again. He pulled back to look into her eyes. The intense blue with violet flecks was his home now. A puffiness let him know that she had cried a lot recently. He twisted a hand into her hair, and pressing another kiss to her lips, he released the charred, tattered thread he'd been hanging on to for two years.

He smoothed her hair back and traced her cheekbone with a shaky thumb. "Where did you go? I needed you so bad." His voice was rough with the yearning he wasn't even trying to hide from her.

Lina softened, practically melting into him. "You needed me?" She placed a palm against his chest. "So did Ruby."

Cody's brows knit together, and he searched her face for meaning.

"I had to go, and I couldn't tell you about it until we were sure it was true … They've been wrong before—"

"Wait, what?"

"They found Ruby!" Lina's eyes glistened with unshed tears.

The corner of Cody's mouth twitched with a tentative smile. "What? For real?" It sounded like the lamest response to his own ears—it must have been even more lame to hers. Cody's heart quickened further. "AbolitionistOps?" He was suddenly surer of his chosen course of study than ever. He gathered her into his chest and their two hearts pounded against each other.

"They found her," she said into his shoulder.

"Is Ruby okay?" he asked, stroking the length of her hair down her back.

"She's alive. I hope she'll be okay soon."

"Lina, you have to tell me more. Everything."

She pulled away and chewed the corner of her lower lip. With a shaky breath, large tears spilled free from her lashes and landed on her cheeks.

"I need to respect her privacy, so I can't reveal anything she wouldn't want me to share."

He nodded, understanding the desire to keep certain things private. He had spent so long being afraid of Mom's illness that he hadn't been honest with anyone about it.

"Okay, whatever you can share is enough."

"She was being held by sex traffickers in Miami." Her voice broke and trembled. "She's been through some … horrific stuff. They got her addicted to drugs to keep her" —she swallowed as she searched for the word—"submissive. That's where she is now, at a drug rehab clinic in Topeka."

The wind was knocked from his lungs as though he'd taken an actual physical body slam. Once again, his own problems paled as he imagined Ruby, broken and alone in Topeka.

"Why are you here? You should go back to your apartment up at school, so you can be close to her," he said.

"She won't be able to have visitors until after the detox, so that's the plan." A fat tear fell on her cheek. "But I need you too." She curled her fingertips to the inside of the collar of his t-shirt.

Cody touched her face. He'd seen enough tears, but these particular tears were so beautiful. Ignoring the saltiness, he kissed the corners of her eyes. "You came back here for me? That's a terrible trade."

"Well, the truth is, I'm headed back tomorrow. I know I can't see her for a while, but I think I'd like to be nearby. Though I'm not sure how helpful I'll be to her. Ruby needs some time. She is only a shell of herself right now. She needs to figure out who she is and adjust to life as a regular girl, and I want to be there for her while she does that."

Cody turned his head at the squeak of a tricycle. The same little neighbor boy passed Lina's house. He slowed to a crawl along the sidewalk and stared at Lina draped across Cody's lap, their hands on each other. He could kiss her again, giving the child something worth staring at, and was tempted to do just that. But he cared more about the girl in his arms than the boy on the tricycle. Only the girl and her sister.

"I'm going to join the Abolitionists one day …"

"Oh, Cody. That means so much to me. You'll be so good with them."

She believed in him. With her at his side, he could face whatever the future held in store. And he wanted to support *her*, have her back and help her through her challenges. "What can I do? What do you need?"

"Will you come see me in Topeka?" Her voice was small, as if she were asking for the impossible.

Topeka was no hardship, but something he already wanted himself. Same with visiting her. "Yes, ma'am. Probably more often than you think."

She gave him a quizzical look.

"Some things have happened here while you were gone." It was time to include Lina in every part of his life. "Do you know how to bake cookies? Because I think you should meet my mom."

CHAPTER 56

Cody

THE RANCH WAS NO LONGER Cody's nemesis. Though he would be stuck there for the time being, it was once again his home rather than his prison. The work was just his job rather than his life sentence. And Mom was his mom rather than his burden.

He looked around her bedroom for anything else she might like to have around her during her stay at the PTSD recovery center in Topeka. He tucked a framed picture of his parents on their wedding day into her suitcase and carried another down the hall, where he hung it to cover the fist-sized hole in the wall.

He lifted the suitcase and the rocking chair into the back of the truck, loaded her guitar case behind the driver's seat, and waved to Eli out at the barn.

"Headed out?" Eli hollered across the drive as he walked out to the truck.

"Yeah. I'm taking her to the PTSD center today. I hope she likes it there."

"Me too. I'll give her a call once she's settled."

"Thanks." He clasped Eli by the hand and pulled him

in for a bro hug. "And thanks for your help with the financial aid paperwork."

"No problem. And remember, it's only temporary until the ranch turns more profit."

"Under your watch, that'll happen sooner rather than later."

"What? My kid brother has confidence in the ranch?"

"In you, man. In you."

"Same thing." Laughing, Eli backed away toward the garage.

At Lina's house, Cody met her at the door and added her two large suitcases to Mom's things in the back of the truck.

Mr. Grant shook his hand. "I hope all goes well today, son."

"Thank you, sir."

"Drive carefully," he said to Cody. Then to Lina: "Text me when you get there. I'll meet up with you this evening."

Cody kissed her when she climbed into the truck with a plate of cookies wrapped in cellophane. She sat in the center seat and kept her hand on his thigh as he drove. It didn't make him nervous anymore. He kissed her at every red light on the way to the hospital.

"Does Topeka have heavy traffic?" he asked.

"At commuter times and in the busier areas. Why do you ask?"

"I wouldn't mind hours of red lights with you." His lips clung to hers until the light turned green. "There just aren't enough of them around here."

At the hospital, Lina waited in the lounge area while Cody rolled the suitcase into his mom's room. Mrs. Bauer sat at the foot of the bed sharing a story about a goat while

Desiree was gathering Mom's few belongings and getting her ready to leave.

"Hi, Mom. Hey, Mrs. B."

"Cody!" The light in his mom's eyes seemed more real than anything about her had been the last two years.

Mrs. Bauer got up and folded Cody into a hug. "Why didn't you call me? I would've hurried right over." She gave his shoulders a little shake. "I had to find out about Rosie's accident from Wayne. And he's *so* stingy with details!"

Desiree held up a laptop. "Is this yours?"

"Yes, ma'am, I wondered where I left it. Been scattered lately." Cody hadn't been interested in his laptop since hearing he'd have to reapply to Washburn.

"To be expected." Desiree gestured him through the door. "If you can give us a few minutes, I'll get her dressed."

Mrs. Bauer already had the suitcase zipped open and was choosing Mom's clothing. "I'll help you, Rosie. Nurses have enough to keep busy."

Desiree shut the door, giving the two friends some privacy.

"Thanks for taking such good care of my mom. I can't believe how much she's improved in just a few days."

"You're quite welcome," Desiree said. "She's still got a long recovery ahead, but the right balance of meds makes a big difference. I'm sorry that Eli won't be coming around anymore."

"Oh, he'll come around if he thinks you want him to."

She wrinkled her nose as she smiled. "I *do* still have his phone number." She sauntered toward the nurse's station. "Give me just a second to print your mom's discharge papers."

Cody returned to the lounge area, and taking a seat next to Lina, opened his laptop. There was another email from the director of admissions at Washburn.

I have reconsidered your request and am pleased to invite you to attend classes this fall. I have consulted with Ms. Jeffries regarding your efforts to receive your diploma, and I would encourage you to retake and pass your statistics exam with a score of at least eighty-five percent or above so you will be prepared for the rigors of a course of study in criminal justice. Registration has already opened. Do not delay your class selections.

For the second time in as many days, the wind was knocked from his lungs. Cody rubbed a hand over his eyes and read it again.

"What …?" he breathed. " How …?" How did they know what he wanted to study? He sat back in the chair, his mind whirling in a thousand directions. Everything he could have dreamed was now possible. Leaving the ranch, pursuing the degree he needed for the career he had chosen, living close to Mom's care center … Lina. He would be with Lina.

"Is everything okay?" Lina wore a huge grin, eyes dancing.

"Yes, ma'am." He pulled her up out of the chair and whirled her around. She squealed, her hair flipping him in the face. With a hand on her cheek, he kissed her and didn't stop until he heard voices.

"This must be the blue-eyed library gal." Mrs. Bauer spoke up first. She wheeled the suitcase while Desiree pushed Mom in the hospital's wheelchair.

"Lina?" His mom looked her up and down curiously. A hesitant smile emerged as she focused in on Lina's face.

Cody set a hand on his mom's shoulder. "Mom, this is Lina."

"I'm happy to meet you." Lina offered the plate of cookies. "And these are for you."

"Well, look at that," Desiree exclaimed. "Rosie, you were right about the cookies." She took the plate and set it on Mom's lap. "Those look delicious."

Cody signed a few papers on a clipboard for Desiree while his mom sampled Lina's cookies. Then he hugged Mrs. Bauer, promised to call her as soon as Mom was settled, and took the suitcase. Lina carried the laptop and the cookies as they all went down to the hospital lobby.

His mom closed her eyes when a block of sunshine fell across her as Desiree pushed her chair up to the automatic glass doors. The doors opened with a whoosh. Cody held his breath.

Escorting the patient out was all business for Desiree. No doubt or concern, just a quick bump of the wheels over the threshold. Then a hand to guide Mom up and into the truck. It was so easy for the nurse to manage what had been so challenging for him.

Cody put his mom in the center seat between himself and Lina. He waved goodbye to Desiree and Mrs. Bauer as he pulled away from the curb, and Lina turned on the Carrie Underwood playlist. Mom started humming before they left the parking lot.

"I think your mom would like karaoke," Lina said as they pulled onto the highway.

"Maybe someday we'll take her to The Bad Bronco."

"Someday isn't far off."

Someday. He would have to learn to be more careful with that word.

CHAPTER 57

Cody

Four months later

CODY KNOCKED on the door of Lina's apartment first thing in the morning.

A voice called out, "Who's there?"

He grinned and waved into the peephole. "It's me, Cody."

"What's the password?"

Cody rolled his eyes. It was fine to require a password, but the password was terrible. "Beware the Cody-bear."

After the deadbolt turned, the door opened a crack and a vivid blue eye peered through the opening. The door shut again, and Ruby released the safety chain. Finally, he was admitted into the apartment.

"Hey, Ruby, how's it going?" Cody asked.

"It's fine. Adeline's almost ready." Ruby returned to a stack of pancakes in the kitchen. "You want some breakfast?"

"No thanks," he said. "Hey, what do you think of that new move we learned last night?"

Since Ruby had left rehab, he and Lina had been attending a self-defense class with her at the community center three times a week.

"It's a little tricky, but I think I've got it. I could use more practice, though."

"How about right now?"

Ruby left her pancakes once more and came to stand in the center of the room with her back to Cody. "Okay, act like you're going to attack me."

Cody bear-hugged her from behind, which was how the most recent password had been coined. Before he could lift her off her feet, Ruby dropped her weight below his waist. He wobbled forward. She elbowed him in the ribs, and turning, braced his shoulder for a knee to the groin. She halted her strike before making contact, but Cody flinched anyway.

"Don't damage him, Ruby. I want babies someday." Lina tilted her head and smiled at Cody with a gleam in her eye.

He exhaled and straightened his jacket that had gotten twisted in the scuffle. Ruby was highly motivated to learn to defend herself, and she didn't do it gently.

Lina hugged her sister goodbye. "Call me at lunch, after your therapy appointment."

After the door shut behind them, the deadbolt thumped into place and the chain rattled as it latched.

"She's doing okay, isn't she?" Cody asked as he helped Lina into the truck.

"Sometimes. I want so bad for her to be the sister I used to know, but I don't think that will ever happen. I need to learn to be grateful for her, however she is today."

"Give her time. After you lost her and then your mom, you became someone else too."

She put a hand on his cheek. "I have a wise boyfriend."

He smiled into her palm.

"With a sexy dimple," she added.

"Better stop that, or we'll never get there. That kind of talk will get us laying down in a meadow somewhere."

They made a stop at his mom's care facility. She was eating breakfast with Darla, a widow who lived in a neighboring room. Mom had a new haircut, and she wore pale pink nail polish to match her floral dress.

"Good morning, Mom." Cody bent to kiss her cheek. He and Lina pulled chairs up to the small table. "What have you got planned for today?"

Darla answered for the both of them. "We're playing bridge later."

Mom smiled at Cody. "I feel lucky."

"Well you should; you beat me every time," Darla laughed.

Cody spotted Dr. Bally across the room. "Excuse me, be right back." He approached the doctor and shook her hand. "Hi, Doc. My mom seems happier lately. Things are going well, right?"

"Come have a seat." Dr. Bally led Cody to an office and invited him to sit in an overstuffed chair. "Rosie is improving. We are still working to find the right balance of meds, but I think we're close."

"That's good news. I can see her getting better all the time. She could barely play bingo when she got here, and now she's playing bridge."

"Yes, but I'm also concerned about her PTSD triggers. She won't talk about the event that took your father, which is understandable—that could be years away, if she ever gets there. But she also reacts unfavorably to discussing the ranch. I think you'd better get used to the idea that she may never go back there. It terrifies her, which is likely the reason she never went outside."

Cody rubbed his forehead. He should've known this about Mom years ago. Like he had shot his father's horse, his mom had similar feelings about the ranch. She'd been suffering the whole time, and he'd only been concerned with keeping her calm.

Dr. Bally steepled her fingers. "You did the best you could with the knowledge and resources you had at the time. You don't need to feel guilty about that."

Eli and Wayne had both told him the same thing. Lina too. He was the only one who still gave himself a hard time when he thought about the past. But he was learning to think more about the future. A future where Mom could be happy and sing and dance, and she was getting there one day at a time. "She goes outside here. Yesterday, I found her outside on the patio. She was playing her guitar in the sun."

"Being outside in general was never the problem." The doctor closed a file folder on her desk.

"So, she'll be here for the rest of her life?" he asked.

"No, I don't think that will be necessary. Depending on her progress, she may be able to move to an assisted living situation, and maybe someday, back to living on her own. It's too soon to know right now, but as she becomes more self-sufficient, the plan can evolve."

Cody nodded his head. *Someday*. As Mom healed, decisions would need to be made, and now that he had power of attorney, he was a part of those decisions.

His phone rang with a video chat from Eli. "Thank you

for the update, Doctor, but this call is for Mom." He answered the chat as he walked back to the dining room.

"Hey, bro," Cody said. He turned the phone around so Mom could see the screen.

"Rosie, I've missed you," Eli said.

"We spoke yesterday," Mom reminded him.

While Eli talked with Mom about her upcoming bridge game, Cody held Lina's hand on her lap under the table. She smiled at him, and his heart flooded. She was the girl who had changed everything for him—her and her alternate ending.

When Eli hung up, Cody checked the time. He and Lina needed to leave, or they would be late. They kissed Mom goodbye with a promise to be back later.

Cody drove them to the Washburn campus and parked in the student lot. He carried Lina's backpack as well as his own as they walked hand in hand.

Trees flamed with the brilliant yellow and orange leaves of autumn. Students hurried through the morning chill as they crossed the quad on their way to class. They passed the family sciences building, and Cody remembered Lina's comment earlier.

"Lina, you told Ruby that you want babies."

"Yeah, someday." Lina stopped walking. She narrowed her gaze as she searched his face.

Cody lifted her chin with two fingers. He saw his future when he looked in her eyes. It was a future much better than anything in his past. He was up to the challenge of having a family with Lina, not afraid or inadequate. Her lips, his kryptonite, curved sweetly within his reach. He pulled her into his arms and kissed her in full view of those milling about the quad.

Forehead to forehead, Cody tucked a lock of her hair

behind her ear and allowed a thumb to trace the length of her neck. "Let's get through school first," he said. "If I've learned anything from you, Adeline Grant, it's that someday isn't far off."

The End

Acknowledgments

Thank you, dear reader. I hope you have enjoyed Cody and Lina's story. Through this journey into authorly life, I've been amazed by the amount of support required, and even more amazed by the amount of support generously offered. Get ready; I've had tons of help.

I am grateful to Michelle Murray of KMP Entertainment and her rigorous Master Writers course. Ms. Murray helped me structure this story on a firm foundation, insisted on my best work, and believed I could do it. Thank you to my classmate at KMP and fellow writer, Sarah Grace, who knew Ruby was still out there and in need of rescue.

I must also thank my editor friends Bethany Cox for hours of sifting through plot holes, and Kathleen Barlow for the final read-through.

Linda Hill has my heartfelt gratitude for all those expert edits, common sense, and for making me laugh along the way.

I couldn't have survived without the love of my writing tribe, Stormy and Emily, and the tough love from my critique partners, Mary Etta, Matt, Dallas, Allan, Gary, and James.

Thank you to Tim Kavmark for the tech and design help, and to Kelly Southwell and Bonnie Moesser for reading everything I've ever written and asking for more.

And finally, I am grateful to my family for being as

excited as I am to see the creation of this novel. Brenna, who encouraged me to take the story out of my head and put it on the page. Lucas, who insisted I read to him the first five chapters and helped brainstorm where to go next. Rory, who enthusiastically, and sometimes brutally, demonstrated Krav Maga techniques for fight scenes.

About the Author

Jan Halen invented her first boyfriend as a pre-teen and has been imagining swoon-worthy heartthrobs ever since. While a firm believer that every story should include a love affair, she writes Sweet with Heat Romance because she still blushes at the sexy parts. Jan is the mother of three and can be found on a Southern California beach imagining backstory about random strangers.

For more Sweet with Heat romance, follow Jan Halen.

Instagram, Facebook, Goodreads, and Bookbub
@authorjanhalen

or visit www.authorjanhalen.com

9 781960 859006